COLD
BETRAYAL

Cold Betrayal

Annalou Mack

*Best Wishes
Anna*

Compass Flower Press
Columbia, Missouri

Published by
Compass Flower Press
Columbia, Missouri

Library of Congress Control Number: 2021901154
ISBN: 978-1-951960-16-2 Trade Paperback
ISBN: 978-1-951960-17-9 Ebook

Foreword

Being an avid genealogist, I had been tracing my family history for years when I stumbled upon this story. The first of my family to migrate to Missouri came to what became Grundy County in 1837 and stayed. Grundy County is joined on the north by Mercer County on the east by Sullivan and Linn Counties and on the south by Livingston County. Since my ancestors lived in the eastern part of Grundy, I was led into Linn and Sullivan Counties in my research.

While searching in Linn County records in the History of Linn County I found the account of the murder of the Meeks Family not far from Browning, Missouri. This intrigued me for a couple reasons. First, I have the surname Meek in my family history, (although it is Meek with no 's' in my family name) and second, this murder occurred within about twenty miles of where I lived as my children were growing up.

I was surprised that my grandfather had not told me the story during one of the many tales I heard while in his company when I was young. Either he had forgotten about it or he mentioned it and I forgot. No matter why I had not heard about it, I now was hooked.

For the next twenty or so years I searched for anything I could find about this terrible murder of a father, mother, and two little girls. I traveled to the Historical Society in Columbia, Missouri and began printing newspaper accounts, then visited the courthouses in Linneus, the county seat of Linn County and to the courthouse in Carrollton, the county seat of Carroll County.

Although I found articles that had been published, I decided to write my version of the tragedy. My first commentaries were a retelling of the basic story. As time went on, I chose to do something different. In my research it appeared that almost nothing had been written about Della, the wife of one of the accused murderers. This then became my mission. To write the story from the eyes of Della.

The facts of the murder and two trials are as outlined in the sources. The spoken words and thoughts of Della and her family are fictionalized since I have found nothing to base them on. The same is true of much of what I wrote of Sheriff Niblo.

As a genealogist, I had to research the families of the main characters in this book. Much to my surprise, after completing the writing of the book, I found through DNA testing that my Meek family and the Meeks family do have a common ancestor. I have DNA matches to descendants of three of Gus Meeks' siblings. At the back of the book I have supplied genealogy lists for the Gibson, Taylor, Meeks and Niblo families. These lists are based on solid research.

Birthdates of the living have been deleted.

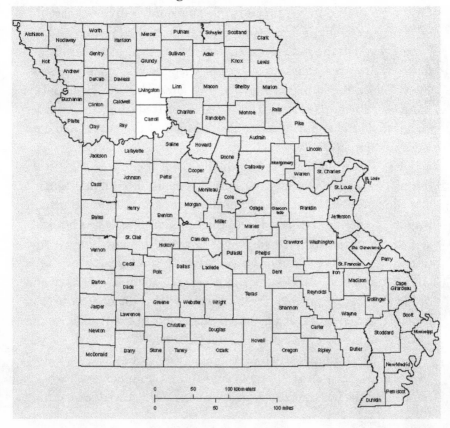

Annalou Mack

Detail North Central Missouri:

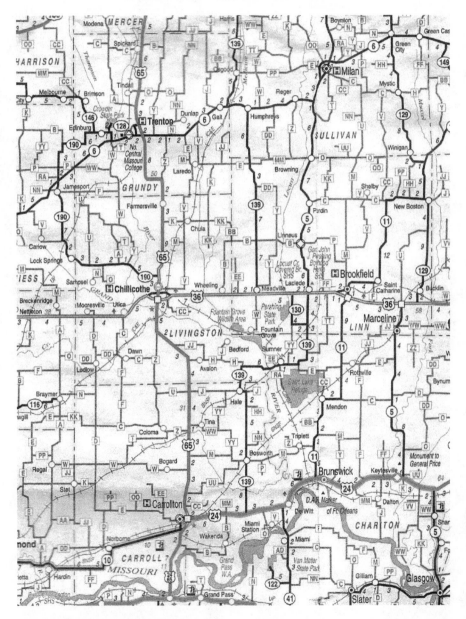

Prologue

September 1893

Three mounted horsemen met at the gate leading into the pasture on the large Warren McCullough farm. Abner Page, Gus Meeks, and Arthur Bingham had been hired by the local banker, William P. Taylor, to relieve his rival banker, Mr. McCullough, of his prized herd of beef cattle. They intended to carry out their job.

In contrast to the criminal duties the men were assigned, it was a beautiful moonlit night with a balmy breeze softly blowing. The sounds of the night creatures in this area were drowned out by the back and forth banter of the men on their nefarious task.

"Come on, Gus, get the gate open so we can be on our way."

"Okay, Abner, don't rush me. It's wired pretty tight. I need a pair of wire cutters."

After working with it a while, the wire was removed; the gate opened, and the trio entered the pasture where, in daylight, the cattle quietly grazed. It didn't take long for the gang to round up the animals and herd them through the open gate. The cattle did not like being disturbed from their night rest, so milled around for a bit. Not sure they should be moving at this time of night, the cows tossed their heads and uttered loud moos, but slowly moved out to the road.

The rustlers had only a short drive down the four miles to the railroad in Browning, Missouri. Just before dawn they reached the station and roused the station master to tell him they were there to load the cattle on the next train.

"I hate to tell you this, fellows," the station attendant told them, "you're too late. You didn't reserve the two box cars you'll need, and the train doesn't have any extras today. You'll have to bring them back another day." The attendant was not pleased at being called out at daybreak so hurried back into the station after delivering his message to the men.

"Hellfire and damnation!" muttered Bingham. "Cousin Bill is not going to like this."

"Now what do we do?" groused Meeks.

Bingham mulled the situation a while then said, "Guess we'll have to take them to my place until we can get further orders from Bill. I'm sure he will want us to finish the job soon."

The three men sullenly turned the herd around and began the trek back up the same road. It was much farther to Bingham's farm; about ten miles beyond the McCullough farm. Frustration showed on all their faces as they quietly made their way to the farm where the cattle would remain for the time being. Each man returned to his home, hoping the job could be finished without the law being involved. Times were hard for farmers and the money from this would give a boost to their meager funds.

A few days later, Warren McCullough, President of the Bank of Milan, Missouri rode out to check on his cows. It was a huge surprise to find the pasture empty. He lost no time in returning to Milan to contact Sheriff Niblo about the theft.

Sheriff Niblo immediately organized a posse to track down the thieves. Cattle rustling was a major crime to a law enforcement officer. Niblo and his men began talking to the farmers living near the McCullough farm. The neighbors thought the cattle had been gone for several days. One man thought he remembered seeing some cattle on the road one night not long ago when he had gotten up in the night.

After listening to what the neighbors had to say about the missing cattle, Niblo guessed the crooks might have been taking the cattle to the train. Going to the train in Browning, the sheriff questioned the train station attendant. "Have you seen a herd of cattle at the train recently?"

"Well, as a matter of fact I have. Just about a week ago three fellows brought cows here to be shipped but there weren't any cars available for them, so they left."

"Do you know who these men were?"

"I'm not sure, but I think one of them was Arthur Bingham."

Following this lead, the sheriff made a trip to the farm of Arthur Bingham where the stolen cattle were found.

In answer to the questions asked by the sheriff, Bingham told how his cousin, William P. "Bill" Taylor, had hired him along with Gus Meeks and Gus's brother-in-law, Abner Page, to take the cattle to the train for shipment to Kansas City to be sold. Taylor had promised the three men a share of the profit from the sale.

A few days later, Sheriff Niblo arrested William P. Taylor, cashier at the Peoples Exchange Bank of Browning along with Bingham, Page, and Meeks. Taylor and Bingham made bail and were released on bond. Page and Meeks did not have the money or assets to make bond so they remained in jail.

Sheriff Niblo had had run-ins with Bill Taylor in the past. The previous year Taylor had been indicted on a charge of arson and prior to that a check kiting scheme. It was no secret that William P. Taylor was not one of the sheriff's favorite people. Maybe he had lots of friends in high places, but in the eyes of the sheriff he was just a common criminal.

A grand jury in Linn County indicted the four men, and a trial was set for each. Gus Meeks was tried first and sentenced to two years in the Missouri State Penitentiary. Trials for the others were delayed.

In preparation for the trial against Taylor, Linn County Prosecutor T. M. Bresnehen convinced Governor Stone to pardon Gus Meeks and in return Gus would testify against Bill Taylor. Taylor was sure Gus would never be able to do that.

Chapter 1

May 1894

Della heard Flossie, her one-year old daughter, whimpering in her cradle beside the bed. Before she could get up to see about her, the baby not yet born gave her a good hard kick. That was enough to wake Della completely. Her new baby was due in a couple of months and it was a good thing Della's mother lived nearby to help out. Keeping up the house, cooking, caring for the chickens, and taking care of two babies was going to be a lot of responsibility for an eighteen-year-old.

Rubbing her eyes, Della noticed her husband George was already up and outside when it was just getting daylight. Her mother had come downstairs about midnight to soothe the crying baby and take her back to the room where her mother and father were sleeping. George wasn't home then, and Della was too sick to think more about it. Della hadn't been feeling a bit good yesterday, and her concerned parents had come over to spend the night with her and help care for the baby.

Della had heard George come in a few minutes later as her mother was bringing Flossie back downstairs. She supposed George and his big brother Bill were out late planning some big scheme. Some of the schemes they had thought up had put them in trouble. She fervently hoped this one was not a repeat.

As she lay in bed, the attractive, young, blue-eyed Della thought back to the first time George Taylor, the most handsome man she had ever seen, noticed her. His lustrous brown eyes and nearly black hair set off his ruddy complexion heightened by his days in the sun. The physical activity of farm work kept his figure lean and trim. George might have been described as a wild young man when he was younger and was definitely a"ladies' man." He was charming and could win a confidence with just a few words.

His movements were quick, and he had an easy laugh. It was said success in his love affairs came easily which gave him quite a reputation. Gossip was how he had narrowly escaped more than one load of buckshot. Fathers in this part of the country didn't like their daughters being dallied with.

For years Della had had a crush on him, but he was so much older—by a full ten years. She didn't think he would ever pay any attention to her. They had grown up in the same neighborhood, and she knew George had an eye for pretty women. There certainly had been plenty of rumors among the community about his roving eye. Being one of the most eligible men in the Browning area he could have had about any woman he wanted. She couldn't help but wonder why he chose her, for she felt most of the eligible girls were prettier than she was. When George began courting her, she was flattered; any fifteen-year-old girl would have been. After a short courtship, Della Gibson and George Taylor were married in October, 1891, just three months after her sixteenth birthday. She was very proud to be the wife of this intelligent and well educated man.

As Della finally crawled out of bed, the sun was just beginning to shine through the east window. It was going to be a beautiful May day in North Missouri. Much-needed rain the previous day had made everything look fresh and crisp. She loved this part of the state with its rolling hills, little creeks, and beautiful timber groves.

While brushing her long brown hair, she heard her father, David Gibson, slip down the stairs and out the door to go home to tend to his animals. Her mother would be coming down soon. They only lived about a hundred yards from her and George, and Della was grateful to have their help on days like yesterday when this pregnancy was about to get the best of her.

Della's mother, Gonia Gibson, started down the stairs. "Little Flossie slept real good after I took her up to my room," she said.

At age forty-four, Gonia was still an attractive woman with long, brown hair showing sprinkles of gray which she wore in a bun on top of her head. Having given birth to six children, she had some extra weight around her middle, but carried it well on her five-foot, seven-inch frame.

Annalou Mack

"I'd better get her fed," Della mumbled as she took Flossie in her arms, "and start breakfast before George comes in."

"Do you feel better this mornin'?" asked her mother. "I'm goin' home now to get breakfast for your pa, Drue and Ivy May and do my mornin' chores. I'll need to get your brother Drue started on his chores, too. I'll be back later this mornin' and we can get those dirty clothes washed up. It looks like a pretty day, so they should dry good today."

"Yes, I'm better, but I sure will be glad when this baby is here. With Flossie the last two months were also terribly miserable. I can't sit for long 'cause my feet swell so much. And standing makes my back hurt. On top of that I'm worried about George. I sure wish I knew what's bothering him. He's been so touchy."

It seemed as though George had been in a bad mood a lot lately. Ever since he had learned the "no–'count Gus Meeks," as George called him, was released from the state penitentiary by the governor. It was rumored Gus had been pardoned so he could testify against George's brother, Bill Taylor, in the cattle rustling charge the previous September. Of course, Bill and George were not anxious for Gus to testify against Bill in the coming trial.

Della fired up the cook stove and had salt pork, eggs and biscuits ready when George came in with Willie, her seventeen-year-old brother, and the hired man, James Harris who had been staying with George and Della. Willie and James had been doing the usual morning chores of feeding the horses, slopping the hogs and milking the cows and were ready to eat. George seemed unusually quiet this morning. Della was sure there was something on his mind he was keeping from her.

"George, when you finish breakfast, would you please chop some wood and draw water for us? Ma is coming back later, and we are gonna do the wash today."

They needed to get a good wood fire going under the big, black iron kettle to boil the clothes. Without a word, George went out to chop the wood and draw the water.

Willie told Della as he left the kitchen, "Me and Harris are going over to James Taylor's where a bunch of us are going down in the timber to cut fence poles."

Della began washing up the dishes and replied to Willie, "Thanks for your help. You all be careful down there in the timber."

She would barely have time to feed the chickens before her mother came back to help with the washing. Flossie came toddling to her mother and raised her arms to be picked up saying, "Up." Della picked her up and gave her a kiss on the cheek.

Carrying little Flossie on her hip, Della went out to the barn to get some corn for the chickens. As she got there, she saw George hitching the team to the harrow. She didn't know what he was up to, but thought it best not to question him right now in his dour mood.

Just as she was finishing her outside chores, Della noticed George had taken the harrow out to the newly planted corn field north of the house. *Now why he would be harrowing up there? The ground is surely too wet, and it will ruin the corn he just planted.* It didn't look like he was laying off regular rounds to harrow but going in sort of a circle in front of the old straw stack in the middle of the corn field. *He sure is acting strange this morning.*

On her way back to the house, Della saw a boy who looked to be a little younger than her thirteen-year-old brother, Drue, walking across the field from the direction of the Carter place. He was too far away for her to recognize him. As she watched, the boy went up to George and began talking to him. She couldn't hear what they were saying, but right away George and the boy came to the barn, so Della went on in the house.

Her brother, Drue had finished his morning chores at home and was sitting in Della's kitchen when she came through the door. A short time later, George came hurrying into the house.

"Drue, go out and saddle my mare for me and unhitch the team from the harrow," George said."I have to go to town to see Bill. I don't know when I'll be back." He gave Della and the baby a quick kiss and rushed out without a word to her. As George rode off, his wife saw the little boy heading back toward the Carter place. She still didn't know what the boy had wanted.

Della checked the time, and it was nearly eight o'clock. *If we're going to get the clothes washed and on the line before mid-day so they will be dry before dark, we had better get at it.* Wash day was a big day on the farm.

Annalou Mack

Drue had built the fire out in the yard under the big iron kettle, and the water was about ready for the clothes. She got the two copper tubs and put rinse water in them. She could see her mother walking up the road with Della's little sister, Ivy. Although only six, Ivy could help with Flossie while the other two did the washing.

Della and Gonia had just about finished with the clothes when wagons and buggies filled with people began to stream in through the gate. They drove across the meadow behind the house, over the cornfield and up to the old straw stack.

What in the world could all those people be doing out in our field at ten o'clock in the morning? thought Della.

"Drue, would you please go out to the field and find out what's goin' on?" his mother asked.

Less than a half hour later, Drue was back. "They say there's a family buried under the straw out there. Looks like they were killed last night, throwed in a shallow grave, and covered with dirt and straw. One of the little girls throwed in there weren't dead. She came to, walked over to the Carter house and told 'em about her family. They ain't sure, but they think it's Gus Meeks and his family."

"My Lord, why would they be buried in our field?" shrieked Della.

Chapter 2

After eating a hearty breakfast of salt pork and eggs, James Niblo, sheriff of Sullivan County, Missouri, walked out the front door of their home in Milan to breath in the fresh morning air and to feel the bright, warm sunlight on his face. As he leaned against the porch railing he took out his tobacco pouch and papers to roll a cigarette. He lit up and was puffing away when his neighbor from down the street came rushing up to him. The man dressed in everyday overalls and flannel shirt was nearly out of breath when he stood in front of the sheriff with words tumbling out of his mouth so fast they were jumbled.

"Slow down, Marvin. What are you tryin' to say?"

"Sheriff, have you heard about the slaughter of the Gus Meeks family?"

Instantly alert, James threw down his cigarette and said, "No. What happened?"

"The family was found in a shallow grave on the George Taylor farm south of Browning. Gus's oldest little girl wasn't dead and got help, so I understand," the breathless man revealed.

"Okay, I'll have to go see what is going on," James muttered as he walked back to the house to summon his son.

"Sam, come on. Let's get saddled up and go see what this talk about the killin' of the Gus Meeks family is all about."

James explained to Sam, whom he had made deputy, what the old man had informed him. "I know George Taylor's farm is in Linn County but let's see where the murders took place to decide if it is my jurisdiction or Sheriff Barton's."

On the road south out of Milan, Sheriff Niblo recalled how he had arrested Gus Meeks, Abner Page, Arthur Bingham and Bill Taylor about two years ago for stealing cattle from the Warren McCullough farm. Of the four, Meeks had been convicted and sent to the state penitentiary. The Governor had issued a pardon to Gus on the promise he would testify against Bill Taylor whose trial was due to start in a couple of weeks. He felt sure this murder had something to do with that case, but why the whole family?

As the two lawmen approached the Sullivan/Linn County line, James cautioned Sam to watch for signs of a struggle. About halfway up Jenkins Hill they saw what they were looking for.

Sam pointed out to his dad where there had been horses standing and tracks of men walking. The light shower the night before was just enough to make the ground sticky.

"You can see what looks like two men walking up the hill, Dad. And look at this dark spot on the ground. It might be blood."

As they moved on, they could see more signs of blood as well as buggy and wagon tracks. Sam found a rock with blood and hair on it, which must have been a murder weapon.

"Well, Sam, we are over the county line in Linn County, so this is Sheriff Barton's case. But let's go on to the George Taylor farm and see what's happening there."

They walked their horses along in silence while they each tried to understand how anyone could kill a woman and little children. What kind of monsters were these men?

Ahead James and Sam Niblo could see George Taylor's cornfield. It held a crowd of onlookers gathered around the bodies at the edge of an old straw stack. They were milling around exclaiming their horror at the scene before them. The bodies were piled up on top of each other in a shallow grave then covered over with straw and dirt.

Both men turned their faces away at the sight of the carnage from the previous night.

"Why have you not taken these people out of this place and carried them up to Milan to Gus's mother?" asked Niblo.

A Linn County deputy answered as he held the crowd back, "We are waiting for the coroner to come."

"These people need to be cleaned up and prepared for a decent burial. I'm an officer of the law, and I want to see them shown some respect."

As if by call, Sheriff Barton arrived with Dr. Van Wye, the coroner. Van Wye swiftly examined the bodies and said, "Gus was shot in the back."

Niblo heard the coroner say, "There is a hole in the baby's head and the mother was also shot. Another small daughter had her head bashed in with a rock."

"Where is George Taylor?" James asked.

"He went to Browning." A neighbor replied.

"I'm going up to the house to see if there is a wagon available to take these bodies back to Milan," said Niblo.

When Sheriff Niblo knocked on the door of the house, it was soon opened by a young woman heavy with child. "Where is George?" asked Niblo.

"He left for Browning early this morning and I haven't seen him since. I'm his wife, Della Taylor. Is it really true a whole family was killed and buried in our straw stack?"

"Yes, ma'am it is. It doesn't look good for your husband, George running off. If you hear from him, tell him he needs to see me or Sheriff Barton and explain about last night."

"I certainly will, but I know he didn't have anything to do with it. George is a good man and he would never be mixed up in something as terrible as this."

"I hope you are right."

The sheriff walked back to the gathering at the make-shift grave. In the meantime, a neighbor had brought a wagon and Niblo, along with Sam and Sheriff Barton, carefully laid the dead bodies of the Meeks family in the wagon box. "I'll escort the wagon back to Milan," Niblo told Barton.

"Thank you for doing this," said Sheriff Barton. "It saves me a long ride up to Milan.

"It's the least I can do for the mother of Gus. She's an old woman and needs a lot of help. I'll be out soon looking for the Taylor brothers," declared Niblo. "How far away do you think they have gone?"

"My guess is they are still in the neighborhood somewhere. They have a lot of family and friends who would hide them," said Barton.

"Well, if we get enough men together, we'll surely find them. Let me know how it goes with your men." Niblo remarked as he turned to mount his horse.

Chapter 3

Serena Idella Gibson was born July 18, 1875 on a farm in Benton Township, Linn County, Missouri, the oldest daughter in a family of six children born to David G. and Aragonia Johnson Gibson. The Gibson family was of sturdy southern pioneer stock.

Idella or Della, as her family had called her since birth, had been imbued with that strength. She was proud of the accomplishments of her Grandfather William F. Gibson. He and his wife, the former Rebecca Brookshire, left Tennessee and moved to Linn County, Missouri in the spring of 1835. He won the respect of his neighbors who elected him to the office of Justice of the Peace for Benton Township where he served thirteen years. He was a pillar of the community. The Gibson family was reared in the faith of the local Methodist Church where William and his family were active members. They were taught to be worthwhile upstanding citizens where a man's word was his bond. Truthfulness and honesty were taken for granted.

The local tales about George clashed with Della's upbringing, but she loved him so much she was willing to overlook the talk she heard about his escapades. The story she was about to hear would shake her to the roots of her beliefs and deliver a serious challenge to her faith.

Della's mother, Gonia, as she was known to family and friends, went over to the Carter farm to talk to Sallie Carter at the neighboring farm.

Argonia Johnson was born in Daviess County, a couple of counties to the west, the daughter of H. D. and Lucy Johnson. The family moved to Linn County when she was young, and a few years later the quiet David Gibson caught her eye. After a brief courtship, they were married on October 3, 1873.

It was hard to imagine it had been twenty years since that day. There had been hardships. One that would always lay heavy on her mind was the death of a baby boy in 1880. Then last year, when the economic slump came, they had lost the farm they had worked so hard to keep. The crop failures along with the high interest on the money borrowed to buy food just got the best of them. They owed a lot to son-in-law, George, who was letting them live on one of the farms he owned. Gonia and David had been extremely pleased when George had asked to marry their daughter, Della. He was quite a catch. Not only was he handsome, but rich, too.

Gonia had to see what Sallie knew about the tale Drue told after talking to the people gathered around the bodies.

By late afternoon, Gonia hesitantly told Della what she had learned from Sallie.

This is the story Sallie Carter told Gonia:

This morning, at just after dawn, a little girl, who looked to be about six years old, came to the door. I had no idea who she was. She had a dirty face and pieces of straw were clinging to her clothes. With her hood tucked under one arm, her long auburn hair, tangled and matted with blood, partially covered her face. The little girl's torn dress was also bloody and streaked with yellow mud. I asked the girl where she came from. The trembling little thing told me she had been asleep in the straw stack and pointed to George's field. She also said her papa and mamma and two sisters were out there, too. She thought they were dead. The little thing begged me to come help her get them out.

I immediately sent my nephew, Jimmie, out to see if he could find anything. While Jimmie went to investigate the story, I began to question the little girl more about who she was. The child said her name was Nellie Meeks. With quivering voice and tears streaming down her blood streaked face, she said her papa and mamma were killed on the hill. Up there on Jenkin's Hill by the cemetery. She said a man hit her on the head, and she went to sleep. When the two men got to that old straw stack, they threw all the family into a shallow grave. Nellie said one of the men kicked her in the back and said, 'Now they are all dead. Get them covered up and we're out of here.'

"The men threw straw and dirt on all the family. Little Nellie thought she might smother, but she didn't dare move or let on she was still alive. She said her little sister had aroused a little and began to cry. One of the men hit her with his gun butt, and she never moved again. Lying very still, Nellie says she stayed where she was until she was sure the men had gone. Clawing the straw and dirt away, she dragged herself free. Looking around, there were lights both to the north and to the west. Nellie first headed toward the light to the north but she was still dazed so she stumbled and fell down. When she got back up she was turned around so instead headed toward the light to the west, toward our place."

Della listened intently as her mother was relaying the story Sallie had told her. When her mother paused, Della said, "But why were the bodies buried on our farm? I don't understand that."

Quietly, trying to spare her daughter as much as possible, Gonia said, "The neighbors are all sayin' the Meeks family was kilt by Bill and George to keep Gus from testifyin' against Bill."

Della could hardly believe her ears. Was her mother telling her that her husband was a murderer? *He may have done some wild things in his youth, but MURDER? Last night?* That was unthinkable. She couldn't help but wonder where he was right now. *George rushed off to see Bill but why hasn't he come back?*

As if to read her daughter's thoughts, Gonia asked, "Hasn't George come back yet?"

"No, I can't imagine where he could be all this time. He'll probably come home soon."

"Well, I have to go home to get my evenin' chores done," Gonia said. "I'll send Drue up in a little while to help James with yours. Before I go, I better get those clothes off the line. A woman in your condition has no business reachin' up to take 'em down. We want this baby to be born healthy without the cord 'round its neck."

The older woman picked up the clothes basket from the floor, turned and went out the kitchen door.

Annalou Mack

"Well, here's the clothes. I'll let you fold 'em while I go on home and get my chores done. I'll come up later this evenin' to see how you're doin'."

After her mother left, Della sat, with twelve-month-old baby Flossie on her lap, and just looked out the window. It was hard to comprehend the story she had just heard from her mother. *George has been acting so strangely for the past few days. Could he and Bill really have done this terrible thing? I wish George would hurry home and tell me he is innocent.*

As the door opened, she turned to see James, the hired hand, come in. "Oh, James, do you know what they are saying about George and Bill?"

"Yeah, there's a lot a talk. And there's a posse from Grundy County and another from here out lookin' for 'em."

"What? Where have they gone?"

"Well, all I know is that this morning while we were down in the timber cuttin' posts, George and Bill rode up, jumped off their horses and walked away."

"You mean they just walked away without saying anything?" This thing was getting more mysterious by the minute. George just couldn't leave without saying anything to her.

Flossie began to whimper. Della stood up and rocked her until the whimpering stopped. "Ma'am," James said, "I better get out there and do the chores. I don't think George'll be back tonight."

Chapter 4

Sleep was impossible for Della this night. She heard the crickets chirping outside her window, and the croaking of the frogs in the little pond in the flower garden. In the distance the far away baying of some hounds announcing they had treed a 'coon mingled with the other sounds in her ears as she listened for sounds telling her George was coming home.

As she tossed and turned, she remembered the evening last September when she first had her apprehensions or maybe it was woman's intuition, how things were not right. The discussion of that September evening was as clear in her mind as if it had been the night before. Supper was over, the dishes washed, and four-month-old Flossie put to bed for the night. Della made sure George was sitting comfortably in his chair before she approached him.

With a worried expression, Della asked, "George, did Bill and those other fellows steal those cattle?"

George turned to Della and angrily replied, "I told you we wouldn't talk about such things, now didn't I? You know how upset I get when I think about how Sheriff Nibo just walked right into the bank and arrested Bill without even asking him any questions about it."

"I know, but your brother Bill has those other charges against him, and I don't want you to get mixed up in this. You won't let him talk you into anything foolish, now will you?"

"Yes, I know, Bill's had his share of problems. You would think after the community thought well enough of him to elect him to the state legislature, the law would not hound him so much. And him

14   Annalou Mack

being a lawyer and all. But maybe they are just jealous and want to bring him down."

"You're probably right," said Della. "I just worry about you. You and your brother have always been so close. And you were implicated in the check forging deal two years ago."

"Oh, well, I'll be cleared of it soon. I have better sense than to get caught up in something like that. Now let me get back to my reading and not talk about unpleasant stuff anymore."

Della recalled how she was darning one of George's socks as she sat in the chair next to her husband. She hadn't asked him any more questions, but she was worried, just the same.

Since sleep was far away, Della's thoughts turned to the Taylor and Gibson families. The Taylors were a well-respected family in the county, being among the earliest settlers to the area. George's grandparents, Isaac and Elizabeth Taylor came to Linn County, Missouri when everyone still referred to it as the "Locust Creek Country."

The lure of cheap land and the rich soil of this area had attracted settlers from the east, many coming from Virginia, Kentucky and Tennessee. Della's ancestors, the Gibsons, were also among the early residents of this county. Her grandfather came from South Carolina, by way of Tennessee and came to what later became Linn County in 1835 where he and his wife raised twelve children.

When their families arrived, about sixty percent of the surface of the land was covered with timber of every description. Some of the trees they found in abundance were white, burr, black, red and pin oak; ash, sycamore, hickory, walnut and elm. There was no want of lumber with which to build their cabins. This rolling prairie land had plenty of small streams, so water was plentiful as well.

Through hard work, these hardy pioneers cleared the land and raised their crops. They had a respect for the land and for each other. Always ready to lend a hand to a neighbor, the community was close-knit, and everyone knew what was happening on the next farm. When there was harvesting to be done, the neighbors all gathered. The same went for butchering; cutting firewood for the winter; building a new house or barn or sometimes just to get together for a shindig.

Both families were highly respected members of the community. The Taylors had done better financially than the Gibsons. They owned much of the land in the area. Her parents, David and Argonia Gibson, lived on one of George's farms. Through the years the Taylors had managed to buy up several of the farms in the area. James Taylor, Bill and George's father, would lend money to farmers with a mortgage on the farm, and when they couldn't pay, he foreclosed on them. In this way, he was able to amass a sizable holding. Each of the sons received a farm as they came of age. With this start, both the sons had been able to increase their acreage.

Della knew that William Price Taylor (Bill, as everyone called him), oldest son of James and Caroline Bingham Taylor and George's older brother, was well thought of in the community. But Della couldn't help but think about the many times Bill had been in trouble with the law. There was the time when Bill had raised a bank draft from $2 to $2,000, and there were rumors he had his younger brother George cash it at the First National Bank of Kirksville. This incident had happened in June 1891, four months before she and George were married. George was arrested, but the cashier at the bank in Kirksville could not be sure it was him. The case had not come to trial yet, and everyone she knew believed when it did, George would be cleared.

Bill was ambitious. He had read law in Judge Brinkley's office in Browning and later attended law school at the University of Missouri in Columbia. After law school, he was employed as bookkeeper in the bank in Browning and soon rose to the position of cashier. He married Maud Leonard, daughter of Morgan Leonard, one of the richest men in the county. In addition to his duties at the bank, he ran a law office. Part of his case load was as an attorney for the Chicago Burlington and Quincy Railroad.

With such an impressive beginning, Bill was easily elected as a representative to the Missouri state legislature by the Democratic Party in 1888 and the same year became mayor of Browning. His family was considered to be one of the most respectable in Linn County, and he had built a firm base of support in the county. He was sure going to need all the support he could get now that he was a murder suspect.

There was also the arson case in which Bill was arrested, charged with burning the lumber and implement house of R. L. Gibson & Brothers. At the same time, a photograph gallery adjacent was burned. Bill carried insurance on the photography building as well as its contents. It seemed clear the equipment from the building was sold to a dealer in St. Louis. The photographer identified some items as his when he went to the store in St. Louis looking to buy replacement for his equipment. The case hadn't come up for trial yet and was still pending after a change of venue to Carroll County.

Della recalled how just a week after their marriage, George and Bill were indicted by the grand jury in neighboring Adair County on the forgery case. They posted a bond and had received a change of venue. The case was still pending two years later, next was the cattle rustling and now the murders. But in spite of these scrapes the two brothers still had friends who thought the issues were just big misunderstandings.

It looked to Della as if Bill was greedy for money and she hated to see her husband get caught up in all this by his older brother. There was no doubt Bill was very intelligent. Some would call him crafty. He was a well-built man, about five feet eight, but not nearly as handsome as George. Bill wore a long, well-trimmed dark beard and always dressed in the latest fashion.

And Maud, Bill's wife. She was too haughty for Della's liking. It seemed to Della that Morgan Leonard's money had gone to Maud's head. Just because her father had been one of the richest men in the county was no reason for her to turn up her nose at Della. Maybe Maud was prettier than Della, with her long brown hair always stylishly done and those large brown eyes. But as Della's mom always told her, "Pretty is as pretty does." Three children had not done much to destroy Maud's slim figure, either. She was still as trim as when she and Bill were married eight years ago. It would have been nice if the two sisters-in-law could have been close friends since their only sisters were so much younger. Della tried to be nice to Maud and offered sympathy when Mr. Leonard died two years ago, but Maud had brushed off Della's acts of kindness.

In her sleepless mind wanderings, Della thought about what she had heard about the cattle stealing. The newspapers had said the thirty-one head of three-year-old steers had been taken out of a herd of over one hundred from the farm of Warren McCullough. They had been running in a wooded pasture on his farm about four miles north of Browning. McCullough had sold the herd to Tom Brandon, and when they went down to get them, they discovered thirty-one head were missing.

A group of men went hunting for the missing steers and found them on one of Bill's farms where he was letting a Bingham relative live. According to neighborhood talk, Abner Page, under an assumed name, ordered some railroad cars. For some reason, the cattle didn't make it to the railroad at the appointed time and had been turned out to pasture to await a future shipment.

Page was taken into custody where he told the authorities the whole story. Warrants were sworn out for the arrest of Gus Meeks, Arthur Bingham and Bill Taylor. Bingham and Taylor made bond, but the other two had remained in custody.

A change of venue was taken to Green City for October 13, 1893, but Bill always managed to get a continuance, so it had not yet come to trial. Gus Meeks and his brother-in-law Abner Page were convicted and sent to the state penitentiary to serve two years. Soon after Gus's arrival at the penitentiary, he made a confession which implicated Bill and agreed to turn State's evidence so Governor Stone pardoned Gus. He and his family were living with his mother in Milan when these dreadful murders occurred.

Late into the night Della kept going over and over these past eight months in her mind. George was not implicated in the cattle rustling, so why would he be involved in the murder of Gus and his family? It just did not make sense. She had heard rumblings how Bill was out to get Gus. *If George is involved in this awful deed, then he was persuaded by his dangerously cunning brother. Maybe George felt obligated because of the case down in Stone County when George had been accused of those killings.*

While Della was in grade school, she knew that George had gone away to the Kirksville Normal School up in Adair County for teacher's training. He then began teaching down in Stone County, in the Ozarks south of Springfield. A rumor had come back to the neighborhood how he had killed a couple men while there. His brother, Bill, a lawyer, and a member of the state legislature at the time had gotten him out of it. She never asked him about it because she thought it was just community gossip.

Without question, Bill is a shrewd man, Della thought. *But would he be clever enough to escape this? And what about George? If he would only come home and explain things to me.*

Chapter 5

Long before the sun rose, after only a few hours' sleep, Sheriff James Niblo quietly arose from the bed he shared with his wife. He was extremely careful not to wake his wife, Ruth, who was not in good health. After dressing in the dark, he rushed to the kitchen. A long day lay ahead of him so a good breakfast was essential since he didn't know when he would have a chance to eat again.

While the eggs and salt pork were cooking, James went to his son's room to wake him. "Come on, son, wake up. We need to be in the saddle by the time it's daylight. Breakfast is about ready."

Sam and James ate heartily then hurried out to the barn to saddle their horses. Unnecessary words were not needed because they both knew the important job that lay ahead.

"Sam, you go spread the word we need a dozen or so good horsemen to form a posse to catch those murdering Taylors. I'll go to the office to see if any messages have come in during the night. We'll meet in front of the jail at dawn."

Just as the sun was peeking over the horizon, James heard the clatter of horses' hooves in the street. Pulling his hat down securely on his head, he went out to greet and give instructions to the men who would be his posse for the day.

"Men, I'm sure all of you have heard of the terrible crime committed by the Taylor brothers night before last. They told me as soon as the bodies of the Meeks family were found, George and Bill Taylor rode their horses to their father, Jim Taylor's place. But they left the horses and took off on foot. We need to find them and bring them back to face a trial. There will be posses from Linn

Annalou Mack

and probably Grundy County out there, too, so watch your step and don't shoot one of your neighbors. We are going to ride east toward the Chariton River. If you come up with the Taylors, restrain them and send me a signal. Be careful and good luck." Without another word, James mounted his horse and led the posse out of town.

They had not gone far when others rode up to join the group. Farmers and businessmen alike left their work to take part in hunting the Taylor brothers. Any male old enough to sit a horse came armed with a double-barreled shotgun or a Winchester rifle ready to pursue the suspected murderers.

It was still early morning when the posse arrived at the George Taylor farm. They all dismounted, rushed up to the door of the farmhouse and began using their fists to pound on the door.

When Della heard this loud pounding on the door, she sprang out of bed and hurriedly put on her robe. Before she could get to the front room, the door burst open. She recognized Sheriff Niblo and behind him were half a dozen men, all looking excited, waving their arms and shouting. The sheriff's loud, angry voice was able to drown out those of the other men.

"Where is George? We've looked everywhere. I'm sure you are hiding him somewhere. You better hand him over if you know what's good for you."

Wide-eyed, scared half out of her wits, Della begins crying. "I don't know where George is. He didn't do this awful thing you are accusing him of." Sobs wracking her body she moaned, "If you did find him, you would just hang him without giving him a chance to defend himself."

The posse members roughly pushed her aside and began going from room to room, searching in every corner. Every piece of furniture was moved, the coats removed from the hall closet, food removed from the shelves in the pantry. Where did they think she could be hiding him? They ignored her sobs and pleading, "Please be quieter, you'll wake the baby."

Sure enough, Flossie began to cry. Della hurried to pick her up and tried to calm her. Meanwhile, the men came back to the front room and told the sheriff they couldn't find any sign George had been there.

Niblo turned to the posse, "We'll search the barn and other buildings. He's a crafty one, so you men spread out and search every inch of the place."

Before he left the sheriff said to Della, "Missy, if George shows up, you had best let me know. If I find you've been hiding him or helping him, I'll arrest you, too."

As soon as all the men were gone, Della put Flossie on the floor, sat down at the kitchen table, put her head down and cried long and hard. *What am I going to do? How can I make it here alone? How long before George will be back?* She didn't know if she was strong enough to make it through this.

She had only been sitting there a few minutes when Gonia opened the door. "I bet I can guess what all those men are doin' out there."

"Yes, they came bustin' in here and ransacked the place trying to find George. They woke up Flossie, but of course, they didn't find anything. George knows enough not to come back here. With their hot tempers, they'll hang him in an instant without trying to find out the truth."

"I'll fix you some breakfast. You just sit there and rest for a while. Maybe some coffee would do you good. Have ya fed Flossie yet?"

"No, I just put her down to play for a little while. I'll nurse her and then go get dressed. The sheriff and posse were so riled up I couldn't do anything but stand there and watch them. They were so rough, pushin' me around. Some of them are our neighbors. You would think they would have a little better manners."

"I know. I'll get the fire goin' in the cook stove and have some coffee and vittles ready soon. You feed Flossie and get dressed."

Della picked up a towel and wiped her eyes, then lifted Flossie to her lap and nursed her. "I'm going to have to wean you," she said to the baby girl while she twisted the child's ringlets with one hand and patted her with the other. "There won't be enough here for you and the new one. Ma, could you stir up some gravy? I'll feed some to Flossie this morning. When the boys get through with the chores, they will want some, too."

It wasn't long before Drue and James came in the house. "Ma'am, those men are sure goin' through everything out there. Do they think

George would be stupid enough to come back here and hide in the barn?" said James.

"I wouldn't want to be around if they caught him," Drue said. "They were throwin' stuff around, and lookin' in everything. Did they think he would be in the rain barrel?"

"Boys," said Gonia, "I'll have you some grub ready in a few minutes. I'm fixin' some gravy for Flossie. Would you two like some too?"

"Yes, ma'am," they both chimed in unison.

"Dellie, the old sow is gonna have pigs soon. Do you want us to pen her up? By the time we finish breakfast, those guys should be gone, and we can finish the chores."

"Yes, James, that would be a good idea."

Della put Flossie down to toddle around the kitchen while she went to her bedroom to dress for the day. Having her mother, brother, and the hired man here with her had settled her nerves a little. She put on her everyday dress and tied an apron over it. Aprons were easier to wash than dresses and didn't take as much material to make, either.

The boys were eating their eggs, biscuits and gravy when Della got back to the kitchen. She picked up Flossie and filled her plate with some of the good smelling breakfast. She was actually too upset to eat, but she knew she had to in order to keep up her strength for the new one. After every two or three bites, she would give a bite to Flossie, who seemed to enjoy eating.

James and Drue had finished breakfast and left the house to make ready the sow for her coming litter when David, Della's father, came rushing in.

"Do you know what that dern fool posse did to me? They came bustin' into the house yelling, 'Where's George Taylor?' Of course, I told them I didn't know anything about George. They didn't believe me. They grabbed me and drug me outside and was gonna lynch me if I didn't tell them where he is. Finally, I was able to convince them I didn't know anything about his whereabouts. Those men are crazy! Were they up here, too?"

"Yes, Pa. They woke me up this morning and searched the house and all the outbuildings. I can't believe some of these men who have known us all our lives would turn on us in such a way. They know what good, upstanding people we are. I don't understand how all this could have happened."

"Well, honey, I'm afraid you may have ta face up to the fact your husband, George, is not as well thought of as you expected. He's been involved in some disreputable dealings, and he is easily influenced by his big brother, Bill. Brace yourself for what may be in the future."

Della just shook her head and said, "No, Pa. I know George couldn't have done this awful thing. He is so kind and gentle. I love him and I won't think he would kill a whole family."

"Dellie, you're young. You have ta know if George is caught he will probably be hung."

"I just won't believe it. I know Bill is a bad influence on George, but George is a good person, and we have to help him. If they are caught and go to trial, we have to say George was home the other night."

"No, Dellie. I'm sorry, but I won't lie. You know he wasn't home, just as I do. I love you dearly, but I will not lie about it."

"Well, we'll talk more about it when the time comes."

"Goni, I'm goin' back home. I hope all those idiots are gone by now. When are you comin' home?"

"I need ta stay and help Dellie for a while. I'll be home later an' fix you some dinner. What're you doin' today?"

"I have to replant some corn. Drue will help me. It may take most of the day, but I'll come in at noon when you call us." He turned and went out the door.

"Ma, you'll say George was home night before last, won't you?"

"I don't know, honey. I'll have to think about it. We'll just have ta take it one day at a time and see what happens."

Chapter 6

Bright and early each morning, Sheriff Niblo rallied his posse of volunteers to lead the search for George and Bill Taylor.

It was common practice for local law enforcement to assemble a group of men who had the mounts and firearms available to help in searching for suspects. The heinousness of this crime was such that any able-bodied man in the four-county area was willing and anxious to join a posse for this task.

The days were spent in combing the timber and hills east and southeast of Milan. This is the prairie area of Missouri, and while it may appear flat, there are small hills and valleys which are rough enough to slow a posse down as they try to search the entire area.

The Chariton River Bottoms include the Locust Creek and Medicine Creek tributaries which contain many small valleys and ravines. Niblo's posse was sure this was the region where the Taylor brothers were hiding. The areas not cleared for farming included not only brush, but stands of cottonwood, oak, maple, hickory, and birch trees. It was not an easy ride for the group.

The mounted horsemen rode through fields where sprouts of corn were just peeking through the ground or gleaming fields of bluegrass which would soon be cut for hay or brilliant green fields of wheat. These were the crops in the sandy-clayey rich soil of the area which the residents depended upon for their livelihood. When possible, the men rode down the rows or along the edges to keep from damaging the spring crops.

At one point the posse surrounded a house where it was thought the fugitives were hiding. Shots were fired, but no one was injured.

It was not the Taylors. The occupants of the house were surprised when they saw this large group of armed men coming toward their house and fired at them. The group returned the gunfire, but it was soon determined the fugitives were not there. The posse disbursed to look elsewhere.

Sheriff Niblo led the group down to Browning where several people told him how last night a couple of horses were stolen east of town. He also heard a story that the fugitives had stayed at a farmhouse last night not far from Browning. Another said four men had tracked the Taylor brothers to their father's house. He refused to allow the trackers to enter and told them not to come around again.

Later the posses from other jurisdictions were seen combing the region for the Taylor brothers. The estimate was as many as a thousand men were in pursuit of the murderers of the Meeks family.

Word also reached Niblo that bloodhounds were being brought from Grundy County to be put on the trail of the fugitives. He was hopeful this would flush out the murderers.

At dusk, the trail weary group led by Sheriff Niblo made their way back into Milan empty handed. It had been a hard day of riding through timber and brush-covered terrain with nothing to show for their efforts. Grumblings came from several members, but most assured Sheriff Niblo they would be back tomorrow to continue the hunt.

Bone weary, James and Sam trudged home disappointed their search for the fugitives had not been successful. James said to Sam, "Even though George Taylor's wife doesn't think he had anything to do with the murders, I'll bet he did. That brother of his is nothing but trouble, and George isn't much better himself. I don't care if Bill Taylor was elected to the state house; he is a bad one. I'll do my best to see the two of them are convicted of this terrible crime. Son, tomorrow I want you to lead the posse, I have some things to attend to here in Milan."

The next morning after seeing Sam and the posse off, James went to the home where Gus Meeks and his family had lived with his mother, Martha Meeks. On a slight knoll, the small dwelling was near the edge of town sitting beside other houses very much like this one. A small wooden porch led to the front door. Along the side of the house James saw a clothesline with a few freshly washed clothes blowing in the light breeze.

Climbing up the wooden steps to the porch, the sheriff crossed the warping boards and knocked on the front door where he was greeted by the elderly woman. "Good morning, Mrs. Meeks. May I come in and talk with you for a spell?"

"Well, I s'pose. What do ya want to talk about?"

"I just want to hear from you about the other night. I am so sorry this happened. I know Gus had been in some trouble but if he wanted to go straight, he could have had a good life here in Milan."

"I told 'im not to get mixed up with the Taylor bunch. Gus was a good boy, but he'd fallen on some bad times, what with the cattle rustlin' deal then the fire that burned down their house. That's why they were livin' here with me. But he thought Bill Taylor was gonna do right by 'im, what with offerin' 'im money and all. I knowed it would not turn out good. Delora, his wife, and I both begged 'im not to go, but he wouldn't listen."

"This was a terrible thing. I'll do everything I can to help bring the Taylors to justice."

"While yo're here I'll give you this note Gus got the morning they left."

Sheriff Niblo took the note and looked at the small scrap of paper written on the letterhead of the Bank of Browning where Bill Taylor was a cashier. It said, "Browning, Mo., May 10, 1894. Be ready at ten o'clock, everything is right."

"This isn't signed. Are you sure it came from Bill Taylor?"

"Yes, I'm sure. I knowed it was him, and I knowed it was him and his brother who came for 'im Thursday night. They didn't want all the family to go, but Delora wouldn't let Gus go without her and the kids. She thought it'd keep 'im safe. Instead, it got her and the girls kilt, too."

"How is little Nellie doing? This is so horrible for her."

"I guess she's as well as can be expected. She woke up with a nightmare last night. I'm an old woman, and I don't know if I can raise her. I'm just barely able to care for myself. And my son George, who lives here in this small house is blind. Do you know if there's anyone who could care for her proper?"

"Let me see what I can do about it. Thank you for your time, Mrs. Meeks, and for this note. I'm sure it will help in the prosecution. If I can be of help to you, be sure to let me know."

He let himself out and started back to his office.

After leaving the Meeks home, Sheriff Niblo stopped by the office of Benjamin F. Pierce, Prosecuting Attorney for Sullivan County. Ben looked up from the file he was reading and said, "Hi Jim. What brings you around here this morning? Have you arrested those treacherous Taylor brothers yet?"

"No, Ben, but we're trying. The posse left again early this morning. I can't believe they've gone far away this quick. Probably some of their family is hiding them."

"You may be right. They still have those other cases against them—the check cashing, the arson and the cattle rustling—which have not been tried yet."

"Yes, I arrested George on the check cashing fraud and Bill on the cattle rustling deal, but the arson case had kind of slipped my mind."

Ben began telling James the details of the arson case. It all started with a disagreement with Beverly Bolling, owner of the only bank in Browning at the time. Bill Taylor was an employee of the bank, but he also practiced law on the side. There were rumors he had defrauded a client who had hired Bill to collect back payment on a pension. The widow's story was how Bill collected the money but did not give any of it to her. Since Bill was the Bolling Bank cashier, this did not sit well with Beverly Bolling, and Bill was fired.

To get even, Bill Taylor convinced his father-in-law, Morgan Leonard, to open another bank in Browning. Thus, the Peoples Exchange Bank of Browning was opened with Bill as the cashier. Even so, Bill still held a grudge against Beverly Bolling and devised a plan to bring down the law on Bolling.

Bill's plan was to burn a lumber yard in Browning and place the blame on Bolling. Bill advanced a sum of money to a young photographer to buy a camera and equipment. He built a structure on the lot next to the lumber yard to house the photography studio. Bill Taylor insured the building and contents heavily in his name. Later the lumber yard and the photography studio burned to the ground. When the photographer looked for camera parts in the remains of the fire, nothing was found.

An acquaintance of Bill Taylor went to the prosecuting attorney saying he had seen Beverly Bolling the night of the fire near the lumber yard with what looked like a lighted lantern. The investigation did not find grounds to charge Bolling.

Hoping to continue his plans for a photography business, the photographer looked at pawn shops in St. Louis for equipment. To his surprise, he found his own camera and instruments for sale. The proprietor of the shop described the person who sold him the equipment. The photographer recognized the description matched Bill Taylor. Bill had already collected the insurance for the building and contents.

Ben continued, "Bill Taylor was indicted by the Linn County grand jury in December of 1892 for the crime, but it has been continued a couple of times since then. It may not matter now with these crimes hanging over his head."

"That's true. Well, I have something which may be of help when the case comes to trial. Mrs. Meeks, Gus's mother gave me this note. Gus received it the day of the murder. Although it isn't signed, it looks pretty certain it was sent by Bill Taylor."

Ben studied the note carefully. "Yes, this looks like a great piece of evidence. Thanks for bringing it to me."

James twisted his hat in his hands, seeming to be not sure how to bring up the next thing he came to see Pierce about. He looked up from his hat. "There is something else I learned from Mrs. Meeks. She is an old woman without much money. Her blind son, George lives with her in a small, run-down, one-bedroom house. They do not have the money or strength to care for a little girl of Nellie's age. Ben, do you know anyone who would be willing to take Little Nellie and raise her?"

"Let me think on it for a while and get back with you."

"I'd be much obliged if you would. My wife is not well enough to take on such a responsibility, or I would take her myself. The poor little thing has had more than anyone should have to bear. No wonder she has nightmares."

"Let me talk to my wife about this. Something can be done to help, I'm sure."

"The funeral is tomorrow, so I'll see you there."

Chapter 7

Sleep was fitful for Della after she finally dozed off. About two o'clock she heard Flossie moving around in her crib. Della got up, fed her and rocked her until she went back to sleep. For Della, sleep was impossible. Slipping on a robe, she walked out into the yard. There was a small stream just behind the barn where Della liked to sit on a log and listen to the water flow over the rocks. Maybe if she sat there for a few minutes it would take her mind off the awful things happening.

Slowly she crept to the log in the darkness. After a few minutes of listening to the stream murmuring and the frogs croaking, she began to relax. She could feel the stress lessening from her. It was peaceful here. Her nerves were beginning to calm.

Suddenly a hand clamped over her mouth. Her heart nearly jumped out of her body as she tried to stand but was held down by the hand of someone kneeling behind her. Whispering into her ear, a voice said, "Don't make any sound. It's me, George. The place is covered with members of the posses. In a few minutes, meet me over by the big, old apple tree in the orchard. Walk slowly and don't act as if anything is unusual. Don't turn around now, you may be watched."

Her breath coming in short gulps, it was all Della could do to sit still. She had to force herself to stay calm and to not turn around to see if it was truly George who had been there. She found it difficult to imagine there were men on her farm watching her but if George said there were, then it was probably true.

After a few minutes, Della rose from the log, stretched her arms up and yawned as if she were sleepy. Carefully she sauntered back toward the yard, meandering through the orchard. When she came to the big, old apple tree, she stopped. The old tree was covered with blossoms indicating there would be a good apple crop this year. It was a huge tree, large enough to hide two people easily.

No one was in sight, so she began to wonder if she had been dreaming that George had actually been there behind her on the log. Suddenly he was beside her. He pulled her to him and gave her a long, hard kiss.

"I'm so sorry to have to put you through this, sweetheart. There is a mob everywhere ready to lynch me and Bill, so we have to leave for a while. We need food and water because we don't know where we're going. The homes of all our families are being watched, so we have to be very careful. Can you go back in the house and put some food in a bag along with a canteen of water? Don't come back here, bring it to the outhouse. Hide it under your robe. I doubt anyone would be suspicious of you going there."

"Of course, darling, I'll gather some meat and potatoes in a bag and fill a canteen with water. George, please tell me you didn't kill those people."

"Honey, how could you even suspect that I did such a thing? They just have it in for us and don't know the whole story. You better go before someone finds us."

Della tried to walk unhurriedly back to the house, but her heart was still beating so fast she thought it would jump right out of her chest. She knew George could not have done the awful things they were saying about him. George had just told her he didn't do it so she had to believe him.

As soon as Della got in the house she lit a small candle in the kitchen. She didn't want much light, but she had to have a little to find the things she needed. She acted as if she was getting herself a snack while she gathered some potatoes from the bin. A slab of salt pork would keep well for George and Bill. Trying to be as surreptitious as possible, she put the meat and potatoes into a clean flour sack she had not yet ripped apart. There was a bucket of water on the washstand. Taking the canteen from the wall, she filled it with clean drinking water, all the while being as sneaky as she possibly could. With those things hidden under her robe, the young mother again went out the back door toward the outhouse.

Della had had suspicions, but now she needed to believe her husband. She loved him so much and with the new baby due soon, it was necessary for her to trust he was truthful when he said he wasn't involved with the murder of the Meeks family. This time she hurried along the path to the outhouse. It was very believable a woman in her condition would need to hurry to relieve herself.

When Della opened the door, she knew George was already inside. Hunting with his friends had taught him how to be stealthy when tracking an animal. Those tricks were of good use to him now as he was outwitting the posse.

George quickly grabbed the items his wife brought him. "Bill and I have to get on our way before daylight. I can't stay now, but I'll see you again as soon as this blows over. Remember, tell everyone who asks, I was home last night so I couldn't have been out killing those people. I love you Della, and take good care of Flossie until I get back."

"George, I love you so much. Come back to your family as soon as possible." She threw her arms around her husband's neck and kissed him. "I'll go out first and hurry back to the house. You be very careful not to get caught. I don't want to see you hanged."

Drawing her robe tightly around her, Della hurried back to the house without looking back towards the outhouse. She felt now as if she could sleep the remainder of the night.

Chapter 8

Early Sunday morning Sheriff James Niblo, his wife Ruth and son Sam, joined a crowd of citizens from Milan for the funeral of the Meeks family. This tragedy had touched everyone who heard of it. The community pulled together to make caskets for each of the family members and because their clothing was missing, provided clean clothes to dress the bodies. By eight o'clock in the morning long lines of buggies, wagons and persons on horseback were seen making their way to the cemetery where the Meeks family was to be buried.

The trek to the Bute Cemetery southeast of Milan was a long one for the group of mourners and spectators. The almost twelve miles distance from Milan to the cemetery was about the same from Browning. No one in the area wanted to miss this gathering. There were probably a thousand persons crowded into the cemetery for the two o'clock services. This murder shook the community as nothing had in the past.

It was a beautiful spring day. The fresh green grass lining the roadway was washed clean with recent rain. Colorful wildflowers bursting with their blossoms would have made for a pleasant trip had it not been for the solemnity of the occasion. Warm sunshine and a soft breeze had quickly dried the roads.

Sheriff Niblo kept a close eye on the carriage in which little Nellie Meeks was riding. As the lone survivor of the massacre of her family, it was possible her life was now in danger. She was the only witness to what happened that fateful night. There was always the possibility with such a large crowd, someone could sneak close to her and make off with her. The sheriff knew he had to find a safe place for her to stay. He would talk to Ben Pierce again.

Farmers living near the cemetery dug the graves where the rough caskets lay side by side. The Reverend Pollard of Milan, with Bible in hand, delivered an appropriate eulogy for the family. He sadly remarked upon the brevity of life and how this family was cut down after such a short time on earth. There were few dry eyes in the crowd during his sermon.

Mrs. Meeks, dressed in black, could not hold back her racking sobs. Little Nellie dressed in a torn dress too small for her, tried to hold back her tears and comfort her grandmother. The wound on her head was covered by her long, blond hair. The only clothes Nellie had were those she was wearing the night of the murder.

After the services, Sheriff Niblo found Prosecutor Pierce. "Ben, have you thought about where little Nellie can stay?"

"Yes, my wife, Sarah, and I had a long talk about it, and we believe we could make a good home for her. Nellie should fit in well with our big brood. We have a couple of daughters a little older who are glad to have a little sister."

"That's great," said Niblo with a nod of his head. "I know you will take good care of her. She is a cute little girl and seems to have a sweet personality. After we get home from the funeral, I will talk to Mrs. Meeks. I'm sure it will be a relief to her."

"Good. Bring Little Nellie by either tonight or in the morning."

"Thanks, Ben. This makes me feel better."

As soon as he arrived home, the sheriff made a visit to Martha Meeks. After this long day, Nellie was already asleep when Martha answered his knock.

"Mrs. Meeks, I know you are having a hard time now with the murders, the funeral, and the long drive to the cemetery today. I won't stay long. I just wanted to tell you Ben Pierce has offered to take Nellie to live with them. He has a comfortable home and will take good care of her. Will it be agreeable to you?"

"Laws a mercy. That is wonderful. I have been wonderin' how I was gonna be able to feed another mouth even though she is my granddaughter. She is a lovely, sweet girl, and I want her to have the best, but I just can't do it. Most every night she wakes up screaming. Hopefully, the Pierce's will be able to calm her and help her through this awful nightmare."

"Then, tomorrow morning I'll come by and take her to the Pierce home. Say about nine o'clock?"

"I'll have 'er ready by then. I'll miss havin' her but she needs more than I can give right now. Thank you so much, Sheriff."

In the morning, at the appointed time, Sheriff Niblo arrived at the Meeks home. As soon as he knocked, Mrs. Meeks opened the door with little Nellie beside her grandmother dressed the same as yesterday.

Niblo kneeled down to speak to the little girl, "Nellie, Mr. and Mrs. Pierce would like for you to live with them for a while. They have kids about your age. They won't take the place of your Ma and Pa, but they are good, kind people and they will give you a good home. Does it sound alright to you?"

"Yes, Sheriff Niblo, it will be okay, but I sure miss my Ma and Pa and little sisters."

Sarah and Ben Pierce opened the door to the Sheriff's knock. "Come in, come in. We've been waiting for you. My, what a beautiful little girl you are, Nellie. My daughters have been so excited since I told them you were coming to live with us. Flora, come here and take Nellie to your room. Sarah, you can help."

Nellie looked around the room and could hardly believe her eyes. *This huge house with all those rooms.* She had never seen a house this big before.

Flora and her sister Sarah came running to meet Nellie and talking as fast as their mouths would move. Shy at first, Nellie was soon talking to the girls like she had known them a long time. In a short while, the three girls trotted off upstairs to the room they would share.

After the girls had left, Sheriff Niblo thanked Mrs. Pierce and hurried back to his office to take care of business. He felt confident Nellie would adjust soon to her new home.

Chapter 9

The dog's repeated barking alerted Della that someone was coming. From the window she saw a horse and buggy approaching. As they get closer, she recognized her cousin; her best friend, Addie. They haven't seen each other since the awful day when the Meeks family was found dead on George and Della's farm.

Addie, the daughter of James Gibson, older brother of Della's father, David, was only a few months younger than Della. They were close from birth and at school had been almost inseparable. A few years ago both were pupils in the school taught by George Taylor, now Della's husband.

Carefully picking up little Flossie and placing her on her hip, Della quickly opened the door and hurried out to the buggy. Addie climbed down and hitched the horse to the rail before lifting out her baby Pearl. Both of them put their babies down on the ground and the two women rush into each other's arms.

"Addie, I am so glad to see you! I've missed you so much. So much has happened since I last saw you. It's been terrible!"

"Oh, Dellie, I've heard horrible stories about what's been happening this last week. It wasn't possible for me to get over here to see you until now. How are you?"

"I'm beside myself with worry. It has been hard with all the turmoil, George gone, and the posse harassing me about where he is. And then the new baby is due soon. I'm so glad Ma and Pa live close. I don't know what I would do without them. Come on in the house. I'll make some coffee, and we'll catch up on what's happening."

"Yes, Dellie," Using her pet name. "I'm so anxious to hear from you about all that's been going on. You must be beside yourself."

The two cousins walked towards the house, Della taking Flossie's hand and Addie carrying Pearl. Flossie had celebrated her first birthday earlier in the month and was just beginning to walk so the going was slow. Pearl would have her first birthday in about six weeks, and although she was crawling everywhere, she had yet to take her first steps.

Addie, a tall and slender young woman, had reddish-brown hair and a face full of freckles. Her bright, blue eyes complemented her pale, creamy skin. Although, at times when they were younger, people may have thought they were twins, no one would make such a mistake now.

Even without the added weight of the baby, Della tended to carry a little too much weight. Her short stature caused any added pounds to make her look heavier. Della's clear complexion set off her beautiful blue eyes, now puffy from too much crying.

In the house, Addie and Della sat the two little ones on the floor where they began reaching for each other and trying to communicate as best they could. Addie settled at the table where they could watch the children while talking. Della fixed the coffee to perk and then sat down to listen to what Addie was saying.

"I have to ask you—did Bill and George commit those gruesome murders? I'm not too surprised at Bill, but it's hard for me to think of George being involved in such a horrible thing."

"The folks around here seem to think they did. I don't want to believe it. George may have pulled some shady deals in the past, but I just don't think he would commit murder. It's awful to have lawmen and their bands of armed men constantly watching, sometimes forcing their way in, questioning me, Ma and Pa and the rest of the family. They even got rough with me one time. Ma came to see what the commotion was, or I don't know what would have happened. I don't know where George is, but the community is so worked up over the murders they will hang both Bill and George in a minute if they find them." Della got up to serve the now ready coffee and continued, "But, Addie, let's don't talk about it right now. I want to know about you and Jim and Pearl. We can talk about something to take my mind off all this trouble." Della slowly rose from the chair to pour another cup of coffee. Putting her hand on her back she said, "This baby is so active it keeps me awake at night, and my back hurts so much. I'll be glad when it gets here. I know George wants a boy, and I do, too."

"Oh, Dellie, I know this is all so hard for you, especially now. Jim and I are getting along fine. Pearl has several teeth which made her pretty cranky when she was cutting them. I'm not ready to have another baby. I hope we can wait a few years. One at a time is enough for me."

"I never expected to have two babies so close together. Flossie is such a good little girl, and I've been weaning her, so a baby won't be much more trouble. At least I hope not. Ma is so good to help, but she has her own house to take care of."

The two women settled in talking about younger and happier days.

Addie recalled the day at school when their teacher, George, pulled Della out of a daydream.

"Della, can you stay after school for a few minutes?"

"Yes, sir, I can."

"What have you done now?" whispered Addie.

"I haven't done anything. I don't know why he wants to see me. He's always had it in for me ever since I caught him kissing Mary one day when I forgot my gloves and came back to school for them. I'm sure it's nothing important."

"Shhh, we better get our noses in this book before he calls us up to the front for talking."

Actually George did not scold Della when they talked. Instead he asked her to go with him to the dance the following Saturday. Della was shocked. George was such a handsome older man and could have his pick of any of the girls in the neighborhood. Why did he pick her? But she was flattered. From then on, George and Della began seeing each other regularly during the summer while school was not in session. They were married in October of that fall.

Addie and Della reminisced about those times when both were young and in love. Addie and her husband, James (Jim) Holding were neighbors when they began dating. It seemed natural for them to marry not long after George and Della. The two couples had babies within months of each other. They grew up from teenagers to wives and mothers almost overnight. The terrible tragedy which recently happened was sobering. The bright future the two women had expected had turned gloomy, at least for Della.

After a couple of hours of sharing talk about their lives, Addie said, "Dellie, I must get home to prepare supper for Jim. I wish there was something I could do to help you."

Addie picked up little Pearl, put on her bonnet and with a parting hug, started out to unhitch the horse.

"Do tell me when anything else happens. Let me know if there is anything I can do to help. And be sure to tell me when the new baby comes. Maybe I can get away to stay with you for a few days. I'll ask Jim what he thinks. Bye, Bye."

"I'm so glad you came. I have wanted to see you ever since this trouble began. Bye now and have a good evening."

Chapter 10

Della's parents, brothers, and sister were nearly finished eating with Della at her house when they saw a wagon and a buggy stop in front of the house. There had been many people traipsing around the farm since the murders were discovered so it was no longer a novelty to have someone snooping around. This time two men climbed down from the wagon and walked up the path to the house. Dave Gibson, Della's father, went out on the porch to see what they wanted. He guessed they were seeking the whereabouts of George and Bill. Because of the newly announced reward, it seemed to be what everybody was concerned with nowadays.

Dave had just read on Saturday morning in *The Brookfield Gazette* this article:

> Governor Stone offered a reward of $300 on the part of the state for each of the two Taylors yesterday. The rewards offered by the county and private citizens heretofore announced amount to about $2000, and the $600 offered by the State swells the total reward offered to about $2600. [1]

The tall man introduced himself as Garnett Atkins, and the smaller one said he was Orville Shelby. "We would like to come in and talk with you for a spell, said Atkins."

Dave ushered them into the dining room. "Have a seat, we have just finished dinner. There is food left if you would like to have a plate."

"No, thank you. We just want some information." Looking at Mrs. Gibson, Atkins said, "Hello, Goni. I haven't seen you for quite a while."

"Yes, it has been a long time since we were in school together, Garnett. What are ya' doin' in this neck of the woods?"

Annalou Mack

"A bunch of men, including the U.S. Deputy Marshall from Kansas City, asked me to bring them by to see if you knew where Bill and George are hiding. Since I knew you folks, I agreed for Shelby and me to come in and talk while they stayed outside with the teams and wagons."

"It seems like every man and his dog from the six-county area around here are out after the reward money," said Dave. "We don't know where those two are and we're getting pretty tired of all the people comin' around and bothering us."

"I'm sure it's getting old. But you can't blame the people for wanting to see them brought back here to face the charges. Goni, I heard you were here on the night of May 10th."

"Yes, Dellie here was not feelin' well, so we came up to stay with her. As you can see, she is in a family way, and we didn't want her to be alone. We knew George was goin' to Browning with some wagon wheels. I wanted ta help Della with the baby, so we came up and decided to stay the night."

"It turned out to be quite a night I guess," said Shelby.

Goni Gibson let out a big sigh. "Oh, the murder of the Meeks family is dreadful. It's hard for me to believe George is mixed up in it. However, I do know he didn't come home that night. He left with his father's team and wagon in the middle of the afternoon saying he wouldn't be home for supper. Dave went upstairs to bed between eight and nine. Since she was not feelin' well, Della also went to bed. I stayed up until about ten o'clock, but George hadn't come home yet so I went up to bed, too.

"Durin' the night I heard little Flossie crying, so I went downstairs to get her from Della's bed. I then noticed George still wasn't home. About four when I heard the wagon, I got up to let him in. I don't know if he had anything to do with the murders, but it doesn't look good them runnin' off in such a hurry."

"No," said Shelby, "it doesn't look good. Governor Stone is very anxious to bring the two of them back for trial. If you have any ideas as to where they might be, we would like to hear them. They will be safer if we can discovers their whereabouts before the mob that wants to lynch them."

Dave was showing his displeasure at the intrusion. "We haven't heard a word from George since he took off that morning. People have been harassing us ever since then. And now we have two farms to tend, with two less men to do it because Sheriff Barton arrested our hired hand the other day."

"Sorry to have bothered you, Mr. and Mrs. Gibson. You too, Mrs. Taylor. We will be on our way now. Thank you for talking to us. Good to see you again, Goni."

The two men walked on out to the wagon where the rest of the group had waited. The others in the room were silent for a few minutes trying to think about what had just happened.

"Ma, I don't think you should have said what you did about George not being home that night. I know he wasn't home, but I'm sure he didn't have anything to do with those awful murders. He will explain it all when he gets back. Until he comes home, I don't think we should be talking to strangers about it."

Mrs. Gibson was taken aback at hearing the criticism from Della. "I was only makin' conversation to let 'em know we didn't know where George is. I've knowed Garnett Adkins since we was kids. He's a good man. If I hadn't talked to 'em, the men with him and Mr. Shelby might have started searching the place. There has been enough of that already.

"Come on now, put Flossie down and help me wash up the dinner dishes."

Chapter 11

Sheriff Niblo was determined to bring the murderers of the Meeks family to justice. Day after day, he saddled his horse early in the morning and led a posse in the pursuit of the Taylor brothers. The perpetrators of this unspeakable crime could not go unpunished.

Rumors were flying everywhere. One said the Taylors were seen at the home of George Leonard, Bill's brother-in-law. When a posse from Brookfield searched his house, it was reported two men were seen leaving a nearby cave and escaped in the dark. Another rumor was that when a stolen horse returned home, they thought the Taylors had ridden it as long as it would go and then released it and took to the woods.

Every county bordering Sullivan and Linn sent men in search of the two men. Guards were placed along the OK Railroad line through the wooded country between Green Castle and Kirksville. Everyone seemed to believe the fugitives would travel eastward toward the Chariton River since it was an exceedingly rough portion of the state. The area was very hilly and covered with woods and underbrush. The strip of timber between the Chariton River and the Mussel Fork was about ten miles wide, reaching north to the Iowa line. It seemed a very good place for fugitives to conceal themselves.

Sheriff Niblo of Sullivan County and Sheriff Edward Barton of Linn County met near Browning a week after the murders to confer. They needed to try to make some organization out of the search, which so far had been futile. The two figured that as many as a thousand men had been in the saddle in pursuit of the Taylors, and no one had found a sign of their whereabouts.

"Ed, what is your take on the situation thus far?" said Niblo with a worried look.

"Well, James, we have run down so many leads that we thought were reliable, I am getting disheartened. Every day there are at least two hundred men out here combing the area for a sight of those scoundrels. Some of the men have given as many as four days for this. This is a tragedy like no other in the history of Linn County." Barton's furrowed brow emphasized his words.

"Yes, I know. It's the same in Sullivan. And those reprobates have many friends who have spread rumors and false reports trying to hinder us in every way possible. I still think George was around somewhere when I searched their house and barn. His wife, Della would hide him if she could, I'm sure."

"Also, I think our not being able to capture them has caused near panic, especially in Browning," said Barton. "People are afraid to open their doors. All are wondering if perhaps their neighbor is hiding the Taylors. And it is looking more and more like it will be a while before they are captured."

The two sheriffs were sure the fugitives were still hiding in the region. They felt they needed to make a more systematic search. Sheriff Barton told James his deputies had arrested Jim Harris and another local, L. C. Phillips. It was thought that Young Harris, George Taylor's farm hand, was an accomplice. The rumor was that Phillips was feeding the murderers. The lawmen seemed pretty sure the Taylors had help in the massacre.

"It was too bad there was no luck with the blood hounds," said Sheriff Barton with a scowl.

"Yes Ed, it would have saved all of us a lot of trouble if it had worked out."

Niblo was referring to how Sheriff Winters of Grundy County had brought his three blood hounds over on Sunday morning even though the trail was cold by then. In spite of the delay, the hounds were making progress when they were approached by a messenger who told the sheriff the Taylor brothers had been seen about a mile southwest of North Salem that morning. Sheriff Winters and the hounds moved up to the place where it was said the Taylors were seen but no trace of them was found.

"You know, James, by Wednesday evening the Brookfield delegation returned home from the chase. Many of them had been in the saddle almost continuously. They had chased false rumors until they were completely exhausted, and returned home to rest, and wait for something authentic."

Sheriff Barton went on, "One thing I will say further, the men who have been riding in the posses are not bloodthirsty mobs. All of the members are genuinely trying to bring the culprits to justice. If there happened to be a lynching, it would not be from citizens of the posse. These men are from all walks of life and are doing it for the sake of law and order. We must give them credit for that.

"I guess you heard how sixty men slept in Mr. Thudium's barn Saturday night. Sunday morning Mrs. Thudium prepared breakfast for all these men. Those are the kind of people involved in this hunt."

During their conversation, the calling of the deputy U.S. Marshall, B. G. Pierman, was discussed. Governor Stone was willing to pull out all the stops to capture the Taylors. He had commissioned six men as special officers specifically for hunting down the criminals. All of the officers had experience with excellent records of finding their man.

"I heard," said James, "that getting the proper arms presented a difficulty since Winchester rifles were wanted, but none could be had. Six-shooters were plentiful and each man was provided with two of enormous caliber. Horses were ordered at Milan for the men and are ready for them. The men will arrive there this afternoon and immediately begin the hunt."

"I wish them luck," said Sheriff Barton with a sarcastic laugh. "I hear they will take with them a guide; a young man who knows the ground of Linn and Sullivan counties like the back of his hand. Pierman thinks that because of the publicity given to their crimes along with their descriptions, it would be nearly impossible for the Taylors to have gone far from this area. There's also the fact they have so many friends around here. Some of them have been involved in their crimes so it would be suicide to betray the Taylors, even if they could. I'm tired, so if Pierman and his deputies can be successful, more power to him. He is going to proceed on the theory that the brothers are still hiding in the woods of either Sullivan or Linn County. Thinking they are being hidden by their old companions, he will not give up the search until he has beaten the woods of the two counties."

"You're right. I'm tired of this daily grind, too but if we couldn't do it with hundreds, how can they do it with just six. I'm skeptical; however, anything to get those two murderers under lock and key is alright with me. One would think with as much reward money as is put up that someone would be willing to turn them in if they are still around here. You know the Sullivan County Court met and are offering $500 for their capture. The full amount allowed by the state, which is $300 each, has been offered by Governor Stone. I understand Linn County has guaranteed $200."

"Yes, James, I even put up some reward for their capture. I think with more reward money offered by private citizens it will soon be as much as $2,000, maybe even more."

After a few more discussions about how they would proceed until the Taylors were caught, the two sheriffs said goodbye and went their respective ways home. It was easy to see the two had been under a strain.

Chapter 12

As the days wore on, rumors flew. All the area newspapers had feature articles about the murders. This tragedy was the greatest sensation to occur in the state of Missouri since it became a state in 1821. The sheriffs of Linn, Sullivan, Macon, Adair and Grundy counties had no trouble in raising posses. Every able-bodied man in the five-county area was willing and anxious to search for the Taylor brothers as suspects for killing the Meeks family.

Their search included the Chariton hills in the southwest corner of Adair County. Also, the homes of George and Bill's parents were surrounded as were Della's parents, David and Gonia Gibson. When Albert Taylor, Bill and George's younger brother accompanied Bill's wife, Maud home from her father-in-law's, he was arrested on the suspicion that he knew where Bill was hiding and was taking supplies to him. It became widely known that James Harris, hired hand for George and Della, was arrested and being held as an accessory to the murders.

By the end of a week, a standing reward of $1,300 was offered with the possibility of it reaching $2,000 within a few days. The community was divided. The Taylor family had many friends who did not believe the two brothers committed this heinous crime. The folk in Milan were convinced of their guilt, as were others in the Browning area who believed Bill, in particular, had done too many things which were not right if not illegal.

The citizens of Sullivan felt the county had spent quite enough money on the murders since they had provided the coffins and clothing for the burial of the Meeks family. Also, hundreds of dollars had been spent on circuit court cases involving either Bill or George Taylor. In spite of it all, the Sullivan County Court added $300 to the reward for the capture of the Taylor brothers.

Della was having a difficult time coping with all that was going on in the neighborhood. She had had no further word from George. She didn't know what to believe. Many of their friends would have nothing to do with her now. Only her parents were openly supporting her in this troubled time.

"Mamma, I am so glad you live nearby. I just couldn't manage by myself."

"Honey, your pa and I will look after you. You have to be strong for little Flossie and for the new one who will be here soon."

"Did you get the newspaper? Tell me what they are writing about George and Bill."

"Your pa says he read in the paper where members of the posse think Bill and George went from the Morgan Leonard place through the fields then crossed West Yellow Creek about a half mile south of the Sandifer bridge. During Saturday about a hundred men gathered there looking for them. Someone reported Bill and George's brother John went to Linneus to talk to their lawyer, Senator Stephens. Some think he was giving Stephens a message and he knows where the men are hiding."

"Ma, I am so afraid for George. People around here are hungry for revenge. I think if they find him and Bill, they will hang them without a trial."

"Yes, honey, I think you're right. Pa heard how Governor Stone has commissioned a party of men, including several deputy United States marshals to look for Bill and George. He read where B. G. Pierman of Neosho, a Deputy U.S. Marshall will be in charge. It seems these men believe the boys are still hiding around here. They think it would have been impossible for George and Bill to have wandered far from here. Your pa and I are pretty sure they are far away from here by now."

"Maybe you're right. If they had still been around here, George would have contacted me again. I wonder if I will ever see him again." Della had to take a couple of deep breaths to keep from sobbing. Her emotions were near the surface as the days unfolded.

About a month after the murders, James Harris came to the house to tell Della about his arrest and his stay in the Linn County jail. For the past couple years George had employed James to help with the farm work. At eighteen years old, James's youthful face had close-set eyes with a strong jaw. His broad shoulders showed the results of heavy lifting often needed around the farm. His thick, brown hair looked as if he hadn't found the comb that morning.

Despite the rumors, Sheriff Barton had not arrested James because he thought he was involved with the murders, but kept him in jail as a witness for the grand jury hearing, which started in Linneus a week ago.

"I hope you remembered how good George has been to you when you testified," Della said to him.

"Oh, sure, I didn't say anything that will be bad for George. You can count on me," James had replied.

He just neglected to tell her he had told the sheriff he had seen blood the morning after the murders on the wagon George had used the day before.

Della couldn't help but wonder about what he had told the Sheriff. *Surely, he would not incriminate George in the horrible crime against the Meeks family.*

James told his story of the grand jury hearing to Della. "It was exciting. I've never seen a grand jury before and have never testified at one."

Della was surprised to hear how James thought this hearing was exciting, but she let him relate what he heard without comment.

He continued to tell Della about the proceedings. How twelve men were empaneled to hear the testimony of the witnesses and seventeen persons were called to tell what they knew about what happened the night of May 10th, including Mrs. Sallie Carter who saw little Nellie Meeks after the murders and Mrs. Meeks, Gus's mother.

Next he repeated the story Nellie told to the grand jury.

Nellie said, "They first shot Papa, and he fell out of the wagon. Then they shot Mamma, and then they hit my little sister with a stone. They kicked me and then struck me on the head with a stone, and then I went to sleep. I did not know anything more until the men threw us all into the hole in the straw stack."

"When the men carried us all to the straw stack, my little sister, Hattie woke up and said to Mamma, who was dead, that her face was bloody. Then one of the men struck Hattie again and said he guessed everybody was dead. I was so afraid he would strike me like he did Hattie so I kept still and never moved.

"One of the men said something about burning the straw pile and someone else said it was too wet. They covered us all over with straw and I thought I would smother, but when they went away I crawled out over Papa and Mamma and went to Mr. Carter's house," Nellie concluded.

"I don't know what will happen next," James went on to tell Della. "Maybe Bill and George will stay away and not ever be found."

"Oh, James, this is all so terrible. What am I going to do? If George doesn't come back, I will have to raise my children alone. But if he is found, arrested, tried and convicted, he may be hanged, and I still will be alone."

"It is too bad this thing happened. But you have your mamma and papa, and I'll still be here to help with the farming. We just hope everything comes out good."

Later that day Della's father read in the newspaper about the hearing and shared it with Della. He said, "After hearing all the testimony of the witnesses, the grand jury issued an indictment for murder in the first degree against William and George. The indictment read in part, 'William P. Taylor and George E. Taylor feloniously, willfully, deliberately, premeditatedly, on purpose and of their malice aforethought, did discharge and shoot off a pistol giving Gus Meeks, a mortal wound.'"

The newspaper related that Judge W. W. Rucker upon hearing the pronouncement of the grand jury issued the following command to Sheriff Edward Barton; "to take William P. Taylor and George E. Taylor, if they be found in your County, and then safely keep, so you may have their bodies before the Judge of our Circuit Court, at the Court House in the City of Linneus within and for the County of Linn on the first Monday in December next, 1894."

"Oh, Pa, what are we going to do? How can I go on without George?" Della sobbed.

David took Della in his arms and rubbed her back to soothe her. "We will go on living. It is not the end of the world. This is a rough time but we can't give up. You have to keep looking for a brighter day because of Flossie and the new baby you got coming."

Chapter 13

On Friday, June 29, 1894, the *Kirksville Weekly Graphic* reported the Taylor brothers were captured by J. C. South of Baxter County, Arkansas at Buffalo City, Arkansas on June 26. William P. Taylor, the spokesman for the two, made the following statement to a reporter for the Little Rock, Arkansas newspaper.

"We met Mr. South last Monday at Buffalo City, at the Hayes house, where we were stopping. He had evidently read of us and the terrible crime attributed to us and on Saturday last, while we were purchasing some shoes in Mr. Hayes's store, he asked us if we were not the Taylor brothers. We told him we were, when he placed us under arrest, and surrendered our pistols without any offer of resistance, and voluntarily accompanied him to this city. We are entirely guiltless of the crime with which we are charged and had intended leaving on a skiff for Batesville anyhow and returning home for trial. We hope to get bail and can give it, any sum—$50,000 if necessary. The murder of the Meeks family occurred on the night of May 10, and we learned the next day that we were suspected of it, and that a mob was after us and would lynch us if they caught us. We immediately sought safety in flight, expecting to return when the excitement died down."

"We came to Springfield, Missouri, where we spent three days and have been in Buffalo City for about a month. Yes, we have heard from home. We both have families whom we are anxious to see and get back to and make an honest living for. We have fared pretty well considering, have had enough to eat, although our clothes became somewhat worn with traveling over the mountains."

"We would not like to say who killed the Meeks family, if we knew. We have heard some very important facts—or circumstances, rather—since we left Browning. We might have been in irons and in jail had a sheriff or ordinary criminal hunter arrested us. But Mr. South has treated us handsomely and we will never forget it. He will accompany us and get the reward and I am glad of it. Sheriff Barton of Linn County is a good man too, and we will get fair treatment at his hands. There is $2,200 reward for us, $600 of which is offered by Governor Stone and the balance by friends of the Meeks family. The $600 Mr. South is sure to get, but I don't know so well about the remainder." [2]

The newspaper commented that one of the interesting facts of the arrest was when the Honorable Jerry South, ex-member of the Arkansas state legislature arrested them, he brought them to Little Rock when he registered with the two at the Gleason Hotel in the city. He is a delegate to the Democratic State Convention, which convenes in Little Rock and he plans for the Taylors to remain with him until the convention adjourns.

It also reported how the two did not deny their identity but did maintain they were innocent of the crimes attributed to them. They said they fled to avoid mob violence but are willing to return to Linn County and stand trial. The paper said W. P. (Bill) intimated to South he knew facts which would clear them of wrongdoing.

The newspaper reported that South was bringing the pair from Little Rock to St. Louis where Linn County Sheriff Barton would meet Mr. South and the Taylor Brothers. It was supposed he would bring them to the Linn County jail.

Upon hearing of George and Bill's arrest, Della immediately wanted to go to the jail—wherever it was—to see George. "Ma, I must go to him to see how he is."

It was hard for Gonia to keep from frowning. She had to remember that Della was still young and did not have the patience of an older adult. "No, dear, it is too close to your confinement for you to be traveling. I know you don't want to have this baby along the road somewhere. You will have to be patient. You'll get a chance to see George after the baby comes. It won't be too much longer."

Della knew her mother was right, but it didn't keep her from worrying about George and wanting the details about what had been happening since they left.

"Ma, I do love him. Do you think he is thinking about me and the baby?"

This was a hard one for Gonia to answer. She wanted to reassure her daughter that her husband loved her, but there were too many doubts in her own mind. This was not turning out to be the great marriage Gonia and David had anticipated for their daughter. Because it was near time for the new baby to make an appearance, Gonia kept the negative thoughts she had about George to herself.

David and Willie decided to go meet the train in Linneus so they could tell Della about it. When they returned, the next day Della's father told her how Sheriff Barton did not take George and Bill to the Linn County jail. The sheriff was so sure they would not be safe anywhere in Linn County, so he made arrangements with the sheriff in St. Joseph to take them there. As predicted, a mob of masked men were waiting at the train station in Brookfield. To their disappointment, the train went on to St. Joseph where they were safely incarcerated.

The Gibson family made a communal sigh of relief when they knew the Taylors would not be in the local jail. At least the local rabble-rousers could not storm the jail and lynch the Taylors without a trial.

"Pa, I want to see George so bad, but I know I can't go to St. Joe. If any of the family goes tell me so I can send a letter and let him know I miss him and want him cleared of this awful mess."

"Yes, honey, I'll let you know if anyone goes to see him and Bill."

A few days later David told Della her father-in-law, James Taylor and Bill's wife Maude were going to see the boys. Della quickly wrote a short letter to be given to George. Before putting it in the envelope, she read it over to herself.

Dearest George,

Flossie and I love you and miss you so much. Things have been really bad here. Friends and neighbors we thought we could count on have turned against us. I am trying to be brave because it is almost time for our new baby to arrive. I so hope it is a boy for you. If it is, I will name him George Edward Taylor, Jr.

You told me you didn't commit those murders, and I believe you. I just pray that when the trial comes up the jury believes you, too.

Be strong and know I am longing for you to be back home with me and the babies.

Love,

Della

It looked good to her, so she placed it in the envelope and sealed it. "Here, Pa, give this to Mr. Taylor. I'll be anxious to hear all about the trip when he returns."

Chapter 14

On July 8th, less than two months after the murders, long before dawn Della woke her mother. "Ma, I think the baby is coming."

"I'll send Drue for the doctor. It'll take a while for him to get to Browning, wake the doctor and get him down here. In the meantime, I'll get some water on heating to have ready."

Gonia sent Drue home to wake his father and Ivy May, his little sister before he went to Browning for the doctor. David and Ivy could help around the house and take care of young Flossie. In a few days, Ivy would be seven, and she liked to watch after and play with the little one-year-old. Flossie was still sleeping in her crib, but she would surely wake soon and want breakfast.

Gonia sat by her daughter's bed, held her hands, and wiped the sweat from Della's brow as the contractions contorted the young woman's face with pain. She knew what her daughter was going through, having given birth to six children herself. The mother was a large woman with strong bones. While Della didn't have the same bone structure as her mother, she was still a good strong girl, so this birth shouldn't be too difficult. Although she was still a few days from her nineteenth birthday, there had been no problems when Flossie was born a year ago, so hopefully, there would be none for this birth.

As the sun was streaking through the morning dew, the doctor arrived to assist in the birth of the baby. By then the contractions were coming more often, and it wasn't long before a baby's cry was heard in the bedroom.

"You have a healthy baby girl, Della," the doctor announced.

Annalou Mack

"Are you sure, Doctor? We so much wanted a boy. George will be so disappointed."

"Just be happy this little thing is healthy. You can have a boy another time."

Tears were streaming down Della's face. "I know. I'll get over it soon. Now, what am I going to name her? We were going to name the baby boy after George. I'll have to think of something else."

Gonia said, "You can still name the baby after George, just make it Georgie."

"That sounds good. I'll think of something to go with it later."

A few days later James Taylor, Della's father-in-law, came by to see the new baby and to tell Della about his trip to see his sons. Even though he was aging, the handsome good looks he had as a young man were still evident through his gray hair and heavy beard. James had a high forehead and a thin, straight nose.

"Della, George sends his love to you and the babies. He so much wants to come home and be with you, but their attorney, Mr. Stephens, believes the feelings here are too strong. There is a chance of a lynching if they are brought back to Linn County."

"Mr. Taylor, how does George look? Are they treating them good in jail? I want to go see him so bad, but I will have to wait a while before I can make the trip."

"Yes, you need to get strong and make sure the new baby grows."

"Tell me about St. Joe and what the jail is like."

Mr. Taylor began to tell Della about how Bill and George were so glad to see him and Maude. All of them shared a long embrace upon entering the jail corridor. Tears filled all of their eyes. Each one was aware there were troubles before, but nothing like this. Their attorney, E. R. Stephens was with them, so they remained in St. Joseph a few days to consult with him as to what future course they should pursue.

"Well, you know, the boys are attracting a lot of attention. Sheriff Carson had to place an extra guard on, not for security from a mob, but to handle the crowds of people wanting to see Bill and George. There are hordes of people coming by the jail to see them. He also wants to be careful of the other prisoners, some who are waiting removal to the penitentiary. Guards are carefully inspecting all packages or things brought to the prisoners. The sheriff says the boys are model prisoners, and he doesn't expect any trouble from them.

"George told a reporter for the newspaper how if they have to be in jail, they have no objection to remaining in St. Joseph because unless things change back in Linn it is the best place for them now. If the prejudice and excitement of the moment were allayed, they would prefer to be tried in their own county."

"Oh, Mr. Taylor, I am so anxious to see George. I can hardly wait until I am well enough to go see him."

Gonia Gibson came into the room carrying the little baby girl. "Here is the new Taylor addition to the family. Della was disappointed it was not a boy, but the baby girl will be good company for Flossie. Would you like to hold her?"

"Sure, I'll hold her for a little while. Della, what have you decided to name her?"

This large man gently took the tiny baby offered him and smiled down on his new grandchild.

"George and I had decided to name the new baby George Edward Taylor, Jr., but since it is a girl I have chosen Georgia as the first name. I can't think of a middle name. Do you have any ideas?"

"Well, let's see. George's middle name is Edward so how about something starting with an E? Have you thought about Ethel?"

"No, I hadn't thought of that, but it sounds good. What do you think, Ma?"

"I like it. Georgia Ethel Taylor," replied Gonia.

Mr. Taylor stood up preparing to leave. "Now, take good care of our baby girl. George will be looking forward to seeing her along with you and Flossie."

"Thank you for coming to see me and bringing me news of George. Let me know when you go again. Maybe I'll be able to go too by then."

"Oh, by the way, he did send a short note for you. Let's see—oh, here it is," handing Della a small folded piece of paper.

As her father-in-law left the house, Della unfolded the note and began to read what George had written to her.

> Dear Della,
>
> It is with a heavy heart that I write you these few words. I want to be there in the house with you and hold you in my arms, but the miles and circumstances prevent it.
>
> By now the new baby will be there. We wanted a baby boy, but as long as it is healthy either one will be fine. Just remember I love you and when this terrible mess is over we will spend the rest of our lives together trying to forget what happened.
>
> Love,
> George

Chapter 15

With the new baby, the family seemed to think it was too much for Della to stay alone in her house. Gonia and David thought the best thing for her and the babies was to move down to their house. In her parent's house there would be several family members to help care for the new baby and to watch Flossie, who was now running all over the place.

Gonia was concerned that Della had become very moody and was just barely able to care for baby Georgia. Ivy May was doing the most to care for Flossie. The toddler was the bright spot in Ivy's life; it was like having a big doll most of the time. Other times Flossie was the little sister she had been craving. The two were inseparable and that was a huge help for Gonia.

"Della, you need something to occupy your time so you don't spend so much of it crying over what has happened and how much you miss George. I think it would be a good idea for you to learn to knit. What do you think about it?"

"Well, Ma, maybe it would be good for me. I can make bonnets and booties for little Georgia to start, and then later when I get better at it, I'll make mittens, sweaters and such for both of the girls. Do you have time to teach me?"

"Sure, I have some scrap yarn and a pair of knitting needles. I'll show you how to do it."

The two of them had only started the new project when Ivy came running in the house saying, "Someone is turning into the lane. Do you want me to go see who it is?"

"Just wait a few minutes, child, we'll know soon enough," said her mother.

Gonia put her knitting away and went out on the porch to await their visitor. "Oh, my goodness, if it isn't Addie. I thought their family had quit speaking to us since the murders."

Addie and little Pearl were welcomed into the house and given a seat in the parlor near where Della had been sitting practicing her new skill. She quickly jumped up and threw her arms around Addie.

"I have missed you so much," Della said with tears streaming down her cheeks. "Why have you deserted me?"

After a long sigh, Addie began to explain why she had not been to see Della. "Jim has forbidden me to have anything to do with you or any of the Taylor family. He's gone away for a couple days, so I thought I would disobey him and come see you. I so much wanted to see the new baby. I had heard you had another girl. How is she?"

"We have named her Georgia. With all the activity and comings and goings of people around here, she has been cranky. I'm not able to get much sleep even though Ma tries to help as much as possible. Flossie thinks Georgia is a doll for her to play with, so I have to watch to be sure she doesn't hurt the baby. Ivy has been a lot of help, especially in watching Flossie. I'm sure you want to see her. She is taking a nap right now, but you can take a peek."

"Good. I've brought her a little present." Addie handed Della a small gift wrapped in bright colored tissue paper.

Della's eyes opened wide when she saw the little bonnet and booties. "Did you make these?"

"Yes, I have been learning to knit from my mother, so these are my first finished items. I hope you like them."

"Addie," Della said with a smile on her face. "This is funny. Ma has just started to teach me how to knit, and I said I would make some booties and a bonnet for Georgia. You did a great job. I don't know if I will ever get that good. Sit down and let's catch up a little."

Gonia went to the kitchen to make coffee. When she returned, Della showed her the pretty pink booties and bonnet Addie had made for Georgia.

"Addie, these are lovely. I'm trying to teach Dellie how to knit. I hope she does as well. I made some coffee. Will you have a cup?"

For the next hour or so the two young women chatted pleasantly about things they remembered from their childhood.

Della brought up their estrangement. "Tell me why Jim has forbidden you to have anything to do with me. I've done nothing wrong."

"Della, Jim is so afraid the scandal will touch him and hurt his business. You know there are some who favor the Taylors and some who hate them. Because you are married to George, he doesn't want me to associate with you or any of the family. I know it seems harsh, but he is my husband, and I have to do what he wants. I hope he doesn't find out I disobeyed him and came here today."

"Addie, I am so sorry he feels that way. Just because George is my husband it doesn't mean I approve, if he and Bill did the terrible crime. Actually, I don't think they did it. I believe some others did it and were trying to point the blame on George and Bill when they buried the family on our farm. We have been talking about hiring a detective to investigate who those others were.

"Of course, Jim is not alone in his thinking. It is hard to go to church and face people who have been our friends for years and see them turn away from me and the babies. We are not to blame, and the babies have no idea of why they are being scorned.

"As soon as I feel strong enough I am going to St. Joe and see George. It is so hard to be without him. Although I am with my family, I miss him so much."

"Oh, Della, I can only imagine how hard it is to not be at home with your husband and children. I do care about you and I always have you in my thoughts even though I can't be here to offer you comfort. Keep your chin up and your head held high. Some day soon this will all be behind you."

The two women continued talking for a while. Then Addie stood up and said, "Well, Della, I had better be going home. Georgia is a beautiful baby. I hope she gets to feeling better and sleeps at night so you can get some rest. I probably won't get a chance to see you again. It grieves me so much to see you like this, but I don't see there is anything I can do. You know my thoughts are with you. Know we are here for you, and know we all hope things turn out well for you. I'll gather up Pearl from Ivy and Flossie on my way out."

Della walked Addie to the door where the two shared hugs. "Thank you so much for coming and for the gift for Georgia. You can't know how much I appreciate your being here. I need all the support I can get. These are truly dark days. Have a safe trip home."

Chapter 16

Since the capture of the Taylor brothers, Sullivan County had been pretty quiet. A few arrests for being drunken and disorderly, but presently the jail was empty. Sheriff Niblo was spending the day going through some papers when a middle-aged woman entered.

"Why, good morning, Mrs. Walters. How are you on this fine September day?"

"Sheriff, I'm tolerably well, thank you. And how are you?"

"As good as I'll ever be, I suppose. What do you have on your mind?"

The room outside the jail cells was not large. There was a large oak desk on which several of the papers the sheriff had been examining were scattered. In addition to his chair, there were a couple others in the room in no particular order. The Sheriff hastily rose to place one of the chairs across from him so they could talk.

"Here, have a seat."

Nema Walters, a short, rather plump woman sat down in the chair the sheriff indicated. With her right hand she smoothed back her slightly gray hair, then made sure her skirt was in place. Hesitant as to how to approach the subject she had come to speak about, Mrs. Walters was silent for a minute. She then said, "Well, I have been hearing a lot about the murder of the Meeks family and they say the Taylor boys are the ones who done it. What do you think about it?"

Niblo had never been quiet about his thoughts in regards to the guilt of Bill and George Taylor in the Meeks family murder. He was certain they had committed the dastardly deed, as he called it. "I am as sure as one can be that those two killed the Meeks family in cold blood. Do you have something which can be used at their trial to help convict them?"

"Maybe."

"Let me hear it and I will decide whether to go to the prosecutor with it."

Still uneasy about the story she was about to tell, Nema sat for a little longer before beginning to talk. "You know if this gets back to the Taylors how I told this, my life may be in danger."

"Don't you worry about it. We will keep your story under wraps until the trial. Then there will be nothing they can do about it."

"Well, if you think I should. You see, it was like this. Bill Taylor came to our house at our farm here in Sullivan County and told me he was planning to kill Gus Meeks in a card game. He said he had convinced Gus to go along with him in a con to fleece some other fellows out of their money during the game. After Meeks had consented to the plot, the details were all worked out. Several of Bill's acquaintances were to be invited to a poker game. After playing a few hands, Gus would be accused of cheating and then shot during the uproar.

"Bill said he was telling me this so I wouldn't scream or raise a fuss. I was outraged and told him I would scream; there would be no assassination in my house. He tried to talk me out of it, but I wouldn't relent. The proposed card game was never played."

Sheriff Niblo was silent for a while letting this filter through his mind. He had to think about this for a while. *Did this really happen?* Struggling to keep his face from showing his questions he sat up straight in his chair. "That is quite a story. Did you tell your husband or anyone else about this?

"No, you are the first one to hear it from me. I don't know if Bill had talked to the others who were supposed to be included in the game. As far as I know, I am the only one who he talked to about it. I was afraid to say anything until after the Taylors were arrested. I'm still not sure you can keep me safe."

Leaning his elbows on the desk, Niblo tented his fingers in front of his face. "Mrs. Walters, give me a few days to mull this over in my mind. Are you sure you are willing to testify to this when the Taylors are brought to trial?"

Annalou Mack

"If I was not willing to testify in the trial, I would not have told you this story. Do with it what you think is best. For now I will take my leave. Let me know if you want me to sign some papers. You know where we live."

Having related what she came to tell, Mrs. Walters rose from the chair and walked out the door of the jail leaving Sheriff Niblo standing with his hands at his side.

If this story were true, it would lend credence to the facts in the case. It was well known that Bill Taylor did not want Gus Meeks to testify against him in the cattle stealing case. There was talk where several men had heard Bill or George say they would see that someone got rid of Gus before he could testify against them. Those statements could be discounted as just idle talk. This was the first account he had heard where an actual plot had been devised. The sheriff wanted to think about this for a while before he passed it on to Mr. Pierce.

After breakfast the next morning Sheriff Niblo headed for Ben Pierce's office. He spent several hours the previous night going over his meeting with Mrs. Walters before he decided the story he heard yesterday was worth passing on. It was time to give it to the prosecuting attorney and let him decide whether to use it or not.

Prosecutor Pierce answered his knock with a cheery, "Good morning, Jim. What is on your mind this beautiful fall day?"

"Ben, we should be out hunting on this gorgeous Indian Summer day. Leaves are spectacular this year with all the red, yellow and orange colors mixing in with the green. It is just too pretty a day to talk about the Meeks murder, but I have a story to tell you."

"Well, Jim, I agree with you. But let's hear what you have to tell me."

The two men found chairs in the prosecutor's office. Ben had a pot of coffee sitting on the heating stove, so he brought out two cups and poured each of them a cup. Niblo began to reiterate the story told to him yesterday by Nema Walters.

When he finished, he said, "What do you make of that?"

"It is quite a story, Jim. I believe before we do anything about it, we should sit on it for a while. What do you know about the Walters woman? I have heard of the family, but I don't know much about them. What is their relationship with the Taylors? Could this be an attempt to get back at Bill for something?"

"Ben, I don't know much about the family either. Which is why I was reluctant to bring the story to you. However, I think we have to give it at least some thought. I have told it to you so you can decide what to do with it when the time comes."

The two men chatted for a while about what was happening in the town. Sheriff Niblo asked, "How is Nellie doing? Is she getting along well with your children?

"Oh, my, Nellie is such a delightful child. She fits right in with our brood. Occasionally she has a nightmare at night, but those are less frequent as time goes on. She is just one of the family now."

"Say, Ben, did you hear the Taylors have hired Ex-Governor Charles P. Johnson of St. Louis to defend them?"

"Yes, I read about it in the St. Joe newspaper. It said Johnson visited them in the county jail where he spent about four hours talking with them. Later a reporter for the newspaper spent some time interviewing Johnson about their talk. According to the reporter, he said, 'Yes, the Taylor brothers have a defense. If William P. Taylor told me the truth today, they are not guilty of the atrocious murder with which they are charged and should not suffer for it.' Johnson went on to explain it was because they believed they would be suspected why they left the area immediately. This will hurt their case. Mitigating circumstances need to be looked into."

Niblo couldn't contain his annoyance at that thought. Giving a sharp rap on Ben's desk he said, "Baloney, what mitigating circumstances are there. Ben, you and I know they are guilty as sin and a high-powered lawyer better not try to get them off. I didn't read the paper. What else did the reporter say?"

"Well, as I recall, Johnson told him he couldn't speak of their defense before it comes to trial. The defense needs to obtain a mass of testimony, so until then it is best to remain silent. Johnson realizes how public sentiment is against them, but the probability of their innocence will be shown in good time. The reporter stated the lawyer said it was not an ordinary case and there are many interesting circumstances. He seems to believe they can show their innocence. He said, 'I have had harder cases.'"

The sheriff listened intently to what Ben told him about the newspaper article. "To me it just looks like the Taylor boys are becoming desperate when they have to hire such a well-known criminal lawyer to defend them. It seems to me they are clutching at straws, like drowning men. Members of their family may say they were home the night of the murder, but it is their only defense."

"Jim, I think the prosecution can make a good case against them. I will certainly try to find as much evidence as I can. We still have a few months to go before the case is brought to trial. I'll keep you informed."

"You do that. One of these days I plan to go to St. Joe to see them. If I learn anything helpful, I'll let you know." After a few more remarks, Niblo rose from his chair and headed for the door. "I best be getting back to the jail. I'll leave this business in your hands. Give my regards to your wife."

On his way back to the jail, the sheriff couldn't appreciate the nice fall day for thinking about the Taylor case. To him it was open and shut. The brothers were guilty so how could anyone think differently.

Chapter 17

Sheriff Niblo had set aside a few days to visit the Taylor brothers in their jail cells in St. Joseph. He decided today was a good day to set the plan into action. He gave some thought to the clothes he would wear and finally determined it would be better to wear jeans rather than his one good suit. Comfort won out over dress. Finding his best pair of jeans, he put them on followed by a clean, white shirt.

After his usual good breakfast of bacon and eggs, he proceeded to the bedroom where his wife, Ruth Ann was still asleep. Waking her gently with a kiss, he told her he would be back in a day or so. One of their two sons would watch out for her while he was away.

As Jim walked down the streets of Milan to the depot on the east side of town to catch the train, he was comforted by the sounds of the birds in the brightly colored leaves on the maples, oaks and hickories lining the streets. His footsteps startled a squirrel who quickly scampered up the nearest tree. This beautiful autumn day made it seem like everything was right with the world.

It wasn't long before the Milan Depot was before him. The train he was about to board for his ride to St. Joseph was commonly called the "Q." In 1870, the citizens of Sullivan County voted to subscribe stock in the Quincy, Missouri and Pacific Railroad in the amount of $200,000. There had been setbacks and financial problems before the rails reached Milan in 1879. In 1882, a depot was erected to accommodate freight and passengers using the railroad. The red clapboard siding with green trim seemed to be in good repair.

The depot was teeming with people waiting for the train to St. Joe when Niblo arrived. He stopped to greet several members of the community before he reached the ticket window. After purchasing the ticket, he found a place to sit on one of the benches lined up in the room for waiting passengers. He looked around and noticed the painted yellow walls above the wainscoting that gave a pleasing warm feeling to those waiting. Although not needed on this warm day, there was a large pot-belly stove standing near the middle of the room which added warmth on the cold winter days common in North Missouri.

The man sitting beside the sheriff began asking him if he had any news about the Taylor brothers and the murders. "I'm on my way to St. Joe today to have a talk with them," Niblo replied.

"You know many of us here in Milan and Sullivan County would like to have a chance at those boys. They are a bad lot, it seems to me. Just look at all those other crimes they have been charged with. Each time it looks like they get off scot-free. It better not happen this time, or there will be hell to pay."

Before the sheriff had a chance to respond, the whistle blew sounding the approach of the train. Everyone rose from their seats, picked up their bags and headed for the platform.

The coach filled rapidly. Niblo was able to find a vacant seat near the back. He was glad no one else was there because he wanted to have some time to himself. He settled into the seat, stretching out his long legs as best he could, and leaned his head back against the seat. His thoughts were currently about his wife. She was not well. It seemed to be one thing after another the past ten years. The doctor gave her some medicine and she got better for a while, then she seemed to take a set-back. He was hoping Ruth Ann would get back to her former self, but it wasn't looking good right now.

James Niblo was the son of a Scottish father and an English mother. He remembered his early life in Pennsylvania where he lived with his older brother, Nathan and younger sister, Mary. Their father, Alexander, arrived in the United States in 1840 and married Elizabeth Melvile a few years later. Alexander was a stone mason and taught his trade to both his sons.

As a young man, James left Pennsylvania and journeyed westward until he came to Illinois. In Richland County, he met the lovely Ruth Ann Phenis who won his heart. Her life had not been easy.

Ruth's mother Catherine Boulton had married Samuel Phenis in Indiana, where six months after Ruth was born, Samuel died. With a child to raise, it wasn't long before Catherine married Abner Bail and they also moved on to Illinois.

James and Ruth Ann were married in Richland County, Illinois in September 1867. They soon became the parents of James Alexander Jr., in 1869; Samuel Lawrence in 1870; and Bessie Katherine, in 1877, all born in Illinois. During this time James Sr. worked as a stone mason in a marble works plant.

As James sat thinking about those past years, he began to ponder why they had left Illinois. They thought that perhaps the dust from James' clothes was contributing to Ruth Ann's illnesses. They came to Milan, Missouri in 1882. Work was not easy to find. James was not a farmer. He had worked as a stone mason since a teenager. Work as a day laborer was what seemed open to him until the job as sheriff of Sullivan County came up. He ran and was elected. Now he was thinking, what did I get myself into? However, he was determined to do a good job. Convicting those Taylor boys for the Meeks family murder was his top priority now.

As the train pulled into the station in St. Joe, James gathered his belongings ready to depart the coach when it stopped. Sitting for long periods of time was uncomfortable for him because he was active for much of the time in his job. He stood as soon as the train quit moving and stretched his arms over his head to straighten out the kinks. This trip was important to him.

Upon his departure from the train, James made his way to the courthouse and jail. His first stop was at the office of Sheriff Charles Carson to visit for a while with him. The sheriff invited him into his office where they sat and exchanged small talk for a few minutes. James then asked, "How are the Taylors doing during their stay here in your jail?"

"They have been model prisoners since their arrival. But the crowds have been huge with people stopping by just to get a glimpse of those two young men. I've had to put on an extra deputy just to contain the mobs of people wanting to see them. The guards have been given orders that no one is to be admitted to the interior of the jail where the prisoners are kept unless a deputy goes with them. All packages have to be submitted for inspection."

Then Sheriff Carson leaned forward with a scowl on his face and continued, "Sheriff Niblo, I have the darndest story to tell you. Last Sunday the jailor, my cousin Turnkey Andy Carson, was given a prescription by the Taylors who asked him to have it filled for them. Andy took it to the drugstore and gave it to James Clark, the pharmacist, to fill. Upon examining the prescription, Mr. Clark decided it was too dangerous to fill. He asked Andy if either of the Taylor brothers was having trouble with their eyes. The jailor told him he didn't think so. The druggist then wanted to know what the Taylors wanted with this prescription. Andy didn't know what they wanted it for and asked if there was something wrong with the prescription. Mr. Clark told him it contained a large amount of deadly poison. The prescription called for "sulphate of morphine two grains, sulphate of atropia [atropine] two grains, lanoline two drachms." Andy then told him not to fill it.

"This prescription was written on a piece of paper and seemed to be written by someone who knew about medicine. We later determined it had been written by Dr. J. G. Walker, another inmate. The druggist said there was enough poison contained in the compound to kill eight men. Now what do you make of that? I am still puzzling over this one," said Sheriff Carson.

Niblo sat back and shook his head. "Whatever they had in mind, it was not good."

"I'm sure you are right, but, like I said, they had been model prisoners since they came. A local physician looked at that prescription and said no competent physician would prescribe it even for external use in the proportions written. He said if ingested it would be sudden death. Do you think they were contemplating suicide?"

Sheriff Niblo thought about that for a minute, "My guess is it was more like an escape plan. You best keep a close watch on them. Now, can I go have a talk with them?"

A deputy escorted Sheriff Niblo back to the area where Bill and George were brought for their visit with him. It had been a year or so since the sheriff had seen the two men. He was struck by their good looks and neat dress. There was no question but what Bill was the leader of the two. He stood straight with about five feet eight inches in height and wore a neatly trimmed dark beard. There was something different about his eyes which gave him a somewhat sinister appearance. One eye looks straight ahead while the other looks slightly upward, making one somewhat uncomfortable when talking to him.

George was a quite handsome young man who appeared to have nerves of steel. Niblo looked directly into his cold blue eyes and found them as unreadable as a blank page. He was clean shaven with wavy brown hair. The impression he gave was that he knew no fear.

"How are you faring here in St. Joe?" asked Sheriff Niblo.

Both agreed they were well treated. George said, "If we have to be in jail away from our friends and family, Buchanan County jail is as good as any."

Bill said, "We would like to come back to Linn County to be with our loved ones, but we know it is impossible until we are cleared of this terrible injustice."

"How can it be unjust for you to answer to the killing of a family in cold blood?" asked Niblo.

"Because we are innocent of this terrible crime. Others committed it and have put the blame on us. Our lawyers will prove this when we come to trial." said Bill.

Sheriff Niblo asked, "Who were your accomplices in this brutal murder? Tell me. If we arrest them, perhaps it will help clear you."

"We had no accomplices because we didn't do this crime." Both were adamant about it.

The conversation continued along those lines for nearly an hour when Sheriff Niblo felt he was wasting his time. He rose from his seat, thanking them for agreeing to talk to him. "If you change your mind, let me know."

Chapter 18

"Ma, I think Georgie is old enough for us to go to St. Joe to see George. She's three months old now. I think she can make the trip. Will you go with me to help care for the girls on the journey?"

"Of course, I wouldn't let you go on such a trip by yourself."

"We can go up to Browning and catch the train. I know it will be long and exhausting, but I want to see George, and I'm sure he wants to see the baby. Do you think we can go next week?"

"The weather is pretty nice these days, so it seems like a good idea. Maybe it would be best to go day after tomorrow before there is a change in the weather. We'll need to make some preparations, so we better get at it."

For the rest of the day, the two women made bread, cooked meat and gathered late growing vegetables from the garden. The next day they laundered and pressed the clothes they needed to take with them. St. Joe was halfway across the state so it would require they have an overnight stay.

Della was so excited to be making these preparations. Staying overnight in a strange place away from family was a new experience. There had been times when she was younger when she and Addie had stayed overnight at each other's homes, but that was family. This was different.

Of course, going to see George was a large part of the excitement. How would he look? Had he lost weight? Were they treating him good in jail? Did he still love her? She hadn't seen him since the night in May when he came by before he and Bill took off. Maybe it was only five months ago, but it seemed like a lifetime to her. Della was a mother now with two babies to feed and care for. Sure, she had her parents to help her, but when she and George married, she had expected to spend the rest of her days with him and their children. This was not what she wanted for the remainder of her life.

Early in the morning the day of their departure, Della and Gonia arose and packed a bag with a few clothes and diapers for the baby. The lunch basket was filled with the foodstuffs they had prepared, and two canteens filled with water. Food was available in the dining car of the train, but it would be expensive. They needed to save their money for the hotel room.

For the trip Della chose a light brown twill suit she had recently ordered from the brand-new Sears & Roebuck catalog. All the weight she had gained during the recent pregnancy was not gone, but the suit, although a little tight, was comfortable. The color was good for her, and the fabric would not show soil. This was important when traveling with two little ones. Another white cotton blouse was packed to have a clean one for tomorrow. Little red string ties completed her outfit with a colorful touch.

Gonia, dressed in a serviceable black and white gingham dress, was ready to go. Both women added small hats to their attire. Flossie had on a cute little red ruffled pinafore with a long wool coat over it in case the October air was too cool. Georgia, at three months, still wore baby dresses. Della wrapped her in a pretty knitted blanket Gonia had made for Flossie when she was a baby.

Dave hitched the team to the buggy ready to take them to Browning to catch the train. He would like to go along on the trip, but he needed to stay home to be sure the chores were done and look after Drue and Ivy May.

"Okay, girls," Della said to Flossie and Georgia, "we are going to have a fun trip today. The big choo-choo train will take us to see your pa. Flossie, aren't you happy to be going to visit Daddy?" Little Flossie, although running around the house as fast as her legs could carry her, was still not talking. Seeing her mother's excitement, she jabbered, "Da-Da."

"Oh, Ma! Flossie just said a word. George will be so happy to hear it."

"We best be going. You don't want to miss the train." Dave said as he waited for them to get settled in the buggy with the children and the baggage.

Annalou Mack

Browning was a bustling community with, among other things, a post-office, general store, two banks and the Jenkins Hay Rake and Stacker Factory. Located on Main Street, it was near the railroad station. More than one hundred men worked here producing hay rakes and hay stackers. The Chicago, Burlington & Quincy railroad, arriving in Browning in 1872, in addition to passenger traffic, did an extensive shipping business.

Going to St. Joseph, the Q connected with the Hannibal and St. Joseph Railroad at Laclede, Missouri. The Hannibal and St. Joseph Railroad was the first railroad across Missouri, completed in 1859. It was said the first train across those lines carried a bottle of water from the Mississippi River where it was poured into the Missouri River in St. Joe to signify the joining of the two rivers by rail.

When Dave pulled up to the railway station in Browning, Della handed the baby to Gonia. Quickly jumping from the buggy, she hurried into the station to purchase the tickets. Dave got out and secured the buggy lines to the railing then went back to help Gonia and the little girls out. He raised Flossie up from the seat and sat her down on the ground. Gonia handed Georgia to Dave and carefully exited the buggy. The two of them entered the station with the toddler and baby.

"We got here just in time," said Della. "The next train arrives in about thirty minutes. I have our tickets. Would you two sit here with Flossie and Georgie while I go for a short walk? I'm too excited to sit still right now."

The couple took seats on the benches provided for the train passengers. Dave held Flossie on his knee bouncing her up and down while she giggled with pleasure. Little Georgia was awake lying peacefully in Gonia's arms. "I'm not much lookin' forward to this escapade, but Dellie's so hooped up about it. Things are likely to get worse before they get better."

Dave, looking down at Flossie on his knee, said, "No doubt about it. There are rough times ahead. All we can do is offer our support to Dellie and the kids. At least they have a good home. The neighbors may be down on her, but we'll see her through this."

"What could those two a been thinkin' to kill an entire family and bury them on George's farm? Maybe they didn't really do it." Gonia said with a sigh. "You know there had to be more than George and Bill involved in it. It was too much for the two of 'em to do by themselves."

"I think yer right. We can hope the law'll get to the bottom of this whole thing."

Della entered the station from her walk. "The train is coming. Let's get out there ready to board when it gets here." She took the baby and Gonia gathered up Flossie. Dave picked up the luggage and food basket to load them on the train for the women.

The platform filled quickly as the passengers hurriedly filed out the station door. As soon as the train stopped, Della and Gonia, each holding a child, climbed the steps into the passenger car where they found seats facing each other. Dave followed behind and deposited their belongings, gave each of them a kiss and turned to exit. "We'll be on the one comin' back tomorrow. So hope you'll be here to get us." said Gonia.

"Of course I'll be here. You take care o' yerselves now. St. Joe is a big city. I don't want anything to happen to you girls." Dave responded.

Without another word, he was out the door. The ladies settled themselves in the seats and quieted the girls who were beginning to get fussy. "Now girls, just hush. This is a new adventure for you. Your daddy will be so happy to see both of you. We don't want you to be all tear stained when we get there. Ma, get that sugar tit out of the bag for Georgie. I'll feed her when we get to the hotel."

Gonia found the small piece of white cotton fabric she had prepared by putting a tablespoon of sugar in the middle and tying it with a piece of string. As she handed it to Della she remarked, "This should keep her quiet for a while."

Soon the train began to move slowly away from the station picking up speed as it rolled along the tracks. The girls quieted down in a short time. Flossie stretched out on the seat with her head in Gonia's lap and Georgia rested in Della's arms. Before long the rhythmic movement of the train put both the girls to sleep. The two women leaned back in the seats and became engrossed in their thoughts.

Gonia leaned her head back, closed her eyes and turned her mind's attention to her family. She and Dave had been married for

Annalou Mack

twenty years. Their family was small compared to some. She had born six children; four boys and two girls. The oldest boy, Clarence Beverly, now had a job with the railroad. It looked like a good start for him which made them proud. For Della, the oldest daughter, everything had looked like it would be a good life when she married George Taylor. He was considered a good catch by the community. Fifteen-year-old Willie and thirteen-year-old Drue were good boys. They were growing into capable help on the farm. Little Iva May had just turned seven in July. She had been a little surprise for them, but Gonia was glad now to have her. With Della and her two little ones living with them, Iva May was helpful with the babies. There had also been heartache when they lost six-month-old Ellis. He was not very strong from birth, and was not able to fight off the whooping cough when it struck.

Now, Della's marriage that she and Dave had thought was such a good thing had turned into a nightmare. All Gonia could think about now was, *how can we get George off from this mess and get the family back on their feet?*

Chapter 19

As the train slowed, Della opened her eyes. The girls were still sleeping quietly and their grandmother had her eyes closed, too. Della looked around to see if anything needed to be replaced in the food basket. Placing her hand on Gonia's arm Della said, "Ma, I believe we are about to the station. Should we get a hotel room, or go to the jail first?"

Gonia opened her eyes, looked around for a minute then looked at Della as if trying to understand what Della had asked. After wiping her eyes with her handkerchief, she said, "Probably we need to get the hotel room so we can leave our bags there. Then we won't have so much to carry when we go to the jail."

The two women gathered their belongings and carrying the little ones, departed the train. George's father, James Taylor had given Della money for room rent and streetcar fare to the jail if they needed it. The two women decided the hotel across the street from Union Station was easy to get to and not far from the jail so they would stay there.

As excited as Della was to see George, she was nearly awe struck by the city. It sure wasn't Browning, Missouri. Union Station was gigantic in Della's eyes. She had never seen so many people in one place, all talking at once, and hurrying to different destinations. Della led the way across the street to the hotel where she approached the front desk to ask for a room.

The clerk said, "How many nights are you staying?"

"Oh, only one night."

"Do you need help with your luggage?

"No, we can make it fine. Just tell us where to find the room."

A porter appeared to show them to the room where he unlocked the door and gave Della the key. Gonia and the two children were close behind. After a quick trip down the hall to the restroom, Della sat down and unbuttoned her blouse to feed Georgie. Gonia opened the bag of food to secure a small piece of bread and butter for Flossie.

As soon as the family finished their quick lunch they were ready to take the short walk to the courthouse and jail to visit George.

The clerk at the hotel gave directions to the courthouse plus a history of the building. He told them the residents of St. Joseph are rightfully proud of the courthouse, calling it "Buchanan's Capitol." Located at Jules and North Fifth Street the courthouse had suffered a devastating fire in March, 1885. The interior was gutted by the fire, but the columns and exterior walls were left intact. After negotiations with the insurance company it was agreed to restore the building to its former grandeur.

The jail, in the same block but separated from the courthouse, was constructed of red brick with white stone trim similar to the courthouse. The eastern section of the jail was two-storied with a hip roof and housed the jailer's family. The western section had a hip and gable roof over the four stories containing the cells. The middle section was the area for offices and visiting rooms.

Upon entering this section of the jail through the south door, Della told the receptionist they were there to see George Taylor.

"Have a seat while we bring Mr. Taylor to the visiting room. It will only be a few minutes," they were told. "While you are waiting a deputy will need to search your bags. It is one of the rules, even though I'm sure you don't have any contraband. We have to be so careful to protect both prisoners and visitors."

Gonia looked around for a chair, but Della was too nervous to sit. Very soon the deputy arrived and asked to see any containers they were carrying. Although Gonia and Della were taken aback at the request, they complied without a word.

In a short time the receptionist returned and escorted the four of them into a small room where George was sitting. Upon seeing them come through the door, George rose and hurried to meet them.

Della rushed to throw her arms around George, careful not to crush Georgie between them. "Daddy, here is your new little baby daughter. She is so precious."

"Oh, Della, I am so glad you made it here with the girls. Mrs. Gibson, thank you for coming with them. It would be such a hard trip for Della alone."

George and the two women sat down in chairs placed around a small table.

"I would like to hold the baby for a while," said George.

Della gently handed Georgia to George with the light blanket wrapped around her tiny body.

Being careful to hold the little one with both hands, George looked at the baby then at Della and said, "She is beautiful like her mother. It breaks my heart I can't be at home with her and the rest of my family. It is my hope it won't be too long before I'll have this behind me, and I can resume a normal life."

"Oh, George, I want you home so bad. I have had to stay with Ma and Pa because I couldn't take care of everything by myself. Your father has been really good to us. But he can't do it alone, either." Della wiped the tears from her cheeks which she couldn't keep from filling her eyes. After a few minutes, she was able to control her emotions and they settled back in the chairs.

Flossie was making it known by her fidgeting and twisting on her grandmother's lap that she wanted down to run. Seeing this, George handed the baby back to Della and reached his arms for the toddler. With a squeal of delight, Flossie jumped down and ran into his outstretched arms. She may not have remembered him, as it had been months since she had seen him, but that didn't seem to deter her.

For the next hour or two, the three of them talked of common everyday happenings on the farm and around Browning.

"The crops were good this year. The boys haven't finished harvesting the corn, but they tell me it will turn out a good yield. We will need it for the animals. Everything is in good shape around the farm, but it won't stay that way long without you there to see the jobs get done. And you probably know how Jim Harris was arrested. We thought he was a good kid, but I'm beginning to question where his loyalties lie. I don't know what he told the grand jury."

Annalou Mack

George told Della about the visit from Sheriff Niblo. "He is a tricky one," said George, "so be very careful around him. He will do anything and say anything to put me in a bad light. If he had his way, he would take me out of this jail today and hang me from the highest tree."

"I know. He and his posse were rough with me, pushing me around, knocking over furniture, and waking up Flossie when they were at the house looking for you." Della sighed at the memory. "I didn't know where you were, and I wouldn't have told them if I did. They would have hanged you right then if they had found you."

"You're right about that. The Sheriff doesn't want to hear a good word about me. But what is the sentiment in the community now?" asked George.

"Not good. I hate to go anywhere because I get these awful stares and know people are saying things about me. I don't even like going to church any more. Hardly anyone speaks to me. You would think they would at least look at the baby. It is hard to be such an outcast. And I was shocked when Addie told me her husband forbids her to come see me. She snuck away once so she could see the baby. I miss her a lot." It was all Della could do to keep the tears in her eyes from falling down her cheeks.

George reached across the table and took Della's hand in his. "Dellie, just hold your head up high. This will all change when we are exonerated and the people know we are not guilty of this despicable crime. I know you think I was not home that night, but when you woke up and I wasn't in the bed, I had gone to the outhouse. Something I ate at Bill's house upset my stomach and I was out there a long time. Just keep that in mind."

"I'm glad you told me, because I thought you were still in Browning, or somewhere."

Gonia sat to the side and only entered into the conversation every now and then. She kept a watchful eye on Flossie who was running around the room on her short little legs. Occasionally George would catch his daughter and hold her for a while. Sometimes he played horsey with her sitting on his foot while he bounced it up and down making her giggle. In another setting it would have seemed like a happy family spending a peaceful afternoon.

"George, are you getting plenty of food?"

"Yes, the meals are quite good and I don't think I have lost any weight."

"You do look as handsome as ever. How I do miss you!"

"This trouble will be over soon and I'll be home to care for you and the babies. We can have a house full of babies in a few years, each one more beautiful than the last. It makes my heart glad you were able to come here so I could see you and hold the girls. The arraignment is in a couple of months. It is in Linneus but I don't want you to be there. The dead of winter is not a good time for you and our girls to be out. Also, you would not be able to talk to me because there will be heavy guards. We will ask for a change of venue for the trial. Don't know where the judge will assign it, but perhaps it will be near enough so you can come to the trial. I would like to have you at the trial to show you believe in me."

"Oh, George, of course, I will be at the trial, if at all possible. I do believe in you and will do whatever you want that will be helpful to you." Della paused for a few minutes then began gathering up their belongings. "Guess it is time for us to be going back to the hotel. We are catching the train back in the morning. Tonight we will spend the night in luxury. The hotel where we are staying has an inside bathroom. There is a toilet in there which flushes water down it after you use it. Maybe we will be able to have one of those on the farm sometime after we get this problem behind us."

"Dellie, honey, don't worry too much. Things will work out. We will all be together soon. Have a good, safe trip back to Browning. Take good care of the babies." He reached over to give his wife a kiss on the cheek then one on each of the girls.

Tears sprang to Della's eyes as they walked out the door after this too short visit. *How am I going to get through the next few months?*

Chapter 20

The arraignment of Bill and George Taylor for the murder of the Gus Meeks family was scheduled for the December circuit court of Linn County. On Dec. 3, 1894, the first Monday in December, court opened with great excitement in Linneus. Not only in the city, but along the route from St. Joe to Linneus, hundreds of people gathered at various stations along the Hannibal and St. Joseph railroad hoping to get a glimpse of the Taylor brothers. For all their effort, the crowds were disappointed because the Taylors did not make the trip that day.

The docket of cases for the December term was quite large. Presiding Judge W. W. Rucker passed over the State vs. William P. and George E. Taylor when it came up on the schedule. It was speculated he did not want the public to know the exact time for the trial because of the fear of danger from the mobs. Definitely Linn County Sheriff Edward Barton was taking as much precaution as possible to prevent violence.

One week later on Monday, December 10, the 12:15 train from St. Joe pulled into the station with the Taylor brothers. The crowd was large, but not nearly as large as it would have been had people known the Taylors would be on it. Sheriff Barton and six deputies were in charge of bringing the brothers to Linneus. When the group departed the train they were met by sixteen more law enforcement officers.

The sheriff spoke to the bystanders in a firm, authoritative voice, "I will maintain order. I expect you people to behave in a proper and lawful manner, and I will not allow any show of mob violence."

Bill and George were taken to the jail where they were served a good meal. Following the meal the defendants consulted with their lawyers before being taken to the courtroom packed with spectators. During the proceedings, Attorneys Bresnehen, Mullins, and Field appeared for the state and Attorneys Meyers, Stephens and Wilson for the defense.

Judge Rucker called the case and a plea of "Not guilty" was entered by Honorable D. W. Wilson, one of their attorneys. Next, Attorney Wilson filed an application for a change of venue from Sullivan, Linn and Chariton counties. The application stated the "minds of the inhabitants of Counties Linn, Sullivan, and Chariton are so prejudiced against said defendants they cannot have a fair trial therein."

Having anticipated this request, Judge Rucker then ruled, "It is therefore ordered and adjudged by the Court that the venue of said cause be and the same is hereby changed to the Circuit Court of Carroll County, Missouri in the Twelfth Judicial Circuit on account of the alleged prejudice of the inhabitants of the Counties of Linn, Sullivan and Chariton." He also ruled the "Sheriff of Linn County having said defendants in custody is hereby commanded to remove the bodies of the defendants to the jail of the County of Carroll."

After the court hearing the brothers were taken back to the meeting room in the jail where their father and brothers were waiting. Neither of their wives was in attendance. The first words out of Bill's mouth were, "Well, the show's over."

In spite of the apparent coolness of Bill, when meeting with his family he shed tears along with the other members of his family as they said their goodbyes. George was as stoic as his usual demeanor, giving the appearance that none of this bothered him.

Soon it was time to leave the Linn County courthouse where they were escorted again by train to the Carroll County jail in Carrollton. During all the time the Taylors were in Linn County for this proceeding there was no violence of any kind. Thanks to Sheriff Barton and his deputies, the crowds were orderly.

Although Della had wanted to go to Linneus for the arraignment, she knew George did not want her to be there. It was clear she would only be able to get a glimpse and might not be able to speak to him.

The cold December weather was not amenable to taking the babies to the courthouse for such a brief encounter. However, the family did want to know about the proceedings, so David, Drue or Willie took daily turns going the twelve miles to Linneus to report on what happened in court.

Della had spent the days knitting a few garments for Christmas gifts for the girls. By now her knitting skills had much improved and the caps, booties, and sweaters she completed were quite nice. She was just binding off the cap she was making for Georgia when her father returned late on the Monday evening of the arraignment.

"Please, Pa, tell me all about what happened. How did George look? I hope there wasn't any violence. Where will the trial be?"

Slowly, David began telling of the day's events. He said, "The trial will be in March in Carrollton. If we go we will need to find a place to stay because it is too far to go every day."

Turning to her mother, Della asked, "Ma, do we have any family members in Carrollton where we can stay during the trial?"

"None I can think of off-hand, but we will find a way to be at the trial when the time comes. We have a couple months to prepare for it."

Through the long cold winter months, Della tried to keep busy to take her mind off the upcoming trial. On some days she went with either her dad or her brothers to George's farm to help with the chores. Taking care of the animals was one of her pleasures. She didn't mind trudging through the snow the short distance from her parent's house to the barn where their cows, pigs, and horses were kept on snowy days.

At other times she was happy to sit after the household chores were finished and take up her knitting. Flossie was growing up, sometimes she thought too quickly. The only word they were sure she was saying was "Ma-ma." Other words were usually accompanied with gestures in order to get what she wanted. And of course, she was into everything like a healthy toddler.

Georgia, on the other hand, gave her some worries. She had never seemed as strong as Flossie was as a baby. It was months after her birth before she was able to sleep through the night. Della felt like she was up all night with her at times. Georgia often was colicky after her feeding and Della had to walk the floor to keep her from screaming and waking the entire family. Those sleepless nights left Della tired and stressed.

The Gibson house was a two story four bedroom home similar to other farm homes of the era. Dave and Gonia's bedroom was on the first floor, while Della and her two daughters slept in a second floor bedroom. The house was not spacious, but was adequate for a family the size of the Gibson's. Iva May, Drue, Willie and Clarence Beverly also had bedrooms upstairs. Beverly as he was called commuted daily to his railroad job in Browning.

Chapter 21

After the long cold winter, Sheriff Niblo was happy to see a nice March day as a harbinger of spring. He was well aware that winter wasn't over yet and there could still be plenty of snow before April or May. The common expression often heard about Missouri weather was, "If you don't like the weather today, stick around; it will be different tomorrow."

The trial for the Taylor brothers was scheduled to begin in a few days. Niblo did not want to miss a minute of the action so he, along with crowds of people from Grundy, Sullivan, Linn and Livingston Counties, packed the trains going to Carrollton. For them, this was the trial of a lifetime. Housing was at a premium with the hotels and boarding homes filling up quickly. Niblo was lucky enough to find a room in a home not far from the courthouse; maybe because he was an officer of the law, but also, he was willing to stay the entire length of the trial. This promised more income for the proprietor of the house.

Not being a native of Missouri, Niblo found it interesting when one of the other roomers filled him in on the history of this area of the state. The man told him Carrollton, the county seat of Carroll County, Missouri, was organized from Ray County in 1833 and named for Charles Carroll of Carrollton. He was told the courthouse where this trial is to be heard is the third one for Carroll County. The first courthouse completed in 1834 was an eighteen by twenty foot building made of logs. The second, completed in December of 1849, was a two-story brick building occupying a forty-foot square in the center of the main square in town. The current courthouse was completed in 1867 and was also a two-story brick building on the town square.

The sheriff knew that Carrollton was a part of the Twelfth Judicial Circuit presided over by Judge W. W. Rucker who also presided over the arraignment. Spectators in the courtroom found Rucker to be a clean-shaven man with a deep dimple in his chin. It was known that the judge attracted attention wherever he was whether in the courtroom or just walking down the street. Born and educated in Virginia, Rucker spoke with a southern accent. The story told was that after arriving in Missouri in 1873, he taught school for two years, and then read law in Brookfield where he was admitted to the bar in 1876. Niblo knew that Rucker was first elected Prosecuting Attorney of Chariton County later in 1876 and was reelected to this office until he ran for the office of Circuit Judge of the Twelfth district. His reputation of being a vigorous prosecuting attorney helped to secure his election to the office in 1892. Despite his youth, he found favor with the inhabitants of the counties in the Twelfth District and Niblo expected he would be a fair and compassionate judge during this trial.

Judge Rucker instructed Carroll County Sheriff Stanley to summons one hundred fifty men from which a jury panel of forty was to be empaneled. On March 18, 1895, the court opened with the attorneys for both the State and the Taylor brothers bring asked if each side is ready for trial. The prosecution and the defense both answered, "Ready."

The crowd got what they came for when George and Bill Taylor were escorted into the courtroom. Neither of the brothers exhibited fear or concern. One would have thought they were just a part of the crowd by their smiling faces. They gave the appearance of two well-dressed, well-groomed men without a care. George sat with a nonchalant look during the proceedings but Bill took a close interest in the inspection of the potential jurymen being scrutinized by the attorneys.

J. B. Hale, Virgil Conkling, E. R. Stephens, D. M. Wilson, and A. W. Meyers were the attorneys present for the defense. Those present for the state were T. M. Bresnehen, A. W. Mullins and L. A. Holliday. During the questioning it was found very few of the panel could answer they did not have an opinion about the case, but if they stated they could give a fair and impartial verdict they were accepted. After several days of extensive questioning of the jury pool, thirty-three members were selected. Judge Rucker ordered all of them to be on hand by Tuesday afternoon for the case to begin promptly at eight o'clock Wednesday morning, March 27, 1895.

When the train pulled into the station in Carrollton on Tuesday evening, three of its large passenger coaches were full of witnesses and spectators arriving with the expectation this trial would last for more than a week. A large part of the crowd were women.

Sheriff Niblo, among the crowd in town, mingled with first one group, and then another to get a sense of the feelings about the trial. Reporters from many cities were on hand to gain as much information as they could for their particular newspaper. If an opportunity arose to interview George or Bill there was always a reporter present. However, the only thing the brothers would say about their case was they expect to be acquitted of all charges. Of other matters, both willingly talked at length with reporters or bystanders but not about the case.

One story that made the rounds of the crowds was one published in local newspapers about Hurley Goin, the fellow on trial for shooting Constable Hall. The story tying Goin to the Meeks murder was that he rode into Chillicothe the morning after the murder on a well lathered horse. The story was disproved, but there were still people who believed it. There was talk the defense would develop a connection to this story.

Prosecuting Attorney Bresnehen and Sheriff Niblo found time to make observations to each other from time to time. "What is your take on what the defense has to offer?" he asked Niblo.

"I think it is a good idea to keep a close watch on their team. I wouldn't be surprised at anything they will try to come up with."

"We believe we have a good case and the jury will find the Taylors guilty, but be prepared for some shenanigans by the defense."

Chapter 22

Della, Flossie, Georgia and Gonia were among the crowds of passengers arriving in Carrollton on Tuesday evening March 26th. The two women were acquainted with some of the others on the train who were also scheduled as witnesses and had spent time chatting with them. Della and Gonia were not familiar with the town of Carrollton and didn't know how to get to the rooming house where the witnesses were to stay. One of the women they had spoken with on the way knew where the house was and told them to follow her.

Della's emotions were on edge. Anxious to see George, but fearful of the trial and what the outcome of it would be were all raging through her mind, making her a bundle of nerves. Still she must appear calm for her daughters because they would sense something was wrong if she didn't hold herself together.

Gonia did her best to keep calm and tried to say soothing words to ease Della's tensions. Dave was not called as a witness, so he and his children remained at home to look after the chores. He was good at making others feel comfortable, so would have been a calming influence, but he really did not want to be anywhere near this trial.

Before nine o'clock on Wednesday, Gonia, Della, and the girls were part of the sea of people pushing to be admitted to the courtroom for the start of the trial. They walked down the center aisle and found seats near the front a couple rows back of the defense attorneys. Gonia picked up Flossie, sat the wiggling toddler on her lap and whispered in her ear, "Now you will have to be quiet while we sit here. Your papa will be coming in soon so show him what a good girl you can be."

At ten-thirty, George and Bill were escorted into the courtroom by Sheriff Stanley. Della was able to see George but could not speak to him. *Oh, how handsome he is,* thought Della when she saw him. She was glad that for the time being, Georgia was sleeping in her arms so would not cause a disturbance.

When the twelve members of the jury were brought into the courtroom, Della saw Bill give each of them close scrutiny, while George didn't seem to care. She sat almost in tears, listening carefully as Prosecuting Attorney Bresnehen read first the indictment and then a statement of the case.

This is the way he told it:

Gentlemen of the jury, we are about to investigate a charge of murder against William P. and George E. Taylor on the night of the 10th of May, 1894, in Linn Co. a short distance east of Browning, in the northern part of Linn county. We submit, gentlemen of the jury, that what shall be shown to you by the evidence to be the most awful and dreadful murder that was ever committed within the jurisdiction of Linn, Chariton or Sullivan counties or within the state of Missouri or any other state. It is the burden on the part of the state to prove to you by evidence that that murder was committed by William P. and George E. Taylor on the evening of the 10th of May, 1894. George Taylor who resided some distance in the country, drove into Browning with a lumber wagon; was seen to have a consultation with his brother William Taylor, and sometime after that in the evening drove up to William Taylor's house to the yard, and ate supper there. That after supper they came out of the house and put some quilts and comforts in the wagon; that sometime after eight o'clock the witnesses will tell you that George, sometime after sundown, after it was growing dark, started and drove across the railroad in the direction, the general direction of which he lived; that after he got east of where the road turned north, turned into the road north toward Milan. That about that time William Taylor was seen to come up through Browning and up the railroad track north. It will be in evidence that the road turning north intersected and crossed the railroad tracks about a quarter of a mile north of

Browning; that by going up the railroad tracks in the direction that William Taylor went, he would intersect the same road the George Taylor was traveling.

Della listened with rapt attention to the telling of the entire story. She had only heard how Bill and George were accused of murdering the Meeks family, but had not heard the whole story of what happened that night until now. Bresnehen went into great detail in his telling.

Continuing on he said:

Gentlemen of the jury, it will be in evidence by competent testimony by the witnesses who saw George and William Taylor several miles north of Browning driving in a lumber wagon with a team they had in town going north toward Milan. It is about twelve miles north of Browning, I believe. They were seen driving several miles north of Browning in the direction north of Milan along about the neighborhood of ten o'clock at night. We will show you gentlemen of the jury and prove to you by witnesses that were seen in Milan; that they went to the Gus Meeks' house; that George Taylor went into the house; that William Taylor stayed outside with the team; that the Meeks family, composed of himself, his wife and three little girls, the oldest probably nine years old, went with George Taylor into the wagon, got into the wagon and that William and George Taylor then in company with the Meeks family drove north. That on the morning of the 11th of May, a little girl, a small little girl, called at a neighbors and imparted to them the information that her father and mother were killed; that her two little sisters were murdered; that she was knocked in the head; that they were buried in a straw stack over in the field probably a quarter of a mile distant from the neighbor's house where she went. That on receiving this information a little boy ten or twelve years old went to investigate and see if it were true. That when he came down to the field where the straw stack was and pointed out to him by little Nellie Meeks, he came across George Taylor harrowing in his corn field; it had been planted I believe but was not yet up; that he said to him that a little girl came to the house and said there was somebody dead over there in that straw stack, and says "lets go and see." Thereupon George Taylor says, "No we haven't time, let somebody else do that, come on to the house. Drove his harrow through the field at a rapid rate and drove on up to the front of the house, told the boy to hold the team, went in and sent somebody out to hitch the team, got a horse, saddled it, and rode rapidly to Browning; had a consultation with William Taylor, his brother, who immediately got a horse, saddled it and both rode rapidly from town in an easterly direction.

It took all of Gonia's patience to keep little Flossie quiet and to not make a disturbance. She was an active two-year-old so she wanted down from her grandmother's lap so she could walk or run around. Baby Georgia had been sleeping but began to stir. Della let her attention slip from Bresnehen as she concentrated on keeping Georgia quiet. When the attorney began talking about the motive for this crime, Della again listened closely so she could better understand why the brothers wanted to kill the Meeks family. This is the way Bresnehen told it:

Gentlemen of the jury, you would necessarily think what was their motive in this terrible crime and dreadful murder. Gentlemen of the jury, it was not for money, robbery was not the cause, but there was a motive on the part of these defendants to wipe out Gus Meeks that is stronger and more potent that prompted the arms of the Taylor brothers in this crime. We will show you that Gus Meeks and William Taylor were friends, had been associated together a great deal; and it will then appear that Gus Meeks on one occasion was brought into court and gave testimony against the defendant William Taylor in a trial in Linn county for a crime in which he was charged, and further gentlemen of the jury, that Gus Meeks was taken to the penitentiary for the crime in which he was jointly indicted with the defendant, William Taylor, for the larceny committed in Sullivan county; that Gus Meeks in this indictment went into court and plead guilty; that William Taylor got a continuance in this case and Gus Meeks was sent to the penitentiary; and further it will be shown to you that Gus Meeks was pardoned by the governor to enable him to testify in the trial of the case with which William Taylor was charged for larceny that happened in Sullivan county; that he lived in Milan at the time of the murder; that he had been back some little time from the penitentiary; we will show you by the evidence here the statements of these defendants, probably both, but at least one of them, that Gus Meeks would never come into court and testify against them. That William Taylor was asked, "Now they have Meeks back here again, what are you going to do about it," that he says "Damn him, he must be gotten rid of, out of the way." This was the motion that caused them to commit this awful crime. We will show you gentlemen of the jury, that on the day of the murder there was received in Milan, through the post office, a letter written to Gus Meeks telling him everything was all right, we will be ready tonight. No name signed to that letter, but it was written on the letter head by William Taylor on the Exchange bank paper, that it was mailed by him and received there. That letter will be in evidence and will be the testimony of witnesses here that that letter was written by Bill Taylor. Gentlemen of the jury this will be the case presented to you.

What the attorney was saying seemed to Della was that Bill was the one who wanted to get rid of Gus Meeks. *Why did Bill have to get George involved in this dreadful crime?* Della was glad to hear Bresnehen close his opening statement for the State with these words:

We submit to your judgment whether or not we establish evidence that the men who committed that crime were William and George Taylor. We said to you in the beginning and say it now that unless the state shows to you these facts that I have stated, that unless we show them to be true and unless we convince you by evidence that they committed this crime, we do not ask for a conviction and do not want one but we believe and know that the state will show to you that no other hand committed the crime than William and George Taylor, and if this is not shown we ask for no conviction. [3]

Annalou Mack

Gonia and Della were happy to hear the defense would not make a statement at this time. The girls were getting restless and it was time to leave the courtroom for a while. Before the break the defense asked that the witnesses not be allowed in the courtroom during the trial and the judge agreed. This meant Della would not be allowed in court except when she was testifying. She wasn't sure if it was a good thing or a bad thing. At least she wouldn't have to listen to her friends and neighbors say awful things about George.

The 12 jurors:

Dave Jamison
Barnett M. Hudson
W. H. Brammer
Benj. Glover
George Fleming
Adolph Auer
Frank Yehle
Elijah Baker
J.T. Noland
James H. Creel
J. A. Rose
Granville Jenkins.

Chapter 23

Sheriff Niblo made sure he was up early and ready to go to the courthouse before the second day of the trial began. The first day was about what he had expected. Before he went to sleep the night before, he went over in his mind the testimony given by Mrs. Martha Meeks on the first day.

Upon direct examination by the State she stated she was sixty-one years old; lived in Milan and was the mother of Gus Meeks. She related that between eleven and twelve o'clock at night on May 10, 1894, George Taylor came to her house. She said that on the Tuesday before, Gus had been to Cora and there made arrangements with George and William Taylor to leave the country for $800 and a team and provisions to last them on their trip. He was to leave so as not to testify against the Taylors in a trial in Sullivan County. William Taylor wrote a letter to Gus Meeks telling him to "be ready at ten o'clock, all is right." She said the letter was not signed but Gus Meeks said it was from William Taylor. She said she didn't read the letter because she can't read or write but her daughter read it to her after she found the family had been killed and she gave the letter to B. F. Pierce. She related she was in the kitchen when George Taylor came in the house; there was no lamp in the room but it was moonlit. He passed into the other room where there was a lamp, picked up one of the bundles where the Meeks family clothes were tied, and carried them to the wagon followed by Gus Meeks. Gus came back and got his wife and children and she heard the wagon driven off north toward the Catholic Church. She could hear it for quite a distance. She said Gus Meeks told her George and William Taylor had come after them to take them away and that the family left with them.

On cross examination she said she had never spoken to George Taylor, but he was pointed out to her in the courtroom in a former trial. He had been at her house a few evenings before and she did not speak to him, but was in the other room, and she looked through the crack in the door and saw him. She heard him talking, and Gus wanted them to give him $1,000 to leave but they would not agree to it. She knew George Taylor before she came in the court room today and also knew William Taylor. She didn't see William Taylor or the wagon on the night of May 10th, but Gus Meeks told her William Taylor was out there with the wagon, and she heard them drive off in a northerly direction toward the Catholic church and that the wagon made a great deal of racket. She heard it for about an hour afterwards. The roads were muddy but were macadamized. She did not want them to go, but Gus said he was not afraid. He was sure they would not hurt him. She told B. F. Pierce and Colonel Butler it was the Taylors who came after them and took them away before they ever told her the bodies were found on the Taylor farm. B. F. Pierce broke the news to her and first asked her where they had gone and she said to the country. After he told her of the murder she said they left with the Taylors the night before. She did not tell Mrs. Johnson and Mrs. Cooper, two of her neighbors, that it was not the Taylors and she knew both of them well enough to recognize them anywhere. [4]

There seemed to be more people at the courthouse this morning than were there yesterday. As Niblo looked around he found it was women who made up a large part of the crowd. Probably half of the five hundred people struggling and pushing to get into the little courtroom were women. If they couldn't find a seat, they balanced on the narrow railing which separated the lawyers from the spectators or on the window ledges or the tobacco-stained carpet. Even on the steps leading to the judge's bench. The object of the women's attention was to get a glance at the handsome face of George Taylor. Niblo saw it was plain the women held as much sympathy for the Taylor brothers as the men held hatred.

Upon entering the room Niblo saw his good friend Ben Pierce in the courtroom and sauntered over to talk to him for a few minutes before court began. Little Nellie Meeks was with him this morning which caused many heads to turn in her direction.

"Ben, is Nellie going to be a witness today?"

"I don't think so. You know all this is a bit much for a seven-year-old. It is traumatic for her and any time she is asked anything about that night, it just brings back the horror she went through. If the case can be won without her testimony it will be better for her. She is doing well in our family and the nightmares are receding a little."

"Well, glad you are helping her adjust to this situation. Looks like it's about time for court to start. I'll talk to you later."

When George and Bill were brought into court, Niblo thought they looked like the trial was having an impact on them. They seemed to be taking an interest in the proceedings. During the testimony of Sallie Carter, they often quietly consulted with their attorneys.

Sheriff Niblo listened intently to Mrs. John [Sallie] Carter as she gave her account of the happenings on the morning of May 11, 1894, to E. B. Fields, the attorney for the State.

> I live in Browning; I am fifty-three years old; the wife of John Carter. I have been in Browning and vicinity since I was eight years old. My husband has a farm about four and a half miles southeast of Browning which joins George Taylor's farm on the west. My husband was in Linneus on May 10th and 11th, 1894, and on Thursday evening, the 10th of May, 1894, I went to this farm about five o'clock, where Frank Carter, a nephew of my husband resided. Frank's nine-plus year old half-brother, Jimmie Carter was there. On the morning of the 11th of May we arose about four o'clock and about five o'clock Frank Carter went up to the timber to finish planting some corn. Between five and six o'clock that morning a little girl

came there crying. I said, "Hello honey, where did you come from?" She replied, "I slept in the straw stack over there." The straw stack was about seventy-five yards from the door of the house, northeast, and George Taylor's dwelling house was about a quarter of a mile from our house. When the little girl got there she had one hand up on her face and her cap in her hand and was crying. I says, "hush up your crying and tell me what you want," and she kept crying and said her little sister was there in the straw stack and I asked her how she got there and she said two men put her there and then she asked me to go and see about her little sister. She didn't tell me her name then. I sent Jimmie Carter to the straw stack to see if he could find anything, and while he was gone I asked the little girl her name and she said it was Nellie Meeks. I went out as far as the barn to call Jimmie and saw him going across the field with a man with a harrow and that they went to George Taylor's barn lot. Jimmie held the horses and the man went to the house and then another little boy came and held the horses and I called Jimmie and he came back and said he could find nothing. This little girl then walked back with him and I sat on the partition fence between Frank Carter's and George Taylor's and told them to holler if they found anything. In a little while they came back and said they found them in the straw stack. I then sent Jimmie to John Gooch to report what he had seen, and then he and Nathan Harvey started to Browning to tell the news. Jimmie got out of the buggy in the road and went through the field and told Frank Carter and the little Harvey boy went to Browning. It was about eight o'clock when he started from the farm. I saw the dead bodies; they were those of a man, woman and two children, one about five years old and another about a year and a half; they were bloody. There was a quilt there partly burned. The child who came to the house was bloody and had a cut on her head. Upon Nellie Meeks being presented to me in the court room this morning, I examined the cut and said that was the child that came to the house at five o'clock on the morning of May 11th, 1894. [5]

Mrs. Carter was cross examined by Colonel J. B. Hale with very little change in the direct examination.

The next witness was Jimmie Carter who was examined by E. B. Fields, attorney for the State:

> I live west of Browning, am half-brother of Frank Carter and Sallie Carter is my aunt. On the morning of May 11th I was at Frank Carter's and was standing in the door and saw a little girl coming up to the house crying and she said her little sister was there in the straw stack and Aunt Sallie sent me over to see what I could find. I saw a man harrowing around there and told him that a little girl had come to our house and said her little sister was in the straw stack and that her father and mother were way up yonder and I said, "let's go and find them." And he said, "No, let somebody else find them. Come up to the barn with me." And he had me hold the horse while he went to the house. The woman was washing and I didn't hold the team, but sat on the wagon box. And there had been shoveled dry dirt and mud over it. He says, "did the little girl say anything about her pa and ma?" and I says, "Yes, she said they are way up yonder in the road." That was before I told him what the child had said about her father and mother. After he got to the house he sent a boy a little larger than me down, and the boy said that he told him to unhitch the team and saddle up a horse. And he started to unhitch the team. Aunt Sallie called me and I went back, and did not see him saddle the horse. I went back to the house and then me and the little girl went back to the stack and at first we couldn't find anything and then we looked on the other side, and saw a white covering and lifted it up and saw a woman's face. We went back to the house and then I got in a buggy with the Harvey boy and he let me out in the road and I went through the field and told Frank and went to town. I did not know at whose house I went where the straw stack was, nor did I know the man that I met in the field, but the house was straight east from Frank Carter's and there was no other house between them. The man that was harrowing had a black mustache about a finger nail's length. I went to John Gooch's to tell him of the discovery and afterwards went to get Frank Carter. [6]

After witnesses, Pierce, Dillinger, Gooch and J. W. Gibson testified for the state, Judge Rucker called a noon recess. Niblo's stomach was telling him it was time to fill it when he hurried out of the courthouse to return to his rooming house for the noon meal. He planned to make it as quick as possible because he didn't want to miss a word of what the witnesses had to say about the crime.

Chapter 24

When Judge Rucker raised his gavel for testimony to resume after the noon break, Sheriff Niblo was in his seat, anxious to hear what the next witnesses had to say. Several of them spoke about whether there was blood on the Taylor's wagon when each of them had examined it. He listened intently as James Harris and his brother John testified followed by John Cornett, E. J. Barton, Peter McDonald, M. L. Gibson, David Beacham and J. D. Jessee. But the one who held his undivided attention was Jerry South, the man who captured George and Bill at Buffalo, Arkansas.

Niblo was not the only one intently interested in the testimony of Jerry South. This soft spoken, mild-mannered, handsome southern gentleman had captured the imagination of the people in and around Carrollton. He was constantly interrupted on the street with warm greetings and questions about the capture of the Taylors.

Jerry South had accomplished a lot in his young life. He was born in Frankfort, Kentucky and was brought to Arkansas by his parents at a young age. He was first elected to public office when only twenty-three years old and had been regularly reelected to the Arkansas legislature at the end of each term.

A. J. Mullins, counsel for the State, called Jerry C. South to the witness stand.

His testimony was this:

> I live at Mt. Home, Arkansas; have been a citizen of that State and county about eight years; am a lawyer; graduated at the University eight years ago and located in Arkansas; I represent my county in the Legislature, this being the third

term. I first saw the defendants about the 20th and 21st of June last at Buffalo City, Macon County, Arkansas, a small town on the river with only one store and dwelling there, situated on the White river. It is a town about fourteen miles from where I live and is nearly seventy miles from the nearest railroad point; the nearest railroad being the K. C., Fort Scott & Memphis. The next time I saw them was on Saturday, the 25th of June, I think. They were in E. L. Hayes' store, his being the only store there, and were stopping with Mr. Hayes. I am acquainted with the people around there and thought these men must be looking for some land business. Since I was interested in such as that, I made inquiries about them. I had a conversation with them at the time and they gave their names as Pierce (Will Taylor's name) and Edwards (George Taylor's name.) They ate at the same table with me and I watched them very closely. William Taylor kept an eye on me rather suspicious and it excited my curiosity. After supper about two hours, I went back to my home; thought of the matter considerably on the way home as to who they might be. Then I thought of the article in the newspaper that the Taylors were going through Southwest Missouri and thinking that if they too saw the same article that they would most likely take the course to that little town. It occurred to me that it might be them. I went to the newspaper office and got some *St. Louis Republicans* and *Globe Democrats* and looked through them and found their description in the paper. In the *Republic* I found pictures of them. Then being satisfied that at least one of them was the man, I determined to send someone to arrest them and tried to get several parties but did not succeed, so I went down there on my way to a Masonic convention, which was eight miles off the road and I couldn't get there until three o'clock in the afternoon. I went to Buffalo City, and got there a little before sundown and found the Taylors sitting in the store. I struck up a conversation with everybody in the store trying to draw them into the conversation; learned several things that corresponded with the descriptions in the paper, among which was that I saw William Taylor buy a pair of No. eight shoes, which corresponded with the number the paper stated he wore. Being pretty sure of the parties, by a little strategy, I secured a gun from Mr. Hayes' clerk and loaded it. Directly they stepped out of the store and started over to the house, and I followed them and when we got up the road a piece I called them to halt, that I wanted to speak to them. They both turned around and I told them to throw up their hands and leveled the shot gun at them. George Taylor threw his hands up readily but William Taylor hesitated a little but in a minute threw his up too. They then walked back to me and we went back to the store, and I had them searched and found Will had a pistol. I had all weapons and knives taken away from them. They asked what they were arrested for and I told them they looked like men that were wanted in Missouri for a crime and showed them the pictures I had of them covering up the names. George Taylor just looked down the road, but William Taylor looked at them and kinder nodded his head and said, "yes, I heard they had those things out. I guess we had just as well give in." In the meantime I had written Sheriff Barton to send me photographs of the men and told him I thought I had them. Capt. Craven helped me watch them that night; he watched half the night and I the other half. I telegraphed Sheriff Barton that I had the men and took them to Little Rock and from there to St. Louis and there met Mr. Barton and Mr. Pierce. We took them on to Macon and I went off to Brookfield and Linneus. We took them to Macon so as to avoid any violence at Brookfield. I had captured the men, and believed them innocent and did not want any harm done them but wanted them to have a fair trial. I did not have any trouble with them at all. I talked with them about the killing and they said they could prove an alibi that although he, William Taylor, did write that letter to Gus Meeks, and although they started away with the family, having given them the $1000 to go, that someone might have killed them for their money after they had left them.

Annalou Mack

Colonel J. B. Hale for the defense conducted the cross examination. During the cross examination, South further stated,

"I got a reward for their capture of $1,500, but it was not understood between me and the Taylors that I was to make a capture of them and then turn over half of the bootie to them. I was friendly to the Taylors when I captured them, and they were friendly to me. I treated them well while they were under my custody. I never entertained any idea of being employed on the defense as has been rumored, and the Taylors did not admit their guilt or innocence to me." [7]

This was the last testimony for the afternoon session. The court took a supper recess then reconvened at seven o'clock. At which time the State announced they would rest. It was then ordered the court would begin at nine o'clock the next morning giving the defense time to arrange their testimony.

Chapter 25

Although Della could not be in the courtroom when the other witnesses gave their testimony, she was not barred from reading the newspaper giving what was said on the witness stand. Upon reading what Martha Meeks said about the night of the murder, Della was sure the old woman had made a mistake. She hadn't actually seen George and Bill; just thought she heard George's voice so she had to be mistaken.

The most surprising testimony was from James Harris who had worked for George for several months before the murders. He seemed to be a nice quiet young man and did good work for them. They thought of him as loyal, so it was hard to believe he was a witness for the State. His testimony did not seem to be favorable to George.

Della shook her head in disbelief when she read what Harris said when questioned by Attorney Bresnehen:

> I live in Browning; lived in Linn county near North Salem. On the 10th and 11th of May; I was at Dave Gibson's the night of the Meeks murder, he lived about half a quarter from George Taylor's south. On the morning of the murder I went to George Taylor's barn tolerably early, about half past five and there saw George Taylor currying his horses, washing their legs off with a bunch of hay or straw and some water which he had there in a bucket. They were Mr. James Taylor's horses. I ate breakfast at George Taylor's and then went to the timber to work in a wagon to which was hitched Mr. Jim [James] Taylor's team. It was the same team that George Taylor was washing off that morning. The wagon to which we hitched

the team was a lumber wagon with side boards. Before we left there he scraped some mud off the wagon and we drove on to Mr. James Taylor's. When we got there we took the bed off, and then went to the timber to work accompanied by Albert Taylor, Bill Taylor and Dave Gibson. I saw blood on the coupling pole of the wagon; was kind of a stream and the blood wasn't exactly dry but kinder dried. I went into the timber to haul wood and when I left, George Taylor was fixing to harrow. I believe about twelve o'clock or perhaps earlier, George and Bill Taylor came riding through the timber where we were on horseback and left their horses there. They talked a little to [James] Jim Taylor and then went through the timber on foot. After I got to the house I examined the wagon bed and found blood on it; a spot about as big as one hand. I also smelt coal oil about the wagon; the top bed was off the wagon; someone took the top bed off before I got there. I was at George Taylor's the evening of the 10th; came there in the afternoon and left about five o'clock and George Taylor was not at home. I stayed at Dave Gibson's that night and Billy and Drew [Dru] Gibson were there with me. Mrs. Gibson and her husband were at George Taylor's. When the team was taken to [James] Jim Taylor's, that team was unhitched and let out in the pasture and another was hitched to the wagon. Albert Taylor unhitched them and let them loose.

In his additional testimony when cross examined by Colonel J. B. Hale he stated,

"When the horses were hitched up that morning, they did not seem to be as pert as usual, but that they did not seem to be so very tired. I had not driven the team for a few weeks. I was bound over to the grand jury about two weeks after the Meeks murder and upon testifying before it was released.

I did not know what I was charged with; the marshal, Jones Wilson never told me. I didn't go to the place of the murder after it occurred, although I was within a quarter of a mile of George Taylor's farm, having gone to my brothers after hearing of the murder. [8]

Della said to Gonia, "How could James say all those things about George after all we have done for him. Ma, we are due in court this afternoon. Are you sure what you will say on the witness stand?"

"Yes, Dellie, I know we have to be very confident in our testimony. We are sure George was at home that night. We both think there is another explanation for what happened the night of May 10. Maybe someday it will all be clear to us; until then we must keep our head high and believe in our hearts this will turn out good."

After a good meal in the rooming house dining room, Gonia, Della and the two babies walked over to the courthouse to wait until each were called to testify. They were seated in a small room away from the court chambers. The courtroom was filled to overflowing with many people in the halls hoping to find a seat or at least get a glimpse of some of the witnesses. This trial had generated a lot of interest. Gonia and Della knew from things they overheard that George did not have much support and it was not going well for him and his brother.

Later in the afternoon Gonia was called to testify. She handed Flossie to Della and with her head held high she walked into the courtroom and to the witness stand.

Virgil Conkling for the defense examined her and she said,

My name is Gonia Gibson, the wife of Dave Gibson. George Taylor is my son-in-law; married my oldest daughter, Della. I live four miles south of Browning and on the 10th of May 1894, I lived about a hundred yards from George Taylor's house southeast. I was at home on the 10th of May, 1894 and saw George Taylor that afternoon. I first saw him at his house when me and my little daughter had started out to hunt turkey nests. I was over to my daughter's and stopped and stayed with her for about half an hour. George was in the house at that time. I did not pay any attention to his dress but he had on his every day clothes and was putting on his shoes. Nobody was there but myself, little daughter [Ivy Mae] and George's wife [Della]. George was going to Browning. I think he started a little after three. He went in James Taylor's wagon and had Mr. Taylor's team. He had wagon wheels in the wagon; all four of them, but he left one of them at home. He was taking them to Browning to have them fixed but threw out one because it didn't need repairing. Albert Taylor put the wheels in the wagon. George was in the house when they were put there. After George left I stayed with my daughter till about four o'clock and then went to my house with my daughter George's wife, my youngest and George's baby; the baby is about a year old. George's wife stayed at my house till after supper. I washed my dishes and she was feeling bad and was going up home so I told her to wait till I got through with my work and I would go with her. My little girl went with us. After a while my husband came up; next to my oldest son was in the habit of sleeping there and it was his intention of sleeping there that night. I stayed at her house that night and so did my husband as she was feeling so badly. My husband and I slept in the north room of George Taylor's that night. My daughter was in a delicate condition and about a month later a child was born. My daughter slept in the south room that night. My husband and I retired to our room upstairs about eight o'clock or a little later. I went down stairs about nine o'clock as I heard George come. I thought I would go down and see how my daughter was getting along. I went in her room and George Taylor, wife and baby were in there. His wife was in the bed and he was on the east side of the room; had off his shoes, coat and hat. I stayed in the room only a minute or two; went back upstairs and went to bed. I came down again about midnight as I heard the little baby crying and stepped out of the door on the step and immediately after this went in my daughter's room and did not see George Taylor in the room as there was no light in the room, but I said 'George give me the baby I will take it upstairs' and he said we had as well worry with it as you. I am familiar with his voice and George Taylor was in the room then in bed; this was about midnight. I took the baby upstairs and went to bed with it and kept it the rest of the night. We got up about daylight; my husband got up first and I got up a little afterwards and went downstairs to my daughter's room and saw Della and George. He was laying over behind his wife and my daughter was in the front part of the bed. I brought the baby down and laid it in the bed with her. He said good morning Mrs. Gibson and I said good morning Mr. Taylor; this was spoken in jest and I then went to my house. [9]

After Gonia was excused she went back to the witness room and breathed a sigh of relief. "I have done my part now. I hope it is enough."

Before it was time for Della to testify, Anna Cooper and Hannah Johnson were called by the defense. Both of these women lived in Milan and were not known to Della and Gonia. Since they were defense witnesses, it was hoped they were saying things that would help the case for George and Bill.

When Della was called, Gonia took Flossie and Della carried Georgia into the courtroom with her. As she approached the stand to give her testimony, she walked over to the defendant's table and handed the nine months old baby to George. He gladly took her; smiled at her and mumbled a few baby words to her. She seemed to like the attention she was getting.

Della stood before the clerk with her hand on the Bible and swore to tell the truth. Just as she said, "I do" baby Georgia let out a loud scream. Nothing George did seemed to calm her down so Della hurried over to remove the baby from George's arms. Georgia's screaming soon quieted to a few hiccups and sniffles as Della took the stand.

Della's testimony was short while being examined by Virgil Conkling for the defense. She said,

"My name is Della Taylor. I am the wife of the defendant, George Taylor. I live five miles south of Browning. I am 19 years old. My mother's name is Gonia Gibson. I have lived in Linn County all my life. My husband went to Browning on May 10th, 1894 to take some wagon wheels starting with four and taking three that were to be fixed. My husband got home that night about nine o'clock and stayed in bed with me all the balance of the night. We got up about five o'clock in the morning."

Annalou Mack

She was cross examined by Maj. Mullins, but before he said anything, the defense objected on the Rule of Law which required the wife of a defendant should not be cross examined. It was allowed and a few questions were asked to which she replied,

> "He went to Browning in his father's wagon and with his team and returned in the same wagon he went off in. His brother, Albert, started with him and he returned alone with the same team." [10]

As soon as she finished her testimony, Della stood up and started down the steps from the witness stand. The clerk moved forward to help her since she was holding the baby. Moving down the aisle she briefly touched George's arm as she walked by. It was all she could do to keep tears from overflowing and running down her cheeks. *Will my testimony be enough to clear George of this awful deed?*

Della, turning her head to the left as she walked down the aisle, saw Sheriff Niblo looking at her with a cold stare. His look gave her cold chills. It was as if he was accusing her of not only being untruthful about the night of the murders, but of being a party to it. *How could he be so cruel?* She quickly turned her head and hurried out the door. It was time for this nightmare to be over.

Chapter 26

The Assistant Attorney General of the State, Morton Jourdan, was seen in Carrollton Monday morning. As Sheriff Niblo talked to neighbors, he heard that Governor Stone had sent Jourdan to determine if there was a need to send the state militia to protect the Taylors. Niblo learned that Mr. Jourdan denied the rumor and was only there visiting friends and to hear the final arguments in the trial. He didn't think there was a danger of mob violence because it was probable that the jury would convict on the evidence. However, Jourdan agreed that should there be a vote for acquittal, the results were unpredictable.

Sitting in the courtroom that morning Sheriff Niblo heard Judge Rucker read the instructions to the jury submitted by the attorneys. When court had convened at nine o'clock, the room was packed with observers. There was not even standing room available. Niblo noticed that on one side of the table Nellie Meeks sat on Mrs. Pierce's lap and Bill and George Taylor on the other. Soon after court opened, Della and Gonia entered with Flossie and Georgia. They pushed through the crowd to sit down near Maude Taylor and her three daughters sitting near George and Bill.

Niblo saw that Bertha Taylor and Nellie Meeks, who were near the same age, sat on opposite sides of the table. At first they just looked at each other. After a few minutes they smiled and seemed to want to talk to each other. To prevent any further communication, Bill turned Bertha around on his knee so her back was to Nellie. It looked obvious to Niblo that this display of wives and children was planned by the lawyers for the defense to have an effect on the jury.

It was a long day for Della with her two children in the crowded courtroom. George occasionally took either Flossie or Georgia on his lap for a few minutes. Della felt almost as if they were a family, even under these trying conditions.

E. B. Fields of Browning was the first to deliver the argument for the state. Most of his speech concerned the harrow tracks that George made the morning when the bodies were discovered. He made much of the fact that the tracks were made several times over the wagon tracks, crossing the corn rows diagonally. That didn't seem to be the way a farmer would have gone about harrowing a corn field.

Conkling spoke next for the defense, taking up the rest of the morning. He spoke to the jury saying, "You have been here now for about five or six days, you have been secluded from the rest of the world; the reason for it was that the duty that you had taken upon yourselves was a solemn and sacred duty. I assure you gentlemen that during these five or six days that you have been resting under the solemn obligation of a juror's oath in a case where life, and death are put in your hands, I assure you that in that time my heart has been as solemn as yours." [11]

Conkling reviewed the evidence in the case and often questioned the veracity of some of the State's witnesses. The attorney was an emotional speaker and at one point during his stirring speech, tears rolled down his cheeks and his voice broke with sobs as did all the Taylor family including Bill, George and their wives. This seemed to be the first time during the trial that George had displayed strong emotion. As he bent over the court railing, his shoulders shook with sobs when he wept. There may not have been a dry eye in the courtroom at that time with sobs being heard all over the room.

Judge Rucker called a ten minute recess to give them time to collect themselves. During the break Bill's daughter, Bertha pulled her knees into the seat of her chair then bent over the back, reached over and touched the hair of little Nellie Meeks. Nellie smiled at Bertha and gave her a piece of the orange she was eating. These innocent ones had no idea of how the proceedings in this court would affect the remainder of their lives.

Following the recess, Conkling spoke for two more hours before summing up his closing statement to the jury with, "Gentlemen I ask you to try this case before Almighty God, let his hand guide you, and if you have any doubt as to their guilt or innocence let them have the benefit of such a doubt. Mercy is asked at your hands, the lives of two innocent men are naked at your hands, and I say to you again that George and William Taylor are asking at your hands a verdict of not guilty." [12] Those words sent tears streaming down Della's face. It certainly was her wish that the jury would find George and Bill not guilty.

At two o'clock court reopened with L. A. Holliday being the first to speak for the State. He spent some time in explaining to the jury the difference between a petit jury and a grand jury. After reviewing points in the testimony of witnesses, he said, "This case is the worst case that ever appeared in the annals of this state, and the most bloody crime ever committed in the state of Missouri, or any other state in the Union. All we ask for is justice and what is right. If the testimony in this case does not develop and prove to your satisfaction that the defendants are guilty of these murders, we do not expect a conviction"

In his argument for the State, Major Mullins retold the story of the murder from the time George left for Browning until he and Bill disappeared into the woods. He was followed by former Congressman John B. Hale for the defense. Gonia listened carefully to his words and thought his speech was the most convincing of all the arguments heard so far. Hale was well known in the area. What might be helpful in this case was his record as a defense counselor in which the twenty cases he had defended none were convicted.

For the night session, T. M. Bresnehen gave the closing argument for the State, and Colonel A. W. Meyers presented the closing arguments for the defense. Della paid attention when Meyers said to the jury, "that upon your decision hang the lives of two human beings; that one little word in the verdict settles the destiny of two of our fellow beings; that this is a case of purely circumstantial evidence and if hung it might in years to come develop that they were not guilty and that their blood would be on your hands." [13]

Annalou Mack

He then referred to the testimony of George Taylor, his wife and that of Mrs. Gibson as to George being home all night, and that although Mrs. George Taylor being his wife and Mrs. Gibson his mother-in-law, that he knew they wouldn't swear to a falsehood, and that the jury should consider their testimony and give it as much weight as that of any other witness. He stated the same in regard to Mrs. William Taylor's testimony as to her husband being home all night, and Bill himself testifying that he was at home all night, and the testimony of two of his neighbors that they saw him in his yard the next morning about five o'clock."

Della was pleased that he had said that about both the testimony she gave and that of her mother, too. Hopefully that would make an impression on the jury.

It was late that evening when court was adjourned. Della and Gonia gathered up the two little ones and their belongings and walked back to the rooming house where they were staying. The trial was nearly over. They now had to wait for the verdict from the jury.

Chapter 27

The hours dragged on while Gonia and Della waited for the jury to reach a decision. Both had their knitting projects with them, so they did not have to sit in their room looking at the four walls. Sometimes they went into the parlor of the rooming house where other witnesses were gathered and made friends with a few of them. Della was especially interested in Alpha Van Wye because she had heard that Alpha testified that she had seen Bill at the bank the night of the murders.

As the women sat around the room visiting often the talk would turn to the trial. Della asked Alpha, "Did you really see Bill standing at the bank door the night of the murders?"

"That's the way I remember it. Mother and I were on our way to set up with my aunt, Mrs. Bertha McCullom who is dying from cancer. It was about ten at night when we passed the bank. Mr. Taylor was locking the bank door and I heard the key turn in the lock. He was still holding on to the door when he turned toward me."

"Well," Della said, "It should show he wasn't in Milan on the night of the murders. I guess you told it to the sheriff?"

Alpha hesitated for a couple minutes before she responded. "Actually I didn't think about it at first. It wasn't until later when Mother introduced me to Mr. Meyers when I remembered seeing Mr. Taylor at the bank on that night. It was a few months after when I went to his office on some other business and he asked me to sign a statement about seeing Mr. Taylor the night of the murder. I'm not sure how Mr. Meyers knew we had seen Mr. Taylor."

Della couldn't help but wonder if Alpha was remembering correctly or if she had been helped in making the recollection. But if it would help free Bill and George, then she was all for it. She missed George so much. It was all she could do to keep the tears at bay.

Turning away from the group Della headed for their room. "I need to go see about the little ones."

Although the girls were taking a nap, she did not want to leave them alone for too long. It was good she did because, Flossie was just waking up. Little Georgia was still sleeping but with Flossie tramping around in the room it would no doubt have awakened the baby soon.

Della took Flossie in her arms and gave her a big hug and several kisses. "I love you so much. We have to be strong now because it is just the three of us. We don't know when or if your daddy will be coming home."

Flossie looked up at her mother as if to say, "Okay Mama." Even at almost two, she wasn't talking much and probably didn't understand what her mother meant. She didn't remember her father because he had been gone from their home since she was a year old.

"It's alright; Mama will take care of you. And Grandma and Grandpa will take care of all of us." Della put Flossie down to play while she picked up her knitting to do another row. It was important for her to keep her hands busy and have something to occupy her mind.

Meanwhile, back in the parlor, Gonia was talking with Anna Cooper who had testified about the talk with Mrs. Meeks the day after the murder. Anna told Gonia, "I was at the Meeks' house the morning after the murders. When I asked her who took her son and his family, she said she supposed it was one of the old Taylors. She didn't see them because Gus went to the door and told the two fellows they were ready. I asked Mrs. Meeks where they went and she told me they had gone to the country."

"I s'pose you are good friends with Old Mrs. Meeks," said Gonia.

"Oh, I always have treated Mrs. Meeks respectfully. We live close together but I don't go visiting. I have to wash for a living and women who wash for a living have no time to visit."

While they were talking, Hannah Johnson came in from taking a walk. She spoke to the others in the room, removed her cape and hat, and then took a seat near Gonia and Mrs. Cooper.

"Is there nothing else to talk about besides the trial?" she remarked.

"Hi, Hannah," said Anna. "What else is there to talk about? It is the biggest story any of us will ever be involved in if we live to be a hundred years old. Gonia and I were talking about the day after the murders. You were there when I was. In fact, there were a lot of people in the house that day."

Hannah put a scowl on her face because she wasn't sure she wanted to go into what happened. Thinking about the Gus Meeks family being slaughtered like animals was painful. Living near the Meeks home, she knew the family well.

"My house was next door to the Meeks place. I saw Mr. Pierce at the door and then Mr. Butler came and there seemed to be a lot of excitement, so I went over to see what was going on. When Anna and I got there Mr. Butler and three or four other men were there. I couldn't hear much of what they were saying and they didn't stay long. I noticed how Mrs. Meeks was frightened and crying. After they left I began to talk to Mrs. Meeks. She was washing so I took it over and hung the washing out on the line," said Hannah

Gonia asked, "Did she tell you the Taylors took Gus and his family?"

"No, she said she didn't see who was in the wagon, but she thought it was the Taylors."

"We won't ever really know, then will we?" commented Gonia.

"Hannah," spoke up Anna, "what is the news about the jury? Have they reached a decision yet? I am tired of staying in this place. I want to go home."

"No, Anna, it looks like the jury hasn't come to a decision yet. The rumor out there is they may not be able to reach a decision. I heard some folks talking how one or more of the jurors was bribed to vote "not guilty." If that's the case then who knows what will happen? I agree with you, I am ready to go home. In fact, I may just pack up and go home anyway. I have work to do and need to be home."

Annalou Mack

Gonia was astonished at this news. *What would happen if there was a hung jury? Would the Taylors be set free or would there be another trial?* "Ladies, I need to tell this news to Della. It's been good to talk to you. Good day."

Georgia had just awakened from her nap and was nursing when Gonia went back into the room she and Della shared. There was excitement in her voice as she relayed the news how there was probably a hung jury.

"I think it is time for us to pack up our things and go home. There is nothing more for us to do here.

"Oh, Ma! Does this mean they will release George and Bill? Will he be coming home?

"Don't get your hopes up. Very likely it means there will be another trial." Gonia thought the chances of the men being released were very slim.

Chapter 28

Sheriff Niblo mingled with the townspeople gathered around the Carroll County Courthouse on Friday, April 5, 1895. The jury had been out since Tuesday trying to come to a decision about the Taylor case. There was much speculation about how the jury would vote, but most seemed to feel they couldn't find the Taylors anything but guilty.

There were others who thought it would be a hung jury and members had been paid to vote for acquittal. So it was with eagerness, when the crowd moved into the courtroom at about nine-thirty Friday morning.

Tom Bresnehen and Colonel Hale followed Judge Rucker into the courtroom. They had been delayed briefly waiting for a deputy to open the door. As soon as Judge Rucker was seated on the bench the clerk arrived and the jury was brought into court. The Taylors were brought in and seated directly in front of the judge, all the time keeping their eyes on the members of the jury.

"Gentlemen of the jury," said Judge Rucker, "have you agreed on a verdict?"

"We have," replied George Fleming, foreman of the jury.

"You will pass your verdict to the clerk," said the judge.

One could have heard a pin drop as the foreman handed the clerk a sealed envelope. The clerk paused a moment after tearing open the envelope and looking at the verdict. Slowly he read.

"We, the jury, can't agree."

Almost as one there was a loud gasp throughout the room upon hearing the clerk's words. The judge banged his gavel calling for order and the courtroom became quiet. Surprisingly, neither Bill or George showed any emotion when the jury's response was read.

"Gentlemen," asked Judge Rucker, "is there any way you can agree on a verdict?"

Foreman Fleming answered, "None whatever."

The judge asked, "Is this what the rest of the jurors' said?"

Several answered, "Yes."

"Is this the way you have stood from the first?"

The reply was that on the first ballot there were seven for conviction and five for acquittal and there had been no change on successive ballots.

"Mr. Bresnehen," asked Judge Rucker, "Do you want the jury to be kept any longer?"

"I think not, your honor."

With a disgusted scowl Judge Rucker announced, "Since the jury has failed to agree in the case of the State of Missouri vs. George and William Taylor you are discharged and the case is continued to the next term of court." [14]

It was evident the people in the court room were upset by the way they hooted, hissed, and yelled vile remarks at the jurors as they left the court room.

Outside the courtroom, Sheriff Niblo heard a newspaper reporter question a member of the jury how they were divided.

"From the first ballot there were seven for conviction and five for acquittal. There was no change on each ballot after that."

"Will you tell me who were for conviction and who were for acquittal?" asked the reporter.

"We think it best to not divulge it to the public."

The strain of the trial was plainly shown on the faces of the jury as they tried to hurry away from the crowd. But Niblo did hear a juryman tell a group gathered on the street how one of the things the jury disagreed upon was whether there was blood stain on the wagon bed. Another was the testimony of blind Mr. McCullom, which made for heated arguments.

During the discussions Niblo heard how juryman Frank Yehle had made each juror promise to not reveal the names of the jurors who voted for acquittal. However, when the seven who had voted guilty saw the state of mind of the public, they feared all the jurors would be suspected of voting for acquittal so they told the names of the five. The five who stood out for acquittal from the first were: Frank Yehle, Barnett M. Hudson, Ben Glover, George Fleming, and J. T. Noland. Those voting for conviction from the first were: J. A. Rose, David Jameson, Adolph Auer, Granville Jenkins, Elijah Baker, James H. Creed and W. R. Brammer.

Sheriff Niblo noticed George W. Meeks, the brother of Gus Meeks talking to a group of citizens, so he went over to hear what he had to say. He knew George was nearly blind and learned he was in Carrollton for treatment for his eyes.

George said, "I don't see how the jury could give such a verdict. Somebody must have been bought. Bill Taylor had a brother-in-law, you might say, on the jury. His name is George Fleming. When I heard the list of jurors read, I said then Bill Taylor had the jury. Bill Taylor and Fleming married sisters. I knew both of them. I don't remember exactly where Fleming lived, but suppose it is in Carroll County. The people will surely lynch those Taylors. I expect to hear in a day or two how they have. The people in this section know them and what they have done before convinces them the Taylors are guilty. I can't see how any juror could doubt that the Taylors killed Gus and his family. Of course, Fleming would favor them, and they must have bought some of the others."

Hurrying from the courtroom, Judge Rucker hung up his robes, put on his suit coat, gathered up his belongings and soon after was seen leaving on the train to Keytesville. This meant there would not be a grand jury called to investigate the charge of bribery in the Taylor jury. It would have to wait until the last Monday of April for the next term to bring it up.

The crowds leaving the courthouse had disbelieving looks on their faces. It seemed impossible to many how the jury could not reach a verdict in the case. There would have to be an investigation into the matter which no doubt both sides would insist upon.

After mingling with different groups of the people on the street and listening to their talk, Sheriff Niblo decided it was time to get to the train and go home to Milan. His firm, square jaw was set with determination. There was no doubt in his mind he would continue to run down leads about the case so that the next trial would have a different conclusion. No way was he going to see the Taylor brothers released from custody because he had no doubts, they were responsible for the heinous crime.

Chapter 29

Things were quiet on this bright, sunshiny April day in Milan. Sheriff Jim Niblo felt too cooped up inside his office so decided to take a walk over to Ben Pierce's office to have a chat with him. The air smelled fresh and clean after the soft rain the night before. He couldn't help but notice the jonquils and daffodils springing up in several yards along the way.

Prosecutor Pierce rose from his desk when he saw Jim enter his office. They shook hands and Pierce indicated for the sheriff to sit in the chair across from him. "What's on your mind, Jim?

"How is Nellie doing after the trial? Did that seem to bother her much?"

Pierce pushed the papers on his desk aside and had a pensive look before he answered. "Actually, Nellie gave no strong indication that she was bothered by the trial. She is much calmer now and has not had any nightmares for a while."

The sheriff looked pleased with that report, but scowled at his pressing thoughts. "I just can't get that trial out of my mind. How could that jury of twelve men not see how guilty those Taylor boys are?"

Pierce gave a small mirthless laugh. "Well, I think it is pretty obvious that there was a lot of skullduggery in the trial. I have been talking with Bresnehen and there is more coming to light every day about jury tampering. You know the five members of the jury who were for acquittal from the very first were Barnett Hudson, Ben Glover, George Fleming, J. T. Noland and Frank Yehle. It seems George Fleming is married to a relative of the Taylors and Yehle has stood by Fleming to hang the jury. I think the prosecutors should have thought about that before Fleming was selected for the jury."

After taking time to roll and light up a cigarette, the sheriff said, "Yes, it would have been good if they had known about the relationship. What do you hear about a grand jury being called to investigate what happened?"

"Jim, I just heard today that Carroll County Prosecuting Attorney, Sidney Miller had asked Judge Rucker for a special grand jury to look into the charge of bribery of the jury. There may be several persons indicted for perjury, too."

"Do you know, Ben, what has been found so far?"

"I don't know much about it yet, but I did hear this story from Bresnehen. One of the older and most respected citizens in Carroll County, John Horning, said Charles Dickinson, who was on the panel of forty men with him, told Horning that after he was drawn on the panel he was approached by Frank Yehle and offered $750 if he would agree to hang the jury. Yehle had accepted the money and agree to vote for acquittal. Yehle also said he had been authorized to get others on the jury to vote for acquittal. After Horning refused the offer, he said Yehle told him he would talk to Barney Hudson."

The sheriff could hardly believe his ears. Did these people have no sense of justice? How could they accept money to let killers of innocent people run free? These thoughts kept running through his mind. He felt he should get some fresh air in order to clear his head for a while. He got so angry when he thought the Taylor brothers might get away with the murders of the Meeks family.

After sitting still for a few minutes continuing to smoke his cigarette, Sheriff Niblo got up and said, "Thanks for the talk, Ben. I'll be back another day to hear what happens with the grand jury."

Prosecutor Pierce rose to shake Jim's hand. "I'll keep you posted.

The walk back to his office didn't feel as pleasant to the sheriff as it had on the way over. His thoughts kept returning to the jurors who had been responsible for the hung jury in the Taylor case. All of them would go to jail if it was up to him.

About a week later, Sheriff Niblo was surprised to see Prosecutor Pierce step through the sheriff's office door.

"Well, hi there. Is everything going good at your house?" asked the sheriff.

"Oh, yes, we are good. You wanted to know about the grand jury proceedings so I thought I would give you a run-down of what I know."

"Good. Have a seat and fill me in."

Taking a deep breath, Ben began his story. "I took a run down to Carrollton because I wanted to see first-hand what was going on down there with the grand jury. Some of the evidence gathered was from James Sparks. He was on the original panel of forty men and he stated that while in Tina on business before the trial began, John Vernard approached him and said Jacob Williams, cashier of the bank in Tina wanted to see Sparks. Curious as to what Williams wanted to talk to him about, Sparks went to the bank. Williams told Sparks that he wanted to talk about the Taylor trial. Sparks told him Judge Rucker told the panel not to talk or read about the case. Williams brushed off the idea by telling Sparks the judge would never know anything about it. Actually what Williams wanted was to get Sparks to hang the jury. Sparks says he quickly closed the conversation with a clear, 'no.'"

"Charles Dickenson also testified that Williams offered him money to hang the jury. Dickenson's testimony was that on the Monday night before the trial was to begin, the same Williams came to Dickenson's farmhouse and told him that if he was selected as a juror there would be big money in it if he would stand for acquittal. Williams said he would see that the money was paid."

The sheriff listened carefully to what Pierce was relating. This was good news, he thought. "So, who were indicted by the grand jury after the testimony?"

Pierce continued on with the news. "Probably because of the marriage relationship, George Fleming was not indicted even though it was investigated. I'm surprised that Yehle was not indicted.

"Williams was indicted and so was Richard Smith for attempted bribery. Smith lives on a farm adjoining Barney Hudson, his brother-in-law. Williams was fined $500, but Smith has not yet been tried."

"In my book they should all have been thrown in jail. A fine is only a slap on the wrist and will not stop them from doing it again," said the sheriff. "Guess you didn't hear anything about witness bribery or perjury?"

Annalou Mack

"No," said Pierce, I think they are still looking into it. There will probably be more indictments later." He looked at his watch and said, "Think I should be getting back to the office. I just wanted to let you know what I have found out."

Rising from his chair, Jim stuck out his hand. "Thanks for doing that. You know how interested I am in this case. Hanging is really too good for those two, but there has to be a jury conviction before it can even be done. Give my regards to the family."

After a firm handshake Ben turned to return to his office. He felt much the same way as Sheriff Niblo. It would be only a couple months before the second trial would begin. Surely it would have a different result.

Chapter 30

Soon after Della and Gonia returned from the trial in Carrollton they were hard at work in the normal everyday jobs on a farm. When the baby chicks hatched they were put in a small brooder house where they could be kept warm and fed. Della sometimes took one of the girls with her when she went to feed the baby chicks. Georgia giggled, clapped her hands and bounced around while watching the little balls of fluff running around the enclosure. When Flossie went with her mother to the brooder house she squatted down to be closer to the little chicks and sometimes tried to catch one when it came close. Della loved spending time with the baby chicks. It seemed to take her mind off the problems which were never far from her thoughts.

Almost as soon as they arrived at their home after the trial, Gonia asked David to plow and work up the garden patch. It was spring, so the warm days meant it was time to put seeds in the ground. With a large family to feed it was essential to grow lots of vegetables to go with the meat which came from the animals raised on the farm for the purpose of providing food for the family.

Della took her turn hoeing around the plants in the garden although it was not her favorite job. A large garden took a lot of work so each of the Gibson family members had a turn at hoeing or pulling weeds.

With plenty of rain the garden plants thrived, and by the first of June the pea vines were loaded with pea pods. One morning Della said, "Iva May, do you want to go with me to pick peas?"

Iva May really didn't want to do it and with a whiny voice said, "Do I have to? Why can't I stay in the house and look after baby Georgia?"

Gonia spoke up about then and said clearly, "Iva May, get your bucket and go help Della with the peas. I'll watch the baby this morning. Flossie, do you want to help your mama? Della do you think she can pick the pea pods?"

"Well, let's give it a try. Come on girls we'll pick the peas. Maybe we can have some for dinner."

Della showed two year old Flossie how to pull the pea pods from the vines. For a while it was fascinating for the little girl, but she soon became bored and everything green was going in the bucket. "No, Flossie, just these big ones."

"No, Mama, these," Flossie insisted.

"Iva May, maybe you should take Flossie back to the house. I'll pick the rest."

"Sure, I'll take Flossie back and play with her for a while."

Della knew this was what her sister had wanted from the first. The two of them had gone over several rows so there was not a lot left to do. Finishing the pea picking wouldn't take much longer.

The rest of the day was spent in shelling the peas from the pods, then canning several pints in the pressure cooker. Iva May was right there to help in the hulling. Gonia took charge of the canning. They left a pan of peas out to cook with some new baby potatoes for their supper.

Daily chores of caring for the chickens, tending the garden, doing laundry and cleaning the house kept Della busy, but in spite of all this she still found time to think about her husband in the jail in Carrollton. *What will be the outcome of the next trial? Will he ever get to come home so we can be a family again? George, did you really do that horrible crime? I love you, and I don't want to believe you could do those things.*

At times it felt like the days were dragging by and July would never come, then other times it seemed like the hours and days were flying by. For a small celebration in honor of Georgia's first birthday on July eighth, Gonia made a cake. Della mixed a frosting for it and asked, "Flossie would you like to put this on the cake?"

"Oh, Mama, I help." Taking the spatula her mother handed her, Flossie began smearing the gooey frosting all over the cake. It didn't matter to her how much she got on herself. This was so much fun.

Flossie was such a lively, happy, rambunctious little two year old.

She loved her little sister, but thought Georgia should laugh and play more. The one year old was just beginning to take a few steps so she couldn't do all the things Flossie wanted her to do.

The birthday cake was a nice change to lighten up the gloomy atmosphere which seemed to invade the Gibson household much of the time. Both the little girls were delighted to dig into the cake with their hands. Neither Gonia nor Della tried to stop them this time. Ivy May and Drue got a big laugh from the antics of the little ones.

One evening toward the end of July as the family was sitting around the dining table, they began talking about the upcoming trial. There was no doubt it was uppermost on the minds of the adults.

David said, "I see in the paper Colonel Myers has been arrested after being indicted for attempting to bribe witnesses for the last trial. I wonder who they have secured to replace him as their attorney."

Gonia said, "Mrs. Gooch told me she had heard the Honorable D. W. Wilson has been hired as the lead attorney for the Taylors."

"What effect do you think the bribery charge will have on the people being picked for the jury?" asked Della.

"I think," responded David, "it will leave an unfavorable impression on them. Really, how can it not? The whole thing with the hung jury, and now the bribery of witnesses; the people in the pool to be selected for the jury are mostly simple, honest, God-fearing people who do not believe in those kinds of things."

"I just want to believe George was not a part of the crime. We owe a lot to the Taylor family. I think we have to do anything we can to see he is not convicted." Della brushed the tears from her eyes.

"Della, I know you love your husband and you feel we owe him for giving us a place to live, but it does not change my mind. I will not lie and say George was here when I know he was not." David was adamant when he spoke.

Gonia said, "Maybe we should change the subject. No need for us to get so upset right now. We'll see how this trial comes out. I think we should go to bed and rest. Tomorrow is another long day of farm work. Della, get your girls, take them up and put them to bed. See you in the morning."

Chapter 31

It was a swelteringly hot July day when Jim Niblo boarded the train in Milan for the ride down to Carrollton. No way was he going to miss a minute of this second trial of the Taylor Brothers if he could help it. The Meeks family were residents of his town and he wanted to see justice carried out for the massacre of Gus and his family more than a year ago. In his eyes it was criminal how the first trial ended with a hung jury. Whatever the punishment was for those who took a bribe to vote for acquittal was not enough. A fine was only a slap on the wrist; they should go to prison.

Niblo knew Attorney Myers was indicted a couple weeks ago for attempting to bribe witnesses in the previous trial. Myers will not be working for them in this trial. The sheriff thought to himself, *I wonder who will be doing the Taylors' dirty work for them this time. I'll keep my ears to the ground and if I suspect anything it will be reported as soon as possible so there is not a repeat of the last fiasco.*

Carrollton was overrun with people as Sheriff Niblo made his way from the depot. He needed to find a room before they were all taken. It took three stops at rooming houses before he found a vacant room not far from the courthouse. He deposited his bag in the room and quickly walked up the street where groups of people were congregating. Just as he expected, the talk was about the trial and he soon learned a pool of forty men had been made. Tomorrow the jury selection would begin from this pool. The sheriff planned to be in the courthouse to listen to everything said by these men.

Sheriff Niblo stopped for a few minutes to speak to Prosecuting Attorney Bresnehen outside the courthouse. Bresnehen said, "We will get a jury because under the law we can accept men who have an opinion if they say they can try the case on the evidence provided. I believe we have plenty of evidence to show them."

"I sure hope so."

"A panel of forty men has been selected. Tomorrow we will begin selecting men for the jury from that group," explained Bresnehen.

"I expect to be there front and center," said Niblo.

"Keep your ears open to the talk around you. If you hear anything which would disqualify one of them, let me or Pierce know so we can take care of it."

"I'll do it, for sure."

On the morning of July 23, just as he said he would be, Sheriff Jim Niblo sat in the crowded Carroll County courthouse which was packed with many farmers and a few merchants who were part of the jury selection pool. The closed room was stiflingly hot, not only because of the summer heat, but because the windows were kept shut to keep out the noise from the street around the courthouse. There couldn't have been more people and noise in downtown Carrollton if the circus had been in town. Music from the merry-go-round filled the air. The streets were lined with vendors barking their wares to the hundreds of individuals milling around. This was the trial of the century, and it had brought in people from all corners of the state of Missouri—and a large number from surrounding states.

Many in the area surrounding the courthouse lounging on the grass in the shade of trees were men and women who were witnesses temporarily excluded from the courtroom. To add to the milieu the Carroll County Teachers' Institute was in session and several teachers were anxious to see the undertakings of the court and to perhaps get a glimpse of the Taylor brothers. They couldn't help but wonder if George Taylor was as handsome as everyone said.

Carroll County Sheriff Stanley brought George and William Taylor into the courtroom at eight-thirty. Niblo couldn't help but notice how free of anxiety the expressions on the faces of the two men were. They seemed to have nerves of steel without a care in the world about what was happening in the courtroom.

After the challenges by the state and the defense were given to the clerk, he read from his list the names of twenty-four men and all others were excused. Judge Rucker asked the group, "Do any of you know of any reason you could not keep an open mind if chosen? Keep in mind the defendants are presumed to be innocent until they are proven guilty beyond a reasonable doubt."

There was no response from the group so now it was time for the counsels for the state and for the defense to begin their questioning. Despite the closed windows, the noise from outside made it difficult for all involved in the questioning to understand what was said. The speaker, either perspective juror or judge or attorney, often was asked to repeat what he said.

One of the first questions asked was if any were opposed to capital punishment. In response six or seven raised their hands and they were immediately excused. The next questions formed in legal language caused a lot of confusion to the men. The trouble was whether when faced with the evidence they could overcome their own preconceived opinion. One man was asked, "Could you find for acquittal if the evidence tended to show the defendants were guiltless?" His reply was "No," so he was excused.

Niblo smiled to himself at the indignant reply by one of the men, "I am an honest man and if I take the juror's oath, I leave my opinions outside."

The questioning continued all day with some excused and others accepted. By late evening after all the questions had been asked and answered, a jury panel was chosen.

E. J. Calloway, a farmer living one mile south of Hale.

F. B. Caesar, a farmer of Hurricane township.

T. N Houghton, a farmer.

John W. Edge, former constable of Hurricane township.

G. W. Shank, a farmer and carpenter.

G. T. Morris, another farmer.

G. W. Craig, a farmer, living in Cherry Valley Township.

W. H. Vaughn, a clerk in the bank of Hale.

George Freeman, an innkeeper and carpenter, living at Roads.

B. C. Dulaney, a member of the firm of Dulaney & Co., Hale.

J. S. Helm, a stone mason.

R. G. Evans, a farmer.

Before returning to his rooming house, Niblo stopped to talk briefly with Ben Pierce. "What do you think about the jury to be seated tomorrow?"

"Well, Jim, I believe we have us a good group of men who will hear the evidence and make the right decision. In looking at the panel, we have a diverse group, which is good. The youngest man is a twenty-three-year old bank clerk and the oldest is a sixty-two-year-old farmer. To me it seems like a good mix."

Chapter 32

By the middle of July, the farm work had slowed down for a while. The crops were laid by and the hay was stacked so it was mostly the daily caring for the animals and farm maintenance, which took up the time for the men of the Gibson family. Gonia, Della and Iva May still had plenty of work caring for the garden, canning vegetables as well as the normal cooking, cleaning and laundry it takes to run a household.

Della looked forward to going down to Carrollton for the new trial one day, and dreaded having to go through what almost seemed like the torture of the trial the next. This July, Della felt like the days were abnormally hot. Georgia was cranky much of the time as she did not tolerate the heat well. Flossie played outside most of the time with her favorite dog and cat.

Gonia and Della were both scheduled as witnesses in the trial, so it was necessary for them to be present when called. Along with the two little ones, the two women boarded the train in Browning along with about three hundred trial witnesses for the trip to Carrollton. Upon arrival they found they were staying in the same rooming house where the witnesses in the previous trial had been housed. It was not large but comfortable and they had become acquainted with the owner during the previous trial.

Soon after they were settled in their room, Della said, "Ma, I want to take the girls over to the jail to see George. I won't stay long, but I want to see him, and I also want the girls to see him. They need to know they have a father. With any luck he will be released soon, and the girls will see what a sweet Pa they have."

"Do you want me to go along to help?"

"No, I think I can handle them both for a little while. Flossie can walk and I'll carry Georgie."

The jail keeper was very kind and made the arrangements for Della and the girls to meet with George in a private room. When he saw them, George smiled and reached out his arms for Flossie to come to him. Flossie wasn't so sure she should go to him. She had seen so little of him during her two years, she really didn't know who he was.

"Go ahead, Flossie, your pa wants to hold you." Reluctantly she went to him and he picked her up and gave her a kiss. He also gave a kiss to Della and Georgia.

The four of them sat at the table in the room while George and Della talked.

"How are you being treated?" asked Della.

"Outside of missing being home with you, we are doing fine. I think this time we will get this taken care of and I'll be home within a month. How does that sound?"

"It will be wonderful. I want this over and you home so we can raise our two beautiful daughters together."

The two talked on for a short time until Della said, "I need to be going. Supper will be served at our rooming house soon and we don't want to miss it. The girls and I will see you tomorrow."

On Thursday morning, July 25, Della and Gonia were up early in order to get to the courthouse before the start of the trial. The morning rituals of feeding and dressing the little ones were completed quickly. Della wore her best dress because, despite the circumstances, she wanted George to be proud of her.

The courtroom was filled with people when the two arrived, but they were able to find a seat near the front of the room. As soon as the defendants, officers, attorneys and the judge entered, the cacophony of noise quickly ceased. Major Wilson, the attorney for the defense immediately asked for the witnesses to be excluded from the courtroom as had been the rule during the previous trial. More than 250 persons stood when the judge asked all witnesses to do so. After all of them left there was room for the persons who had been waiting outside in the hallway to find seats.

Della and Gonia decided to go back to the rooming house because it didn't look like they would be called as witnesses for some time. First the attorneys for the state and for the defense would make their opening remarks before any witnesses were called so it would be another day or two before Gonia or Della were called on to testify.

The next day Della found the Carrollton newspaper which had articles about the trial. She read with particular interest what the reporter had to say about the defense statement made by Colonel John B. Hale.

The reporter told how for twenty minutes during his opening remarks, Colonel Hale ranted and raved about the newspapers of the country trying his clients as they did all criminal cases. He was called down rather sharply by Judge Rucker and told to keep with the law. Even after being told to stick to the law Hale went on to decry how unscrupulous and merciless the state had been in trying to crush the Taylors. He said the Taylors fleeing the country was not because of guilt, but to escape the mobs who were out to get them.

The article told of how Colonel Hale had expounded upon the good qualities of Bill Taylor including his family background, good education and his good record in the legislature. At the end of nearly two hours of speaking, the reporter went on to say that Colonel Hale, "… indicated as a line of the defense of the flight of the Taylor boys as necessary to avoid death at the hands of the mob and not as an evidence of guilt."

The reporter said Hale had, "adroitly taken up each point in the evidence given at the last trial and showed it as a natural act on the part of one or the other of the Taylors and not tending to show guilt." Hale also said there had been an attempt to intimidate the witnesses for the defense.

Della couldn't keep the tears from rolling down her cheeks when she read, "Colonel Hale indicated one of the leading theories of the defense would be how Meeks was murdered by someone, not in any way connected with the Taylors, to secure $1,000 which Meeks was to have received from the Taylors for leaving the country. In closing his statement to the jury, he made an eloquent peroration on the horror and gloom of death and especially the end of a man sent to his death in expiation of a crime. During this speech tears filled the eyes of Bill Taylor and rolled down his cheeks. He hid his head and wiped his eyes with his handkerchief. George was unaffected." [15]

Reading these words puzzled Della. *This couldn't be right. Why was George unaffected?* This was a mystery to Della. *Was it because George was sure he would not be found guilty?* Della hoped it was true, but she was not sure it would happen.

Annalou Mack

Chapter 33

Day after day, Sullivan County sheriff James Niblo sat in the courtroom in Carrollton listening to the witnesses testify in the second trial in the case against the Taylor brothers. It was inconceivable to him how the first trial had ended with a hung jury. Why would otherwise good honest citizens condescend to taking bribes to vote "not guilty" when it seemed so obvious to Niblo how guilty the two defendants were.

Gus Meeks was not exactly an upstanding citizen since he was involved in some shifty deals in addition to the cattle rustling scheme, but how could anyone stoop so low as to attempting to wipe out an entire family. Killing a man was one thing, but also killing his wife and two children was unthinkable. No doubt the crime would have been successful had Nellie, the eldest daughter been killed instead of just knocked unconscious.

Niblo wondered if little Nellie Meeks would be called to the witness stand. In the previous trial it was thought it best if she was not subjected to the stress of testifying. Also, since she was living with Ben Pierce one of the prosecutors, no one wanted it to be said her testimony was tainted.

He learned the attorneys for the State in this case were: Prosecuting Attorney Bresnehen from Linn County; Major A. W. Mullins from Linneus; Les Holliday, Mayor of Carrollton; James I Minnis, also from Carrollton; E. B. Fields of Browning; and Prosecuting Attorney Pierce from Milan.

On the first day of the new trial, Bresnehen made the opening statement for the State. Niblo watched the Taylors as the Prosecuting Attorney detailed in graphic detail the killing of the Meeks family. Bill showed very little emotion except when the speaker told of the threats to get rid of Gus Meeks. The whole time George sat emotionless—seemingly indifferent, as if he wanted the whole thing to be over quickly.

During the first trial the defense did not make an opening statement, but for this one Colonel John B. Hale made the opening statement for the defense. Other defense attorneys were: D. M. Wilson of Milan; Virgil Conkling, Ralph Lozier, and James F. Graham.

All afternoon witnesses were called to the stand to testify. Most of what was said was a repeat of what had been related in the first trial. Again the finding of the bodies of the Meeks family in the shallow grave beside the small straw stack was repeated as well as the examination of the wagon tracks in the cornfield where it was speculated George Taylor had attempted to remove them when he was harrowing along the same lines. Several witnesses were called to discuss whether there was blood on the wagon bed or the coupling.

The repetition of the statements by the witnesses was interrupted when one of the jurors became ill and the judge called a halt while a physician was called to examine him. Nothing serious was found so the proceedings continued until smoke began pouring into the room. The cause was from an awning under the window where the jurors sat, catching fire. It was quickly extinguished by a deputy sheriff when he leaned out the window and poured a bucket of water on the fire.

Soon court was back in full swing when W. J. Freeman was introduced as a witness. Niblo did not know Freeman, so listened carefully to his testimony.

"I reside at Brunswick; was born and raised there; moved to the city of St. Louis about ten years ago; have been in the National Cash Register business; have been in no other business since I went up there; was never in the saloon business in my life; have done detective work two years and ten months; was on the police force in St. Louis about three years and nine months; I retired from the service three years ago; I then came back to Brunswick; since coming back I have been traveling for the Cash Register company; I am now deputy Game and

Fish Warden for the state of Missouri; was appointed to the position on the 12th day of this month; that required most of my time; there is no salary attached to this office; went to Brunswick on Tuesday following the murder; went down to the neighborhood of the killing the next morning; Jimmie Fleming was with me." [16]

Freeman brought in new testimony when he told of how he found on the morning following the murder in the pasture of James Taylor where a fire had been. He found clothes, a piece of burned trousers, bedding, the clasp of a pocketbook and some feathers. This unexpected evidence caused a sensation in the courtroom when the burned fragments were introduced.

Virgil Conkling on cross examination attempted to show how Freeman had tried to intimidate Mrs. George Taylor when he led a crowd to her house to get her to tell where George was when the posses were searching for him.

Mrs. Meeks was called to identify the burned fragment of trousers as belonging to her son, Gus. She said the fragment was part of the trousers Gus had worn the night of the murder. She was not able to identify the clasp of the pocketbook but said the bedding was what the family had taken with them the night of the murder. This was difficult for her and as the articles were passed to her she burst into tears.

This poor woman has suffered so much the past two years, thought Niblo. *Just being here in the court room brings all the feelings to the surface, then seeing items belonging to her dead family cause intense emotional pain.* He wished there were something more he could do to help her with these troubles.

Niblo found it disgusting the way defense attorney Virgil Conkling kept bullying the witnesses. Numerous times Judge Rucker told him to stop, but the attorney seemed to not understand what the judge was telling him as he repeatedly disobeyed the orders to stop. At one point it was so bad the judge told the witness to leave the stand. Conkling accused the judge of depriving him of the right to defend his clients.

After this episode Judge Rucker took a few minutes to sternly lecture Conkling on his behavior in the court. The attorney saw he had made a mistake and apologized to the court. Then Conkling relented and Colonel Hale handled the cross examination of witnesses.

The rest of the afternoon was spent in the testimony of Jerry South. Niblo did not find anything new in what South said.

Annalou Mack

Chapter 34

The rooming house where the female defense witnesses were housed was modest, but clean and tidy. The proprietor was a kindly older woman who had lost her husband several years ago. The meals she served were not fancy but were simple and filling. Gonia and Della found her pleasant to talk with and easy to be around. Georgia and Flossie were the only children in the home and the women there seemed to enjoy having the little ones around. Most missed having children around, whether it was because their children were now adults, or were left at home, or they never had children.

One or two of the women had been in the same rooming house during the previous trial so Della and Gonia renewed acquaintances. Mattie Van Wye and her daughter Alpha were occupants. Alpha had testified in March, but Mattie had not. Della was anxious to discuss the testimony Alpha gave at the previous trial. This discussion would probably not be allowed if the lawyers knew, but who was going to tell them. If what Alpha and Mattie said was reliable then it was an alibi for George and Bill.

"Alpha, are you going to testify this time that you saw Bill the evening of the murder?" asked Della in the evening as they were seated in the parlor on the sofa.

"Of course. I plan to give the same testimony as I did before. Mamma and I were going to my aunt's house to dress her cancer. On the way we walked by the People's Exchange Bank and I saw Bill in front of the door. We spoke to each other before we passed on. It was sometime between nine and ten o'clock at night."

"So, you are sure you saw and spoke to him at that time of night?" Della wanted to make it clear how important it was for Alpha to be sure of what she was saying.

"Yes, very sure. "Alpha seemed a little nervous when she replied. Della wanted to believe it, but she was somewhat skeptical.

"Then there is no way he could have gone to Milan later is there?"

"I don't see how it would be possible."

Della was happy to hear how Alpha seemed sure of what her testimony would be. This alibi coupled with what she and her mother were going to say, should carry some weight.

During their conversation Della learned Alpha and her mother no longer lived in Browning as they did at the time of the earlier trial. After the death of her sister, Mrs. Blythe McCollum, Mattie and Alpha had moved to Brookfield.

Della asked Alpha, "Did you tell anyone about seeing Bill Taylor in Browning the night of the murders?"

"No, I never told anyone, not even my uncle. I didn't think it was anybody's business. He and my mother talked a lot since we were there every night. They talked about the murders but our seeing Mr. Taylor was never mentioned." [17]

On occasion, Gonia and Mrs. Mattie Van Wye had conversations about the trial. One thing of special interest to Gonia was what Mattie had to say about being approached by Dr. Van Wye.

"You know," Mattie said, "it seemed strange to me how Dr. Van Wye came to me and wanted me to leave the country. When I asked him why he would ask such a thing, he told me they didn't want the truth for the Taylor boys. If we testified on behalf of the Taylors the prosecuting attorney would prosecute me, blacken my character and send me to jail."

"Oh, my," said Gonia, "What a terrible thing to say to you. How did you answer him?"

"Why, naturally I told him I wouldn't swear to anything but the truth. If they wanted to put me in jail, at least they would have to feed me while I was there." said Mattie with a smile.

Gonia grimaced at that thought. "Well, it sounds to me like the prosecution is trying to railroad Bill and George. Maybe your testimony along with what Della and I have to say will swing it the other way."

Mattie couldn't keep the tears back when she said, "You know, Gonia, times have been hard for me the last year or so. My sister who Alpha and I had been caring for at the time of the Meeks murders passed away not long after. My father died in December and I have been real poorly the last while. I'm ready for this trial to be over so maybe I can get my health back."

"Yes, Mattie," said Gonia as she handed her a handkerchief. "This has been a terrible year for us, too. We moved Della and the babies in with us and my husband, Dave and the boys have been trying to care for both our farm and George's. We want this over with and George back at home taking care of his family. Your testimony should help as it will back up what we will swear to."

On Monday morning Della and Gonia prepared themselves and the girls to go to the courthouse for their testimonies. After testimony by Dr. M. F. Craig, Jessie Bailey and Albert Taylor, Gonia was called to the witness chair. V. M. Conkling conducted her direct examination where the court reporter transcribed her testimony as follows:

> I am the mother-in-law of George Taylor; he married my daughter [Della]; my daughter lives with me now; we live on George's place; on May 10th, 1894, we lived on George Taylor's place; don't know just exactly how far it is from George's house; about 120 yards south, on the east side of the road. George Taylor's house is on the west side of the road. I remember of being over to George Taylor's house on May 10th, 1894, on Thursday afternoon; George was at home at that time; George went to his father's [James Taylor] in the afternoon sometime; don't know when he came back; he went to Browning that evening; he went in his father's wagon; he went to Browning to take his wagon wheels to the wagon shop to get them fixed; he went about three o'clock in the evening; Albert Taylor went with him; he had the wagon wheels in the wagon; after he left I staid there at George's house until about four o'clock and then I went down to my house; my daughter went with me; I staid [stayed] there until after I got supper; George Taylor's wife was with me at the time; after supper we went back up to George's house and I staid [stayed] at my daughter's house all night; my

daughter was feeling badly at the time was the reason I went home with her; she was in a delicate condition at the time and I concluded to stay all night; we went to bed just as soon as we got there; we went to bed about eight o'clock or a little after; George had not got home from Browning at the time; he got back about nine o'clock; I was upstairs when he came back; I heard him open the door; was up during the night; slept in the north room upstairs; came down about nine o'clock; I heard George come home and I went down to see how my daughter was feeling; I heard them talking and I came downstairs; saw George when I came down; I then went upstairs again; came down again about midnight; I heard my daughter's little baby crying; came down stairs and stepped into the door; went back into the room and told her to give me the baby; we passed some words between us; we were talking about the baby; at that time he was laying over behind his wife in the bed; took the baby upstairs with me; I staid [stayed] the rest of the night upstairs in bed; got up the next morning about daylight; it was just getting day light; went downstairs and went into the room where George Taylor was; saw him at that time; he was in the bed in his room; passed some words with him at the time; I then went down to my house; my husband's wagon was at his own house that night.

Major Mullins conducted the cross examination.

My husband did not have any stable where his house was; he kept his horses at George's; my husband went up to George Taylor's a little after dark. He never left there until the next morning; he went down stairs just a little before I did the next morning; he went down to his own home; he went on a little ahead of me; in passing from the room upstairs downstairs, we had to pass through the room where my daughter was; that was the only way down stairs; don't know whether my husband is here in town or not; I suppose he is at home; he was there when I left; have not heard any complaint on his part since I left; my husband was there at George Taylor's as long as I was; he went up there a good while after I got there and left a little before I did; he was there all night until after sunrise the next morning; during the night I never saw anybody but George Taylor; did not see Albert Taylor; never paid any attention to the wagon in the yard the next morning; did not look to see where the mud was cleaned off; was back at my daughter's the next day; was there when the gentlemen were there looking at the mud that was cleaned off the wagon wheels; don't know just how far it was to where the men were standing; it was between the barn and house; did not go to look at the mud myself; don't know exactly what time I saw the people gathering in the field on George's farm; think it was about ten o'clock; did not go down myself; my husband went down there and my son; I have three boys, they were all there; I returned to my daughter's that morning about eight o'clock; there was no one in the yard when I returned to her home; did not notice anybody over there from the time I got up and went over there, but the home folks saw George Taylor chopping wood at the wood pile out at the barn; did not notice him hitching up a harrow; don't know anything about the harrow; did not see the harrow in the yard; never noticed about the wagon and harrow tracks; staid [stayed] at my daughter's after that most of the time but did not go out to look after them things; saw my boys that morning; they staid [stayed] at my house that night; saw Jim Harris that morning; he also staid [stayed] at my house that night; when I went home they got up and went out about the farm; don't know whether the sun had come up or not; Jim Harris, Willie and Drury came up to the barn; Jim Harris was sitting in the room at my place when I got home; just as soon as the boys and I came down, they all went over to George Taylor's barn; saw George about the barn and yard; about the time they took the wagon away, Willie and Jim Harris drove the wagon away; they drove the wagon out at the east gate and turned north and went a right smart piece and went into the gate and over to Mr. [James] Taylor's. My husband, Dave Gibson, drove his wagon away that morning; do not know just where he went; think he went the other way, south; he came back, I think, about ten o'clock; it might have been a little later; don't know exactly what time Jim Harris and Drury and Willie drove the wagon away that day; it was after breakfast when they left with the wagon; I don't know whether George Taylor had come down or not; saw him when he left; he went horseback; it was about seven o'clock or a little later when he started; he went north; could not see him but a little piece up the lane; guess it is about five or five and a half miles from there to Browning; that is the last I saw of him; don't know whose horse he rode off; I first heard of these people being killed and down in the straw stack on my son-in-law's place about eight o'clock; my son-in-law George Taylor had been gone over an hour before that; saw the people gathered there about nine or ten o'clock; did not see George Taylor after that; I was first told of the dead bodies by my little boy; he had not been down to the straw stack; he had got it by hearsay; me and my daughter done some washing the next morning; we had not got through the washing when my little boy told me the information; that was Friday morning; was doing the washing out in the yard; George had been gone about an hour; I am not acquainted with Hiram Atkins' son Garnett; don't know whether I would know Hiram or not; Garnett and I were reared in the same neighborhood for a little while; have seen Garnett Adkins since this murder; he came to George's house with a United States Marshal and detective; that is what they said he was; he was not in the house but a few minutes; did not talk about the murder; the boys names were not mentioned when he was in the house; did not tell him that I saw George Taylor the next morning; did not tell him that I knew about his coming home; never said anything about it; did not say that it was after four o'clock when he came home the next morning; had no talk with him at all; did not tell him that I got up and let him in the house when he came home and that it was between four and five o'clock in the morning; did not tell him that they were charging him with the murder; did not say whether he was guilty or not or whether he was innocent.

Annalou Mack

Gonia responded to the re-direct examination questions by M. V. Conkling with :

> My husband was not downstairs that night; had no opportunity to see George Taylor that night; my husband's wagon the next morning was down at our house; my husband's wagon had been used the day before for hauling water; we had no well; there was a barrel of water in it that morning; I was in Browning the next day; have seen Mr. Bresnehen before; have seen him at Linneus; court was in session at the time I was there." [18]

As soon as Gonia finished her testimony she stepped down from the witness box. Silently she breathed a sigh of relief. She hoped she had been enough in control of her emotions on the stand so that what she said was believable. Della smiled at her as Gonia picked up Flossie and took a seat beside her daughter.

Chapter 35

Following the noon recess Della was called to the witness stand. Her direct examination was conducted by V. M. Conkling. She said in her testimony:

I am the wife of the defendant, George E. Taylor; I live in Linn county, about five miles from Browning, southeast; I was at home on the day of May 10, 1894, excepting a little while in the afternoon; my husband went to Browning; he went to take his wagon wheels to get them fixed at the wagon shop; he took his father's wagon because he had no other wagon but the one with the wheels off; he took his father's team because his team was not fit to work; he started to Browning about three o'clock; his brother Albert went with him; after he left I went to my mother's; I staid [stayed] there about an hour or two; came home a little after sundown; after supper my mother came up home with me; my mother staid [stayed] at my home all night; I was sick and my mother came home with me on that account; I was feeling badly that evening; my husband got home that night from Browning about nine o'clock; after he came home he went to bed with me; he was there all night; my mother was down stairs shortly after my husband came home; she came down again about twelve o'clock; she came down to get my little girl; I have another child older than this one. [19]

Major Mullins led her cross examination to which she answered:

I saw my husband at nine o'clock; he staid [stayed] there all night; I saw him the next morning until he went off; he went north on horseback; he rode a horse that he had there of his brother William's; he was keeping it; I got up the next morning about five o'clock; I got up after my mother did; did not see my husband when he saddled his horse; I saw him when he started off towards Browning; [19]

Since both Gonia and Della had given their testimonies they could remain in the courtroom. They listened to George and Bill's brother Charles and mother Mrs. James Taylor then to Della's brothers, Beverly and William.

The direct examination of Willie Gibson was done by Senator Stephens. These are his answers to the questions:

I was living at my father's house on the night of May 10th 1894, about a hundred yards from George Taylor's; I went to George Taylor's early the next morning; I saw George Taylor at his home the day before that; I helped him do the feeding the next morning; saw George Taylor's horses at his house about three o'clock; I never saw them the next morning in the barn; saw nothing wrong with the horses at all; they looked to me just like they always did; I saw them just about sun up the next morning; I saw George Taylor at that time; he was feeding the horses; we curried the horses that morning; I curried one horse and he the other; before we curried them they had some manure on their hips and their legs were a little muddy; after we curried them we harnessed the horses; we did not do anything more to them then; we then went to the house and ate breakfast; after breakfast we bridled the horses and hooked them to the wagon and drove them over to Mr. James Taylor's; after they were hitched up they looked like they always did; there was nothing about them to indicate usage that day or the night before; I saw nothing unusual about George Taylor that morning; he acted and looked just about the same way he always did; I drove the horses over to Mr. Taylor's; did not see anything about the horses that indicated that they had been washed; Jim Harris was in the stable the morning we were at George's he did not do anything in particular. [20]

Della listened closely to what her brother Willie was saying. It sounded good to her. It followed nicely with what she had said on the witness stand. Hopefully it would help clear George of these accusations. She needed George home with her to raise their two babies and maybe several more.

Next Willie was cross examined by Major Mullins. In answer to his questions he continued with what happened the morning after the murders:

> Jim Harris and my brother staid [stayed] at my father's house that night and my brother, Drury [Dru]; nobody else was there besides us three boys; we got up about sunup; I saw my mother that morning; she was down at our house; it was just about sun rise; I went immediately over to George Taylor's; Jim Harris and my brother went with me; Jim Harris and I took breakfast at George's; my other brother went back home; my mother prepared breakfast for my father and brother at home; Mrs. Taylor, my sister, got breakfast over at George Taylor's; my sister was up when I got over there that morning; George Taylor was at the barn; that was just after sunrise; don't know just exactly what time it was when I got to the barn; we got our breakfast and I don't know just what time it was when me and Jim Harris started over to Mr. Ja. [James] Taylor's; I never saw any mud cleaned off the wagon wheels; I saw where the mud had been cleaned off after I came back from the timber that day; did not notice it that morning; I was with George Taylor nearly all the time that morning; I was in the barn cleaning out the stables; did not see where he was; did not see whether he was cleaning the wagon wheels or not; I don't know just exactly how far the wagon was from the stable; the wagon was sitting to the northeast from the stable, between the stable and the dwelling house; it was nearer to the stable; don't know just how far it was from the dwelling house; could not give you any idea of how far it was. I saw the harrow that morning; it was sitting there by the barn; George Taylor was not fixing up his harrow to go to the field when I went there; I did not know that he was preparing to do some harrowing; we harnessed his

team before breakfast; I never asked him what he was going to do with the team; did not hear him say what he was going to do with the team; I did not see him do the harrowing; my brother Drury got there at George's that morning; he went home to get his breakfast; I ate breakfast with my brother and Jim Harris; as soon as we got breakfast we went to Jas.[James] Taylor's with the wagon; I did the driving; we went through the field; did not go around the road; did not notice whether the harrow was ready to hitch on to or not that morning.

Upon re-direct examination by Senator Stephens, Willie further explained how he heard George come home the night of the murders:

I heard George Taylor come home that night; the north window was up where I was sleeping and I heard the noise of the wagon when it came down the road; that was about nine o'clock; the road passed right down the house; the public road that he came down was about fifteen or twenty feet from where I was sleeping; did not see him anymore until the next morning after sunrise. [21]

Della was pleased with her brother's testimony. Albert Taylor, George's brother was the next to take the stand. His testimony was pretty much a repeat of what Willie had said. One statement he made was to refute a previous testimony.

"My brother George did not tell me after I had gotten out [of the wagon] to go and do what I told you or don't forget to do what I told you." The rest of his testimony spoke of how he spent that night and the next day.

After Albert Taylor finished, Beverly Gibson, Della's eldest brother was called to the witness stand. Although Della listened to what he had to say it repeated much of the previous testimony about whether or not there was blood on the wagon bed and about the harrowing around the straw stack.

George and Bill's mother had started her testimony when it got suddenly dark. The old courthouse vibrated with each clap of thunder. Many of the people in the room grew restless and headed for the door. The lawyers tried to continue with the case, but the wind and lightning was so disconcerting it was hard to ignore.

At about four o'clock in the afternoon Judge Rucker said, "The building is not very safe. If the counsel wishes, court will adjourn until the storm shall be over."

Almost everyone was happy to hear him say that and quickly gathered up their belongings and escaped the courtroom. However, Della and Gonia did not want to take the girls out into the pouring rain so they chose to remain in the courthouse until it was safe to return to the rooming house.

Chapter 36

Wednesday morning Della, Gonia and the two little ones were back in the courtroom listening to the testimony from witnesses. This morning the State was calling rebuttal witnesses and the testimony of Garnett Atkins sent chills up Della's back. The things he was saying were in direct contradiction with both Gonia and Della's testimony. They listened carefully to his words.

Garnett Atkins testified as follows:

I live at Green City, Sullivan Co.; I moved there in January 1894, from Browning; I am a son of Hiram Atkins and have known Mrs. Dave [Gonia] Gibson twenty-three or four years; I had a conversation with her at George Taylor's house and she stated in the conversation that this murder was a sad affair and that they had George implicated in it; and she stated that the night of the murder that she set up waiting for him until ten o'clock and he didn't come and she went to bed and that she let him in between four and five o'clock that next morning; she said she did not know whether he was guilty or not; she said she was awake before he came in that morning and it was after four o'clock not yet five; she said she let him in; that was at George Taylor's house on the 11th day of May, 1894.

Upon cross examination by Colonel Hale, Atkins answered his questions like this:

Mr. Gibson and Mrs. Gibson and George Taylor's wife and Mr. Shelby were there with me; I guess they heard what was said; I had quite a conversation with her; [Why did you go there?] three people sent me in there; it was a matter of business; I was in the livery business and I took a party out there to get what information I could; I wasn't looking for the Taylors myself; I was tending to business; [who was with you?] these people I had with me were a U. S. Deputy Marshall from K. C.; we went in to talk with them; I went in with Mr. Shelby and left the rest of the party out on the road; Mr. Farris, Joe Bryant and James Wilson and Mr. Shelby were in the party; the rest stayed out to the road with the team; we were sent in and Mr. Shelby and I both talked; I commenced talking and asked her how she happened to be there that night; I had heard she was there; she told me why; I didn't know that she testified before the coroner's jury at that time; I hadn't heard anything about it; I didn't live down there; [Why did you ask her about George?] I heard that day she claimed to be there that day; I had heard she was at George's that night; that was the reason I asked her that question; she told me because her daughter was sick; she said she didn't know whether he was guilty or not guilty; said it was a sad affair and they had George implicated; said she sat up until ten o'clock and waited for him to come in but he didn't come and she went to bed; I have never testified before in this case; nor I wasn't here at the last term of this court; I never forgot about this conversation; I never asked her anything about her husband or where they slept and she never told me; she said she got up the next morning between four and five o'clock and let George in; [Where were you during this conversation?] we were all in the same room; the south room; Dave was talking in that conversation too; they both talked; when one said anything the other agreed to it; Dave said he was asleep when George came; didn't know anything about it; they said they both went to bed about the same time; [Who introduced you to Mrs. Gibson?] no one introduced me to Mrs. Gibson; she called me Garnett and knew me and shook hands with me; it had been about a year before this that I had seen her; I met her and Dave on the road to Browning and talked with them; these people came from K. C. and hired two teams; a buggy and wagon and I drove the wagon for them; I went in and come back and told them what he said; they went for information as to the Taylor boys; I suppose they were hunting the Taylor boys and not evidence; I did what they told me to do; they told me to go in and talk to them and get what information I could; I never thought anything about any evidence; I was trying to find their whereabouts; I went in and talked to her; I told the boys that I knew her; I tried to find out what they knew about the Taylor boys; I wasn't thinking about the trial; that was my purpose to find out the whereabouts of the Taylors; I had heard of the murder of course; I went in to see if they knew anything concerning the whereabouts and to talk with them; we talked about everything; I went in to get what information I could of the Taylors; I went there and was recognized as an acquaintance; I told these parties before that I knew her; she was several years older than I; I went in there to talk with these people and they talked. I didn't find out where they were and went out and told the people outside just what they had said to me; that wasn't the information they wanted and they left; they were all armed; Mr. Shelby did not take his Winchester in the house with him; the others were all armed and could be seen by the family from the house. [22]

Colonel Hale tried his best to shake Atkin's testimony, but he held firm to his statement.

Following Atkins' testimony, Gonia was recalled by the state.

Major Mullins asked, "Did you tell Garnett Atkins that George Taylor had arrived home between the hours of four and five o'clock that morning, and that whether innocent or guilty, he did come home at that time?"

This visibly riled Gonia to which she hotly replied, "No!"

Looking over the shoulder of Major Mullins she angrily said to Prosecutor Bresnehen, "You have a heart of stone. Have you no common decency?"

After Gonia was released, Della was recalled on rebuttal.

Upon direct examination by attorney Conkling, Della said,

I was present at my house on or about the 21st day of May 1894, at the time Garnett Atkins and the detective and the United States marshal came to the house; Garnett Atkins and my father came into the house at that time; I was present during conversation that occurred between Garnett Atkins and my mother, Mrs. Gibson; there were very few words said. There was not a word said about my husband; my mother did not say a word to Mr. Atkins or in his presence or hearing on that occasion about what time my husband George Taylor came home on the night of May 10th, 1894; there was not a word said about it; he never said a word." [23]

In the afternoon the defense rested its case. Judge Rucker adjourned court until the next morning to give the attorneys time to prepare their instructions. It was expected the closing arguments would take most of the next day. The judge gave each side five hours to argue their case. The speeches for the defense will be given by Colonel Hale, Virgil Conkling, B. F. Lozier and Ex. Senator Stephens.

Chapter 37

In Della's mind July had been a hot, uncomfortable month, not only as far as outside temperature but the pressure of the trial made it even hotter. She was glad August had arrived. Maybe things would be better this month. The hope the jury would find George and Bill not guilty of the horrible crime was the only way she felt she could get through the days. The jury finding the brothers guilty was an idea she pushed away from her mind. To even think of it was too distressing. *How can I go on living without George? I am too young to be a widow. What would become of our two girls?* Those negative thoughts were pushed away as Della and Gonia went through the morning tasks of feeding, grooming and dressing the girls for the trip to the courthouse.

Long before they arrived at the courthouse square, the two women clinging to Della's little girls were nearly lost in the large crowd which filled all empty space in the area. When the courtroom doors opened, Della holding Georgia, and Gonia leading Flossie proceeded down the aisles to the front of the room. Bill's wife and three daughters walked a few steps in front of them and both families found seats in full view of the jury.

At a few minutes before nine o'clock the attorneys began reading their instructions to the jury. The meaning of willful and deliberate murder was stressed by the attorneys for the state as well as the terms "provocation and malice." The defense attorneys called attention to the action of witnesses as well as their testimony. This was probably in relation to the bullying of witnesses by Virgil Conkling.

Next Judge Rucker instructed the jury to take into consideration how the defendants were only charged with the murder of Gus

Meeks and not any member of his family. He told the attorneys that each side could have no more than seven hours for their arguments. It was up to them to determine how they would allocate their time.

The mayor of Carrollton, L. A. Holliday made the opening arguments for the state. At one point in his remarks Conkling objected to the way Holliday was describing the murders. Della was glad Conkling had interrupted the speech because she was stunned by the way Mr. Holliday was painting such a horrible picture. She couldn't hold back the tears.

Ralph Lozier, the youngest attorney in the case, was the first to speak for the defense. He was noted for his orations. People in Carroll County believed he could speak on any occasion and called him the boy orator. He accused the prosecuting attorney of exceeding his authority by asking the jury to commit judicial murder. He said, "The public clamor demands their lives, but, if the Taylors are hanged on this demand, the life of no man will be safe."

By now Della's weeping had become sobs. Sensing her mother's emotions, baby Georgia began crying loudly. Gonia reached over, picked up the baby, took Flossie's hand and walked out to the hallway. The movement and secure arms of her grandmother soon calmed the baby girl. Flossie was finding it hard to understand what was wrong. She asked Gonia, "Momma okay?"

"Yes, your mama is all right. She is sad right now. Just remember she loves you and Georgie. And I love you, too. We will go back in the room soon."

The last speaker in the morning session was Benjamin Pierce the prosecutor of Sullivan County. By the end of his speech, Della had regained control of her emotions. It was bad enough for her to break down crying but then with the baby crying so loudly all heads had turned to her. She knew they were thinking, *Can't that woman control her baby?* She was so embarrassed she bent her head down and put her hands over her face. George would never understand what she was feeling.

Pierce's speech was not long, so Gonia stayed out in the hall with the little ones until court was dismissed for the noon meal.

As soon as Della saw her mother she said, "Ma, I'm so sorry for the display. Thank you for taking the girls out. I'll try to do better."

"It's all right. Those speeches were emotional. I even got a lump in my throat when Lozier was talking. We'll go eat now. You'll be better this afternoon."

The meal at the rooming house was tasty and filling. By time to go back to the courthouse, Della was ready to face the afternoon speeches. It was painful to listen to the words of the state's attorneys, but she had to be strong for her daughters. As they walked back into the courtroom Della could not help but see Sheriff Niblo right up front. Even though he glared at her when she took her seat, she tried to remain calm. He had no right to look at her in such a way.

During all the long day, Sheriff Niblo sat as if turned to stone while listening to the closing arguments delivered by the attorneys. It had disgusted him when Della began sobbing and her mother had to leave with the toddler and crying baby. At least after they left it he could hear what the lawyers were saying.

He, along with half the courtroom, went to a nearby café for something to eat while the court was taking the noon break. As soon as he finished eating, he returned to his seat, not wanting to miss a word of the speeches.

The first attorney to address the jury in the afternoon was E. R. Stevens of Linneus. Niblo was amazed at this peculiar looking man and his extremely disturbing remarks. How could he find anything to joke about in this serious situation? It looked to Niblo at one point in Stevens' speech as if Bill Taylor stretched out a hand to get Stevens to stop, but he continued to shake his head and to teeter back and forth on his toes.

Stevens has been Bill Taylor's lawyer for a number of years. He seemed to eulogize Bill when he said "I leave it to you as businessmen, if he is not all right. Why, he was cashier of a bank for a long time in Browning and you know what a bank cashier is."

To Niblo it didn't seem like a good recommendation.

The next speaker was Sidney Miller, a young prosecuting attorney for Carroll County who spoke briefly for the state. He stuck to the evidence in the case and asked only for justice. Niblo found his words quite convincing.

The rest of the afternoon was taken up by arguments by Brindley for the defense and J. I. Minnis for the state. Both tried to make their case by attempting to convince the jury of their side of the story.

After listening to the speeches of Brindley and Minnis, Della and Gonia were very tired. Flossie was restless and Georgia was fussy, so they decided to return to the rooming house and not stay for the night arguments. It had been a long day trying to keep the two little ones occupied and relatively quiet.

Chapter 38

Although it had been a long, hot day, Sheriff Niblo could not tear himself away from the arguments which had gone on all day and was now into the evening.

He thought Minnis for the state had made some good points. In his opening words he had said, "Gentlemen of the jury, if I were to consult alone your personal comfort or that of the court or myself, I would contribute the time allowed to me in this discussion to shortening your labors and the hours of responsibility; but the vast importance of this case to the people as well as to the defendants makes a thorough argument of the facts; a duty that should not be shirked. Gentlemen this is an important case; it involves the lives of these defendants and that is an important feature in the case; it also involves the lives of innocent children and an innocent woman." [24]

He went on to say how it was the fear of death which caused the defendants to enter a not guilty plea. If they had not been afraid of death, they would have entered a guilty plea to avoid all the trouble of a trial. He remarked how it was the duty of the law to punish the guilty to preserve the safety of the innocent. These sentiments were basically along the same lines as the sheriff's. Niblo thought the jury surely would see it this way.

Minnis touched on the fact that the crime had stirred up a mob. He thought it was a natural reaction upon the discovery of the murders. He said, "A man who would not become interested in the search of the guilty parties at the sight of this great crime would not be worthy of the protection of the law, and not worthy of our citizenship."

The argument of Virgil Conkling for the defense did not sit so well with Niblo. He thought Conkling was a bully and the way he treated the speech of Mr. Minnis was unethical and demeaning. Conkling called Minnis his friend, but his words did not imply they were friends.

Conkling said, "I believe I know the effect of an appeal to passions of men as was made this evening by Mr. Minnis; I fear if I were on that jury I would not be able to sit unmoved when a lawyer appealed to my passions and my revenue as my friend appealed to you this evening. I don't complain of Minnis for doing so, he and I have practiced law here in this bar together, and I have learned to know him; I have learned to know how well the man can argue and I have learned to know that in one case he is far superior to myself; I have learned to know that Minnis can do something that few men can do; argue on both sides of a criminal case."

He went on to say, "I don't care if Minnis is a little jealous of Colonel Hale, I don't care if Minnis is trying to get ahead of him and if there is a little rivalry on the part of Minnis, I don't think it is fair to make reflections and try to prejudice you men against old Colonel John B. Hale."…. "I don't think it is right to come before you men and attempt to poison your mind against Colonel Hale and his arguments and efforts in behalf of these defendants; it is not right."

Niblo noticed Conkling touched on the exchanges he and the judge had engaged in at some points during the trial. He indicated he felt humiliation and regret for those moments. He said, "I know His Honor on the bench has not tried to treat me unjustly in any way and therefore I must say it must be my shortcomings that the deep thrusts have found their way to my heart. I know another thing, gentlemen, I know that I have occupied a position in this case that is a little bit unusual." He explained it was because he considered himself a friend of the defendants.

Near the end of his speech he said, "I am their friend; I will stand by them and take their chances here; you twelve men go into your room and if you bring in a verdict of guilty in the first degree, if you place the rope around their necks, I will be found standing by their side. If I don't do anything else, even though I be in the wrong, I intend to stand by them." Ending with, "I tell you men now I believe they are innocent. The Almighty God direct your verdict aright. I thank you for your time." [24]

After the closing, Niblo was ready to retire to his rooming house for a good night's sleep. On the way out of the courthouse he encountered his friend Ben Pierce.

"Well, Ben, what do you think of the speeches tonight?"

Ben rubbed his chin with his hand giving some thought to the question before he attempted to answer. "I naturally think the state has a good case. Minnis is a good man and does not deserve those critical remarks by Conkling. If Conkling considers the Taylor boys his friends he has made some poor choices for friends."

"You're right. Conkling is a bully and if like personalities attract, maybe that is why he is friends with the Taylors."

"Tomorrow Breshnehan will close it down," said Ben. "I think we can count on him to give a good closing. He is a good honest man who wants these criminals punished for the terrible things they did to the Meeks family. It is hard to imagine the jury will not return a guilty verdict. We should be prepared for violence if they don't."

"I think you are right, Ben. How is Nellie holding up?"

"Actually, she is doing very well. She isn't having nightmares now and she gets along well with our family. I am surprised the trial doesn't seem to affect her. She is such a sweet little thing. I'm glad you thought to ask us to make a home for her."

Niblo raised his arms to stretch then reached around and rubbed his back with his hands. Being an active man, it was hard for him to sit so many hours without getting up and moving around. "Guess we had better be getting back to the rooming house for some sleep to be ready for the rest of this in the morning. Have a good night, Ben."

"See you in the morning, James."

Chapter 39

Friday, August 2, 1895 dawned a normal, bright, sunshiny, Missouri summer day without a clue as to what the day held for the Taylor brothers' case. Della tried to be optimistic about the outcome, but there was the dread in her mind how it would not go the way she hoped. *No matter what happens, I must hold myself together when the verdict is announced,* she vowed.

After the girls were fed, the women ate a good breakfast along with the other occupants of the rooming house. It would probably be their last day in Carrollton. As they made their way to the courthouse, Gonia said, "I'll be glad to get back to the farm to some sense of normalcy. The circus atmosphere in this town is terrible. All around the courthouse square there are people selling everything imaginable from medicine, soap, cigars, canes, and lemonade. There are even men running around singing and playing a guitar or violin. People from all over the country are here appearing to enjoy this merriment. It seems almost blasphemous in this serious situation when two men's lives hang by a thread."

"I know, Ma. It makes my heart ache to see all this laughter and fun when George and Bill are fighting for their lives."

The courtroom was packed with spectators when Della and Gonia arrived. It was good that seats had been saved for them up front. The little girls were comfortable on Grandma's and Mamma's lap. From time to time, Gonia bounced Flossie up and down on first one knee then the other much to the delight of the little girl. Georgia was satisfied to sit quietly at least for the time being on Della's lap.

When Bill and George were brought into the courtroom, Della wanted to say something to George but thought perhaps it was better if she kept her seat. She loved him so much it was hard for her to keep her hands away from him.

"Georgia, that's Papa down there." Della whispered, "Wave to him." Even though Georgia didn't really understand what her mother meant, she waved her little hands and made gurgling sounds until Della had to shush her when the Judge signaled it was time for Colonel John B. Hale to begin his closing argument for the defense.

Colonel Hale knew he had to put in a strong plea for his defendants. He tried to make the jury comfortable by indicating he realized it had been a long trial and they probably were as weary as he was after the extended days of testimony. He said, "I will therefore try to give you a calm, quiet and candid statement of the points in this case as I understand them... ...I will be compelled to address you in a calm and quiet manner. I shall not attempt any flight of oratory or eloquence as if I was a young man in the springtime of my youth."

He went on to describe his years as a defense attorney, emphasizing he had never been a prosecuting attorney. He also touched on the speech of J. I Minnis and how Minnis seemed to be critical of him, but Hale said he was sure the remarks were intended to weaken or destroy his argument. In Colonel Hale's opinion the words of Minnis were unkind and unfair.

Della listened carefully to Colonel Hale's speech knowing he was giving it his all. If she had a pencil and paper Della would have listed some of the points he was making: They briefly were these:

1. *The jury must be satisfied that both Bill and George are guilty.*

2. *There is no question the murder occurred on Jenkins Hill, but was it Bill and George?*

3. *The brutality of the crime, which has been dwelt on in the arguments, does not assist you in determining who committed the murders.*

4. *They fled the next day because of the danger to themselves from the mobs and not as evidence of guilt.*

5. *The distance supposedly covered by the wagon at night—to Milan then Jenkins Hill and to George's farm—is too great to have been covered in such a short amount of time. And no one saw Bill come into town that morning which is unreasonable.*

6. Why was no blood found on their clothes if they committed the murders? None found when the houses were searched. For such a violent crime there would have been lots of blood.

7. Did the state have a fear of conflict if they had allowed Nellie to testify?

8. No conflict in Gonia's testimony before the immediate grand jury until they brought in Garnett Atkins who saw her several days later.

9. This point was closest to Della's heart: Damage to the families of Bill and George if they are convicted; the fate of the innocent children.

Colonel Hale closed by telling the jury the fate of these defendants is in your hands. "I say deal with them as you would wish to be dealt by under similar circumstances. When you retire and bring in your verdict, make such a verdict as would justify you in returning to your homes and spending the remainder of your days in peace and contentment, with the conviction you had done your duty to both the state and these defendants. Do that and all will be satisfied. Gentlemen, I thank you very kindly for your attention."

In Della's thoughts, *Oh, if the jury would only listen to Colonel Hale, George would be saved. Can't they see George is a father with children of his own? How could he kill someone else's children?* Della was ready to leave, but they would stay until the end. She tried to think of other things while Bresnehen for the state gave his closing arguments. She did not want to hear again about all the violence of that night. By playing with Georgia and thinking of other things Della was able to block out most of what he said. Near the end of his speech, Della heard Bresnehen mention her name along with her mother and father. This brought her fully alert to what he was saying.

"Where was George Taylor that night? Mrs. Dave Gibson says George was at home; that he came home that night about nine o'clock and got up about four the next morning; she swore to that in the court room. Gentlemen what is the testimony? You saw Garnett Atkins here. You talked with him and heard him talk. You know what he said. She told him in the presence of Dave Gibson, who was at that time sitting here in the courthouse when he swore it. Dave heard that talk, the father-in-law of George Taylor and the husband of Mrs. Gibson heard him swear that. Garnett Atkins says Dave was there, Mrs. Gibson was there, and George's wife was there and Mr. Shelby was there. You say where is Mr. Shelby; Why ain't he here, if a prosecuting attorney had a thousand brains and a thousand eyes, it would be impossible for him to know all the facts and bearings in a case of this kind. Many of the witnesses were never brought into the court room; we have no means to know what every witness will testify to until he comes in court. I ask you gentlemen, and I ask you Mr. Conkling, when Garnett Atkins said that Mrs. Gibson said that she sat up and waited until ten o'clock for George Taylor to come home and he didn't come and she got up the next morning and let him in, in the presence of Dave Gibson; I ask you sir, where was Dave Gibson, the father-in-law of the defendant at the bar; stood there and heard the contradiction according to Garnett Atkins. Gentlemen, I ask you why was he not here to give his testimony. He stayed there and heard this talk and knows something of these facts. You know just how that matter stands, you know that Garnett Atkins told the truth; Mrs. Dave Gibson here swearing for her son-in-law, I have no harsh words to say against her, not a thing on earth, I wouldn't say it. I say it is commendable in a relative, in a father or brother, wife or mother-in-law and near and dear friends and relatives, I say it is commendable in them to come and stand by their relatives while there is life and hope and I would not say, taking into consideration the weaknesses of mankind the emotions of sympathy, love and relationship, I would not say an unkind word against them for coming into court and telling untruths in order to save their relatives, their husbands, their son-in-laws, their father-in-law or their brother, their wives or husbands. But the court gives you an instruction on that question. The court instructs the jury that under the law of this state the defendants and Della Taylor, wife of George E. Taylor, who have testified in this case are competent witnesses so to do, but the fact that they are the two defendants and one of them is the husband of Della Taylor may be taken into consideration by the jury in determining what weight, if any, shall be given to their testimony. You therefore take into consideration the fact that they are the defendants and that Della Taylor is the wife of George Taylor and the interest she or they all have in the result of this case, and determine what weight, if any, shall be given to their testimony.

"The jury are the sole judges of the credibility of the witnesses under the instructions of the court. Their relation to the defendant, George Taylor, his mother-in-law, his father-in-law and his brother-in-law; his father-in-law don't testify; the mother-in-law does; take into consideration the relationships. Did she tell the truth or did Garnett Atkins, the man who came down there on a matter of business, running a livery stable in Green City; who told it? You know Garnett Atkins told you the truth. That Mrs. Gibson did say on that day of May that George was gone and they waited until ten o'clock for him to come and he didn't come until four or five o'clock the next morning and that she let him in; that's what she told Garnett Atkins, and gentlemen that's when she told the truth; they did set up waiting for George to come that night. [25]

As she listened to what Bresnehen was saying, Della's heart sank. It sounded to her like a death sentence for George and Bill. Why couldn't they believe what she and her mother told in their testimony? She was both relieved and sad when Bresnehen closed by saying,

"Colonel Hale committed the defendants into your hands for their safety and deliverance. Gentlemen, I now commit into your hands the safety of the people; we commit into your hands your honor and your integrity to say whether such crimes proven shall go unpunished." . . . "You gentlemen do right; do right under your oaths to the commonwealth and to the defendants and the State is satisfied."

After his closing, Della said, "Ma, do you think George and Bill have a chance of being found not guilty?"

"No honey, it looks bad for them. Let's go get something to eat and then come back for the verdict."

Chapter 40

The past two weeks had been hot and exhausting for all those interested in the Taylor case. Sheriff Niblo was glad the trial was coming to a close and sincerely hoped the jury would find the defendants guilty. The closing arguments delivered by the attorneys on both sides were noteworthy. His thoughts naturally were with the side of the prosecution who he thought had done a good job of proving their case.

Tom Bresnehen brought out the discrepancy between the testimony of Mrs. Dave Gibson and Garnett Atkins. In Niblo's opinion it should have discounted the case of the Taylors having an alibi. He had no sympathy for Della Taylor or her mother. He was sure they were lying and, if he could, he would see they were arrested for perjury.

There was a little excitement when Bresnehen said, "Last night Conkling asked why the state had not produced Orville Shelby." Turning to Conkling, he said, "Where is Dave Gibson?" and Conkling shouted back, "Where is Orville Shelby?" [26]

This brought on a stir in the courtroom, so Judge Rucker banged his gavel and demanded silence.

Sheriff Niblo noticed as Bresnehen talked about the murders, Bill appeared nervous and his face was very white, while George's face was fiery red. The jury looked to be strongly affected by the story of the crime even though it had been told to them many times.

Toward the end of his two-hour speech, Bresnehen knew the jury was very tired and he felt he should close before he lost their attention. Most of the jury members were used to an active life so this confinement was hard for them to take. Niblo knew that, like him, the jury had sat for twelve hours yesterday with only an hour at noon and an hour for supper. He also was ready for this trial to end.

Niblo agreed with Bresnehen's closing words, "The doubt of the guilt of these men is the dream of a dream. They are guilty; do your duty, jurymen." [27]

After those words the courtroom burst into a roar as the people knew the trial was over except for the verdict.

Judge Rucker gave the jury their instructions and since it was noon the members were allowed to have their noon meal before they began deliberating. After eating his meal, Niblo hurried back to the courtroom to find a seat in order not to miss the verdict. As soon as it was suspected the jury was in, the courtroom was inundated with upward to a thousand persons trying to get into a room that should hold no more than three hundred people. Niblo thought it was a good sign the jury only deliberated an hour and a half before they sent word to Judge Rucker they had reached a verdict.

The main reason Della wanted to go back to the courthouse after the noon recess was to see George again. She wanted to embed his handsome face in her memory because she didn't know when she would see him again if he was convicted. Little did she know how true it would be.

It was good that their seats had been saved for their return, since there was only standing room when Gonia, Della and the little girls entered the courtroom. They settled in their seats and played with Flossie and Georgia to keep the thoughts of why they were in this place from their minds. Flossie was such a pretty little two-year-old with her silky blonde hair and clear blue eyes. The two girls were quite different, as Georgia had hazel eyes and might have brown hair when her baby fuzz was replaced. Flossie was always on the go, at every chance she got while Georgia was very laid-back with a sweet smile. It was all the two women could do to keep the little ones quiet when the judge took the bench and called for the defendants to be brought in at 2:35 p.m.

When George and Bill entered the courtroom, Della was surprised at how pale and haggard Bill looked. George's color was good, and he didn't seem to be as affected by the trial as his brother.

Maybe it's a good sign, thought Della.

Immediately after Bill and George were seated Judge Rucker asked the jury if it had reached a verdict.

"We have," said Foreman Craig.

"Are all the jury present?"

The circuit clerk called each name who answered, "Present."

George W. Craig, the foreman took the verdict to the clerk who read it. "We, the jury find the defendants, William P. and George E. Taylor, guilty in the manner and form charged in the indictment. (signed) G. W. Craig, foreman." [28]

As soon as the verdict was read the crowded court room erupted in pandemonium. With that announcement, Della knew what she had thought might be a good sign was not. She erupted along with the crowd, but with a different sound. "Oh, no, no, no, no! It can't be." She began sobbing with tears streaming down each cheek. Gonia tried to comfort her by reaching over and encircling Della in her arms.

"Ma, what will I do now? I can't go on without George."

"Yes, honey you will go on. You have two beautiful children to care for. You and the girls will have a home with us. Pull yourself together."

Judge Rucker began banging his gavel for order, but nobody seemed to pay any attention to it. Finally, he said, "I want this noise stopped or the room will be cleared. Sheriff, arrest any man who applauds."

This caught the attention of the crowd, so they began to rush out the doors. Many were rushing to the telegraph office to send messages throughout the country as this famous case was now over. After order was restored, Attorney Conkling requested the jury be polled with each juror answering in the affirmative.

The verdict had a different effect on Bill and George. Bill started to rise in his seat and gasped as in shock. He looked haggard as the gravity of the situation dawned on him. The jury was discharged, and the Taylors were given to the charge of the Carroll County Sheriff.

Gonia was surprised at the lack of reaction the guilty verdict had made on George. *Did he have a heart of stone?* He just stared off in the distance as if it was of no concern what the jury had decided. No doubt

Della loved him, but Gonia, who had been so pleased when George and Della were married, was sure now it had been a mistake. It was time to go home and try to forget this terrible ordeal.

"Let's get out of this crowd, go pack and catch a train back to Browning. There is nothing more we can do here."

The two women did not tarry long outside the courthouse. The roisters in the streets around the courthouse were too much for Della to take. She wanted away from all the shouting people who were so happy her husband would be put to death while she would be left a widow, and her daughters without a father.

It was sometime after the court had adjourned before the sheriff took the Taylors to the jail. One reporter asked Bill, "What will be your course, now?"

Bill replied, "I have nothing to say to anyone."

Sheriff Stanley had received a tip how friends of the Taylors would try to make a means of escape possible for the brothers. With this information in hand the sheriff searched the building carefully but found nothing amiss. He, along with five officers escorted the Taylors to the jail through a crowd of nearly 5,000 people blocking the street completely.

Sheriff Niblo joined the crowd around the courthouse square to learn the public thoughts about the verdict. What he heard was jubilation when the verdict was "guilty." He heard B. C. Dulaney and George Freeman, two of the jurors say the verdict was reached on the first ballot.

Ben Pierce had not yet gone back to Milan when Niblo came out on the square. They greeted each other with a handshake while Pierce said, "Do you think the verdict was just?"

Niblo's response was, "Oh, my, yes! I don't see how they could have reached anything else. I would like to arrest half or more of the witnesses for perjury; especially that wife of George Taylor. How could she get up on the witness stand and swear George was home when she knew he wasn't?"

"Well, James, you know she has two little girls now to raise alone. You can't really blame her for wanting George to be set free. I'm not sure how she will manage. Her parents don't have a lot of money so it will be hard for them, too. Bill's wife also has children, but her mother has money and can take care of her family."

"But I think George is a cold-blooded killer who really deserves to die for killing the Meeks family. How could he kill those little girls of Gus Meeks? You know how it has affected the one Meeks girl left you are helping."

"Yes, Nellie is doing very well now. She will never get over the massacre, but she is strong and will survive."

"Do you think the attorneys will file for a new trial as is usual?"

"Yes, no doubt they will, but probably the motion will not be granted. I think the trial was conducted according to the rules and Judge Rucker is known for being a stickler to the law protocol."

"Ben, it was good talking to you. Have a safe trip back to Milan. I'll see you in a few days."

Chapter 41

It was a rather sedate homecoming when Della, Gonia and the girls returned to the Gibson home. The family and especially Dave were glad to have them back. Della's sister, Ivy Mae, although only eight years old, had done a good job of caring for the house with help from her brothers. Actually, her father, Dave was pretty much in charge of the cooking, but she was a good helper. It might take a few days, but soon things would be back to normal, if there was such a thing, after all that had happened.

Della was depressed and found it hard to do the every-day chores which were needed as her part of the household duties. She kept thinking about what life would be like without a husband and a father for the girls. *How am I going to show my face in the community? It was bad enough before, but with the guilty verdict no one would want to associate with me or the girls. The girls would be known as daughters of a murderer which would destroy their chances for happiness in their home community.*

She just couldn't believe George was guilty of the horrible crime of trying to kill a whole family. Maybe the attorneys were right; it was done by someone else who had framed George and Bill. It didn't seem reasonable the two of them could have killed the entire family without help.

This theory was brought forward again when it was learned of an anonymous letter sent to the sheriff of Carrollton. The Gibsons found a copy in one of the local newspapers. It brought a little cheer to Della as she read it.

> We the undersigned, do solemnly swear that the Taylor brothers are not the murderers of the Meeks family, as the majority of the people think, but the men who committed the

deed are as follows: Varney Taylor, Bill White, Enos Williams, Tom Williams. We heard that the Taylors had given $1,000 to Gus and we took this method of getting the money. By throwing them in George Taylor's hay stack all the suspicion would be thrown on him, thinking he could clear himself. We have been wanted for murders, robbery, and a number of other crimes but have never been caught. We are now on our road to New Mexico, and if you can catch us you may have us. You will hang two innocent men. We have no relatives and if we come to the gallows it won't be as bad as if the Taylors do, for they are innocent. Hoping that you will not hang the innocent brothers for that crime, we bid you adieu. [29]

Surely the law would investigate this letter. Della thought it made a lot of sense, but what would Bresnehen do about it?

In another newspaper Della read where the defense attorneys in the Taylor case had filed a motion for a new trial. They listed thirty reasons why there should be a new trial. She was not a lawyer, so the explanations seemed reasonable to her. Perhaps there was still a chance for George yet, but it would have to be soon because Judge Rucker had set October 4, 1895 as the date for the hanging of the Taylor brothers.

Della knew the attorneys would make all the appeals possible, even up to the Missouri Supreme Court. She could only hope something would come up, so George was set free. She loved her parents and they were very good to her and the girls, but she had married so she would have a home of her own.

August was a slow month for farm work so the men were kept busy by caring for the animals, repairing machinery, and restoring the buildings. Mr. Taylor had agreed to let the Gibsons remain on the farm if they would continue to plant the crops and care for George's animals. It was a big farm which kept all the Gibson men busy with a little help at times from George's brothers.

For the women, it was a very busy season. The big garden planted in the spring now was yielding forth its plenty. Each day saw another vegetable harvested, cleaned, packed and canned in quart jars to have in the winter after the garden was depleted. It was good for Della to be engrossed in this work during the day. At least it took Della's mind away from her grief.

Clarence Beverly Gibson, eldest brother of Della was working for the railroad in Browning which put him in a position to hear news from all over the state. If one looked closely at his face, they could clearly see his excitement as he returned home from work this bright, September day. This news would surely excite Della. Bev, as he was called by the family, could barely keep still as he waited until the family finished their evening meal to tell his story.

"Folks, you won't believe what I heard today. Sheriff Stanley of Carrollton has learned of a plan for George and Bill to escape from jail. Bill had approached the night watchman Brown and offered him a lot of money if Brown would help them break out of jail. After hearing and agreeing to their proposition, Brown approached the sheriff who told the night watchman to continue listening to their plans."

"They agreed to write letters back and forth. Bill Taylor wrote a letter outlining escape plans and gave it to Brown who later took it to the sheriff. Sheriff Stanley copied the letters so Brown could give them back to Bill."

"One of the surprising things in the letters was when Bill asked Brown to become a partner in counterfeiting gold and silver coins. Bill said before their arrest he had cleared $5,000 from this business and Brown could be a partner after their jail escape."

Della's face turned deathly pale after hearing her brother's words. "Do you believe any of that, Bev?"

"It sounds fantastic to me. Did you ever hear George say anything about such a thing?

"No, and I don't think George was involved in it any more than I think he committed those murders."

"At least, I hear," said Bev, "Sheriff Stanley has put on extra guards so I don't think the plan will work."

As color began to come back to her face, Della wiped her face with her sleeve. She couldn't imagine what would happen if George and Bill did break out of jail. *Would George come and get me and the girls or would he run away by himself? How should I react to this?*

Young Drue could hardly hold his tongue as he listened to his brother tell of the new developments in this seemingly never-ending saga. Drue Green Gibson since he was only now fifteen, was not called on to testify at either trial. His brother William Isaac Gibson was at George's place helping with the chores the morning the victims were discovered so he had things to say on the witness stand. Willie was almost a man at age eighteen. Drue was feeling a little jealous at not being involved in any of the action in the case. Maybe, if George escaped from jail, he would come here to get Della and the girls. Then, in Drue's imagination, he could help George, Della and the girls get away. In Drue's eyes he was almost a man so he could be a big help. These thoughts were running rampant through his mind as Bev was telling his story.

When Bev finished telling what he had heard at the railroad, everyone at the table started talking at once. Gonia raised her hand and said, "Now, let's just stop right here and quit all this jabbering. It is not likely George and Bill will escape from jail. Sheriff Stanley seems to have a good grip on the situation, so we just as well not think about what 'might' happen. We need to get to bed soon because there is a lot of work to be done tomorrow."

Chapter 42

Sheriff Niblo also heard about the Taylor's plan to escape. This infuriated him so much he decided to go to Carrollton and have a talk with Sheriff Stanley. Maybe he could offer some support or at least advice.

The two sheriffs greeted cordially and after a few minutes of small talk, Nibo asked, "What do you know about this escape plan of the Taylor's?"

Sheriff Stanley said, "Here, James, take a look at these letters. Their plans are pretty well laid out in them."

Niblo carefully read the letters Bill Taylor had written,

"I think it simple and safe. I notice the padlock at the top of the door inside of the box is not locked, but simply hanging in a slot. I notice there is a hole running through the top of the box where the slide bar that unlocks the cells passes through the wall. I can easily arrange a wire with a hook in the end and pass it in through that hole and the inside padlock can be hung on the hook at locking up time. That disposes of the top lock. Now, the bottom one. If you can get the keys a few minutes during the day and unlock it but turn it so it will stick on and not be locked but appear all right. Then we are safe as to the exit. If that lock cannot be unlocked during the day and left apparently all right, then we should have a saw and cut it off or get duplicate keys, but I much prefer to have it unlocked on account of noise and possible detection by some of the family." [30]

In another letter Bill wrote how Brown could divert attention away from himself.

> "How to set yourself right and leave no possible suspicion, you do this: You come in and walk around till near morning and begin to shout and halloo and run outdoors and shoot. That of course will arouse the entire house. Then you can say that when you came we ran out over you, knocked you down and made the run, and to show you took great chances and did all you could, you fire one shot through some part of your clothing and say we shot at you. Then the work is done. We will be gone some time before you do the shooting and you can say we ran just the opposite way we expect to go. That will put them off our course. We will go to some friends for a few days and arrange our means of travel, and when sufficiently quiet we will join and go quietly to some jungle or mountain gorge." [31]

"That is some plan," said Niblo. "What do you expect to do about it?"

"Oh, I have already put on extra guards. There have been other plans since I received these letters. So far, I have been able to discover them and put a stop to their escape plans."

"I certainly hope so. Bill Taylor is one devious crook and his brother George will go along with anything his brother proposes." Sheriff Niblo lamented. "It looks like you have things well in hand. If you need me to help in anyway, just telegraph me and I'll get here as soon as I can."

"Thanks for the offer, James. I believe we have it well in hand at this point. We are keeping a close watch on things. You know the hangings have been postponed while the appeals are making it through the courts. It will probably be later next spring."

"Too bad it couldn't be next week." With this, Sheriff Niblo said his goodbyes.

Through the winter Jim Niblo kept in touch with his friend Ben Pierce and when they met the talk usually turned to the Taylor brothers.

"You know, Ben, it was quite a plan Bill came up with for an escape. Sheriff Stanley showed me copies of the letters exchanged between Bill and Officer Brown when I was down there in October."

"Oh, Bill Taylor is a crafty one, Jim. It's too bad he didn't use his smarts for good instead of evil."

The sheriff sighed, "Yes, he was just too money hungry for his own good. I can't help but wonder how George got mixed up in all that. Bill must have had something over him to get him to help in the murders. George is a cold one. Maybe he has a bad streak, too."

"Well," said Ben, "the lawyers are keeping busy making their appeals. How much longer will old man Taylor's money hold out do you reckon? The last appeal is to the State Supreme Court. I don't think they have a chance, but they do have to do it."

"I told Sheriff Stanley when I went down there, I would give him help if he needed it. So far, I haven't heard anything from him. Let's hope they are able to keep those two in jail until the hanging."

"Jim, I'm sure if he needs you, he will let you know. Surely they have things in control down there by now."

"It's been a long winter, but Spring is here now so I hope the hanging goes off as it's supposed to. I better get back to the office. See you later."

A few days later Sheriff Niblo received a telegram telling him of the attempted escape of the Taylor brothers on Saturday night, April 11, 1896. The telegram said Bill was caught but George escaped so his help was needed to find George.

The sheriff lost no time in saddling his horse. He knew exactly where he wanted to go first. It didn't take him long to arrive at the Gibson place. Niblo jumped off his horse, ran up to the door and started pounding on it. David opened the door as quickly as he could.

"What do you mean trying to break down the door?"

"Where is that no-good son-in-law of yours?"

"In jail, I suppose. Why are you here?"

"That's a likely story. Wouldn't the first place he would come after breaking jail be to get his wife and babies?"

"What?" gasped David. "Did he really escape from the jail in Carrollton?

Sheriff Niblo was still not sure he believed that David didn't know about the jail break, so he pushed his way in the door and began looking around. It was early on Sunday morning and the family had not been up long.

Della heard the noise and came rushing down the stairs to see what was the matter. When she saw Sheriff Niblo she knew something was terribly wrong.

Her father said, "Dellie, George escaped from jail and the sheriff thinks he's here."

Hearing that, Della burst into tears, "Oh! No! And Bill, too?"

While nervously pacing back and forth, Niblo told the family how Bill and George and another inmate had attempted to escape Saturday night. Bill and Cunningham, the other inmate, were captured when they climbed down off the roof of the jail, but somehow George had gotten away.

David said, "There is no way George would come here. He knows this is the first place you would look. By now he is probably long gone from the area. If the escape was Saturday night, George probably jumped a train and is in another state by now."

It seemed as if there was nothing else he could do here so reluctantly Niblo left the house and got back on his horse. Before leaving he said, "I'll be watching you and the Taylor families so if you hear anything from George you had best let me know right away."

Chapter 43

After Sheriff Niblo left their house, Della didn't know whether to laugh or cry. George was free! What would he do next? "Pa, do you think George will come to get me and the girls?"

"No, Dellie, you know he won't come around here. If he is free, he will keep on going because he knows there will be law officers all over this part of the country. Maybe after things calm down, he might send for you, but don't get your hopes up too much. He is a convicted murderer and the law will always be on the look-out for him. You had best convince yourself he is gone for good."

Before Sheriff Niblo left, Gonia came into the room in time to hear what Niblo said about the jail break. She now took Della in her arms trying to comfort her. "Honey, we will look after you and the girls. We'll take it one day at a time and see what happens. Right now we better get breakfast on the table for this hungry family. We'll talk about it later."

It was impossible for Della to keep the tears from running down her cheeks, but she put on her apron and from time to time brushed the tears away with a corner of the apron. She knew it was important to be strong for the girls because sensing her feelings would make them nervous. By the time breakfast was on the table, Della had pulled herself together, but she still couldn't eat much. After each bite she took a long drink of milk to wash the food down her tight throat.

If the family had planned to go to church today, those plans were soon canceled. The tension was noticeable in the congregation when they did attend the local services. After this jail break no one in the Gibson family felt like being around their neighbors. Maybe it would get better in time.

Annalou Mack

Somehow Della made it through the day without a breakdown. There was plenty of work to keep her busy even on a Sunday. After doing her chores, Della spent much of the day playing with Flossie and Georgia. The girls played well together. Flossie, with an increasing vocabulary, was trying to teach Georgia everything her big sister knew. It could be quite laughable at times.

Each day Della insisted the family get a newspaper to learn what was happening with the hunt for George. The family didn't have access to all the papers with articles about the Taylor brothers because this was big news all over the United States. The Gibsons took a couple local newspapers; one of the newspapers related how two days after the jail break, Sheriff Stanley took Bill Taylor to the county jail in Kansas City for safe keeping. Della also learned the Gibson house was not the only one visited by searchers as the Taylor homes were searched also. In addition to fifty to a hundred men out hunting for George, bloodhounds were brought in to search. The bloodhounds had followed the scent for a ways, then they lost it near the Wabash and Santa Fe railroad tracks.

The feelings were so strong that even though he had put extra guards on duty there was danger of a mob coming for a lynching if Bill had remained in Carrollton. Citizens of Browning were very angry about the jail escape and blamed Sheriff Stanley and his Deputy Sheriff Lon Shelton for what they thought was their negligence. Before Bill was transferred to Kansas City, Linn County Deputy Sheriff Wilson went to Carrollton and demanded the sheriff turn Bill Taylor over to him to take to the Linneus jail. Sheriff Stanley refused which made Wilson very angry and he accused Stanley of taking money to allow George to escape.

Discussion about the jail escape was about all anyone talked about when two or more people met in the Browning neighborhood. Naturally there was a lot of talk at the train depot where Bev Gibson worked.

"Today I learned a new version of how George escaped from the jail," said Bev one evening as the family sat down to eat.

"So how was that?" said Willie.

Bev continued, "Bill told a reporter this story. At about eight o'clock on Saturday evening, after Deputy Shelton had made his rounds and left the jail, the loose bars of the cell that were previously sawed through were pushed down so the three, Bill, George and Cunningham, another inmate, could get out. They found a rubber hose, quickly picking it up they went up the stairs where they cut through the tin roof.

"Deputy Shelton had not gone home and was back of the jail talking to another by the name of Eisenhour. When Bill saw the deputy, he told Cunningham to lie down. But Cunningham was anxious to get away, so he threw the hose down on the roof which made a noise. Cunningham insisted on going down the rope first and when he did Deputy Shelton was there at the bottom to seize him. Bill came down next and was also caught, but George seeing what happened with Bill and Cunningham ran across the top of the jail and made his way down the smokestack of the furnace on the opposite side of the building.

"Bill lamented to the reporter how after he did all the preparation for the escape Cunningham caused it all to go bad. Bill was sorry they allowed Cunningham to go with them."

"Bev, what a story," said Drue. "Do you think that is the way it happened?"

"Yes, it makes sense and the sheriff's wife and young daughter were sitting outside enjoying the lovely spring night. When she saw the men on the roof, the daughter may have been the one to call the deputy's attention to the escapees. They tell the same story, so I hear."

"Well, said Della. "I can't help but be glad George got away. I am sorry the way things are he can't come home so we can be a family again. I can't help but feel betrayed. I have stood by him through the escapes, the trial, the community contempt and what do I have in return. I am left alone with two babies to bring up. How am I supposed to feel?"

"Della," said David, "it certainly has not been what we expected when you married George. We all just have to continue on each day. You know you have a home with us as long as you want to stay."

"Yes, Pa. I know. You and Ma are so good to me. I just can't bring myself to face what is down the road. I'll try to get myself together soon. I know I must be strong for the girls.

Chapter 44

The execution of Bill Taylor was rescheduled for April 30, 1896. The day before the hanging crowds of people began streaming into Carrollton from all over Missouri and surrounding states. It was more than a circus; it was like a political convention and a holiday celebration combined. The hotels and rooming houses were full while people tried to locate accommodations anywhere they could, even going to neighboring villages to find a place to sleep.

On the train from Linneus and Milan were two mothers who, although they knew each other, they did not speak. Mrs. James Taylor was coming with the intention of taking charge of the body of her son after the hanging. Mrs. Martha Jane Meeks, mother of Gus Meeks, came only for the purpose of seeing one of the men who murdered her son hanged. Accompanying Mrs. Meeks was her blind son George. Also, on the train was John Page the brother of Delora Page Meeks, wife of Gus. and her cousins R A. Page and J.A. Page.

Sheriff Niblo was on the train, too. He heard Mrs. Meeks talking with the passengers seated near her. He sympathized with her when he heard her say, "My only regret is I probably will not live long enough to see George Taylor and the others involved get what they deserve."

Someone said, "You think there were others involved?"

Mrs. Meeks looked around, "Of course there were others. Little Nellie told me there was a Bill and a Will because she heard one of them call another Will and there were other voices besides George and Bill Taylor, Nellie said. It's too bad I didn't get to tell Nellie's story on the witness stand. They said they wanted to catch the others so for me to keep quiet about it. But they have never caught anyone else yet."

A passenger across the aisle asked her, "Do you have any idea who the others are?"

With a shake of her head, she replied, "I think I know, but I won't say anything right now because they are not far from here and I think George is nearby, too. There's no doubt some of them helped George get away. I wouldn't be surprised if they didn't try to stop the hanging of Bill tomorrow."

Sheriff James Niblo had some of those same thoughts as did many others from Linn and Sullivan Counties. He knew there were several men who were on the look-out for any suspicious activity around the jail in Carrollton. In the evening about 250 men from those counties went to the jail. Sheriff Allen with ten Linn County deputies went into the jail with the intention of seeing that Bill Taylor stayed in the jail.

As the group was talking, Sheriff Niblo began telling the story of the crimes committed by the Taylor brothers. There were stories of forgery, of arson and, of course, the cattle stealing. He told of how Bill had collected a premium on an insurance policy he had issued but when the man's house burned there was no such insurance company. Niblo continued for an hour telling of the crimes committed by Bill Taylor to anyone who would listen to him.

The reporters from various newspapers throughout the area were in abundance all evening. At about midnight several were admitted to the jail. They noted that Bill Taylor was in his little cell lying down in his clothes as he tossed and turned on his pallet. When Colonel Hale appeared, Bill gave the attorney his gold watch and chain, his pocket comb and his silver match box to give to Maude, his wife.

One of the reporters asked Bill the next morning, "Do you plan to make a statement before going to the gallows?"

Bill's response was, "I am innocent, so I have nothing to confess. All the statements necessary I have already made so I have nothing to say."

A couple hours before the hanging, Colonel Hale, Virgil Conkling, Russell Kneisley and Ralph Lozier were admitted to the jail. Bill thanked his attorneys for their work on his behalf. "Mr. Conkling," Bill asked, "is there any hope of a last-minute respite?"

"No, there is not."

Annalou Mack

"Well, they are hanging an innocent man. If I had had another thirty days I would never be hanged." responded Bill.

As they left Bill gave Colonel Hale a letter. Bill said, "That's my last and only statement."

This is the letter Bill had written:

> To the Public.
>
> I have only this statement to make. I ought not to suffer as I am compelled to do. Prejudice and perjury convicted me.
>
> By this conviction my lovely wife is to be left a widow. My babes are made orphans in a cold world, my brothers to mourn and friends to weep. You hasten my gray-haired father and other to their graves.
>
> The mobs and that element have hounded me to the grave. I had hoped to at least live till the good people realized the injustice done me, but I am prepared to meet my God and I now wing my way to the great unknown. There I believe everyone is properly judged.
>
> I hope my friends will all meet me in heaven. I believe I am going there.
>
> Goodbye all.
>
> W. P Taylor [32]

At nine-fifteen o'clock on the morning of the 30th, the mother of Gus Meeks along with George W. Meeks, her blind son, asked for permission to witness the hanging. At first the sheriff did not think it was a good idea, but later he acquiesced and said, "You may stand in the passageway in full view of the scaffold while Bill is hanged."

"I am so afraid," Mrs. Meeks said, "there will be trouble."

"The only trouble will be for Bill," said her son George.

There were several women in the building. In the sheriff's parlor they sat laughing and chatting as if all of this was for their entertainment while Bill paced back and forth in his cell. Once Bill looked out through the bars to the crowd across the street and it appeared his lips quivered as he saw how packed the crowd was.

When the coffin was placed under the scaffold the crowd burst into a cheer mingled with jests and laughter. At ten o'clock about three hundred spectators with tickets were pressing to be admitted to the stockade after waiting about two hours or more. The estimate was there were between 1500 and 3000 men, women and children in the area around the stockade where the gallows were built.

Just prior to the execution, Bill had accepted the Catholic religion so shortly after ten o'clock, Father Kennedy along with a few other men and women entered Bill's cell to offer extreme unction. The onlookers heard Father Kennedy's voice as he told those listening to take the righteous path to avoid the penalty about to be administered to Bill Taylor. Mrs. Taylor, Bill's mother was not there, but Mrs. Meeks was by the door listening to the ministration of the last rites.

At 10:40 Sheriff Stanley read the death warrant then strode to the gallows where he said, "Gentlemen, please make an aisle for the advance of the prisoner. Please remove your hats when he comes and remain uncovered while the body is suspended and until pronounced dead." [33]

Following this Bill Taylor came out the side door of the jail holding a crucifix to his breast as he walked between Linn County Sheriff Allen and Carroll County Sheriff Stanley. He mounted the steps and stood in the middle of the trap. At 10:57 Sheriff Stanley pulled the trap and in a little more than thirteen minutes, Bill Taylor was pronounced dead.

None of the Gibson family was at the hanging of Bill Taylor. A couple days later Della read about it in the newspapers. Thinking this is what would have happened to George had he not escaped brought tears to her eyes. It had crossed her mind how George might come back and try to get Bill out of jail. No doubt it would have led to his being caught.

As Della held her daughters, she gave them both hugs and a kiss for each. She was getting resigned to the fact that it was just them now. It was highly unlikely George was coming to get them. The thoughts of how he had told them he would always be there for them and take care of them were uppermost in her mind. It was hard not to feel bitter at his betrayal. He had told her he was not guilty of the crime and she believed him. Now she was left to face the future alone.

EPILOGUE

Life was not easy for Della following the murders, trials, and the hanging of George's brother, Bill. There were some friends and neighbors who stood by her, but there were others who wouldn't speak when they saw her. This hurt her to the quick. How could they think it was her fault what happened to the Meeks family? Through it all she held her head up high and took care of the girls. She longed for George to pay her a visit, but knew it was impossible. Never a word from him.

It was another blow when little Georgia became sick and died in December, 1898. She had never seemed as strong as Flossie so any disease going in the community she was sure to get. After a bout with measles she came down with pneumonia and died suddenly.

Della decided to get away from the Browning community after the death of Georgia. Without much education she didn't have many job skills but she was able to find a position as a waitress in the Jefferson Hotel in Macon, Missouri. She had to leave Flossie with her grandparents, but Flossie was good with that because she had spent most of her life in the Gibson home.

A couple of years later, Della moved on to Kansas City where she worked in the West Ninth Street restaurant. One of her customers was a handsome man of about her age. He came in more and more where he always found a table in her waiting section. It wasn't long before he asked her out.

They talked and talked about their past lives which in some ways were similar. Ernest Mabe was born in Germany and came with his parents to the United States as a child. He served in the military during the Spanish-American War then married a St. Louis woman. They had a son. The marriage was not a success so after the divorce he moved to Kansas City.

Della and Ernest were married in February, 1907. Ernest took a job with the Kansas City Fire Department and he and Della made a home for Flossie in Kansas City. But Flossie had close ties to Linn County and in 1912 she married Guy Thomas Carter from Browning. During the next nine years Flossie and Guy were the parents of three daughters before Flossie died in February, 1923.

Only a year after the death of Flossie, Della died in March 1924 without ever hearing a word from George Taylor after his jail escape.

There was much speculation about what became of George. Many news articles wrote about sightings and investigations, but nothing was ever proven. This article seemed to be a good possibility.

Tulsa, Oklahoma — July 1926

Leaving his job at the Post Office, C. E. Kennon, walked along the banks of the Arkansas River. This warm, humid afternoon made the odors from the trash scattered along the bank almost overwhelming. It was his first time to venture this far into the area which often contained hobo tents and camps.

Spying a makeshift hovel, completely encircled with tin cans, trash and four mangy dogs, C. E. came close enough to see an emaciated man barely clinging to life.

"Hi there. Can I be of some help?"

"You best stay away from me," came the low growl from the form. "I don't need your help."

"Okay, suit yourself. I thought maybe I could offer a little water and maybe a bite or two of food." Kennon took a step back from the door. As he turned to walk away, the man moaned and gradually sat up.

"Maybe, a drink of water."

"Sure, take a sip from this canteen. I have a few crackers in my pocket you can have, too."

The man greedily grabbed the canteen and crackers without a word.

"I don't take kindly to strangers. That old crone who came around the other day almost got a knife in her gullet for disturbing me."

"Would you really kill a person for just looking at you?"

"You don't know me so you don't know what I would do, now do you?"

"No, I don't. Why don't you tell me about yourself? How did you end up here on the river bank?"

"Well, now, maybe I just might do that. There are not many days left for me on this earth so telling you about me may ease my conscience a little."

The old man ran his fingers through his long, straggly, dirty grey hair. His beard, the same color as his hair, hung nearly to his waist. It was clear that neither had seen soap and water or a comb for days, perhaps even months. His blue eyes seemed to come more alive as he began the tale that took well into the evening.

"I was once a well-off farmer in Missouri with a young wife and two beautiful baby girls. Unusual circumstances caused me to leave them. Williams is what people now call me. I have wandered the world since leaving, never able to go back, even for a short time, to see my family.

"During the Spanish-American War, I bravely fought without fear, taking chances where I might have been killed. Much to my sorrow, I survived. The awful crimes I have committed haunt me to this day. Going from one country to another trying to find peace has consumed my life. I have never told anyone what I am telling you. Perhaps this will bring me the peace for which I have been seeking."

Kennon listened carefully. He had heard the story of the "unusual circumstances" to which the hermit referred. Could this really be the one who had been sought for so many years? Be that as it may, he needed to get this man to the hospital as soon as possible. It was clear the hermit was near death.

In spite of getting help as quickly as possible, the old hermit died in the hospital a few days later without revealing anything else about himself. [34]

Acknowledgments

This book would not have been possible without the help of many people throughout the three decades it was in the research and writing.

The first to give me a boost in the research were the County Clerks in both Linneus and Carrollton in Linn and Carrol Counties of Missouri. These clerks were extremely helpful in not only helping me find the information I needed, but in copying each document for me to peruse.

The staff of the Historical Society of Missouri in Columbia helped me find the film and copy multiple pages of newspaper articles during numerous trips to their facility. Without those papers I would not have been able to piece together the happenings that are the basis for this book.

After the research came the writing; this was the hard part. I joined writer's groups who gave me insight through their comments. Two members from those groups come to mind—Terri Lynn Cobb and Deni Phillips. My two daughters, Leanna Eversmeyer and Linda Kay Crowe read and gave observations to help in the proofreading. Also, my friend, Mark Starkey, was a willing proofreader with helpful comments. I am incredibly grateful to Trisa Hudson who helped make the book more readable. Without her clarifications and notes it would be much more garbled than it is.

I would also like to thank Mike Trial for his remarks on the back cover. Of course, it goes without saying how much I owe to my editor, Yolanda Ciolli. It is only through her that the book has seen the light of day. She is such a talented artist which shows in the cover design for the book.

I owe much to each person who helped bring this book to fruition.

QUOTE SOURCES

Chapter 10
    (1) The *Brookfield Gazette*, Brookfield, Missouri, Saturday Morning, 19 May 1894

Chapter 13
    (2) *Kirksville Weekly Graphic*, Friday 29 June, 1894

Chapter 22
    (3) *Thursday Morning Democrat*, Carrollton, Missouri, Thursday, 28 March 1895

Chapter 23
    (4) *Thursday Morning Democrat*, Carrollton, Missouri, Thursday, 28 March 1895
    (5) *Carrollton Morning Democrat*, Carrollton Missouri, Friday, 29 March 1895
    (6) *Carrollton Morning Democrat*, Carrollton Missouri, Friday, 29 March 1895

Chapter 24
    (7) *Carrollton Morning Democrat*, Carrollton Missouri, Friday, 29 March 1895

Chapter 25
    (8) *Carrollton Morning Democrat*, Carrollton Missouri, Friday, 29 March 1895
    (9) *Carrollton Morning Democrat*, Carrollton Missouri, Friday, 29 March 1895
    (10) *Morning Democrat, Carrollton*, Missouri, Saturday, 30 March 1895

Chapter 26
    (11) *Wednesday Morning Democrat*, Carrollton, Missouri, Wednesday, 3 April 1895
    (12) *Wednesday Morning Democrat*, Carrollton, Missouri, Wednesday, 3 April 1895
    (13) *Tuesday Morning Democrat*, Carrollton, Missouri, Tuesday, 2 April 1895

Chapter 28
    (14) *Kansas City Star*, Friday, 5 April 1895

Chapter 32
    (15) *Carrollton Daily Democrat*, Carrollton, Missouri, Friday, 26 July 1895

Chapter 33
    (16) *Carrollton Daily Democrat*, Sunday, 28 July 1895

                                        Annalou Mack

Chapter 34
  (17) *Carrollton Daily Democrat*, Sunday, 28 July 1895
  (18) *Carrollton Daily Democrat*, Carrollton, Missouri, Tuesday, 30 July 1895

Chapter 35
  (19) *Carrollton Daily Democrat*, Carrollton, Missouri, Tuesday, 30 July 1895
  (20) *Carrollton Daily Democrat*, Carrollton, Missouri, Tuesday, 30 July 1895
  (21) *Carrollton Daily Democrat*, Carrollton, Missouri, Tuesday, 30 July 1895

Chapter 36
  (22) *Carrollton Daily Democrat*, Carrollton, Missouri, Thursday, 1 August 1895
  (23) *Carrollton Daily Democrat*, Carrollton, Missouri, Thursday, 1 August 1895

Chapter 38
  (24) *Carrollton Daily Democrat*, Carrollton, Missouri, Saturday, 3 August 1895

Chapter 39
  (25) *Carrollton Daily Democrat*, Carrollton, Missouri, Sunday, 4 August 1895

Chapter 40
  (26) *St. Joseph Weekly Gazette*, Tuesday, 6 August 1895
  (27) *St. Joseph Weekly Gazette*, Tuesday, 6 August 1895
  (28) *The Morning Tribune*, Trenton, Missouri, 4 August 1895

Chapter 41
  (29) *The Morning Tribune*, Trenton, Missouri, 6 August 1895

Chapter 42
  (30) *The Leader Courier* (Kingman, Kansas) 19 September 1895, Thursday
  (31) *The Leader Courier* (Kingman, Kansas) 19 September 1895, Thursday

Chapter 44
  (32) *The St. Joseph Weekly Gazette* (St. Joseph, Missouri) 1 May 1896, Friday
  (33) *The St. Joseph Weekly Gazette* (St. Joseph, Missouri) 1 May 1896, Friday

Epilogue:
  (34) *Tulsa Daily World*, Tulsa, Oklahoma; 9, 10, 12, 13, 15, 17 July 1926

BIBLIOGRAPHY

Birdsall & Dean, *The History of Linn County, Missouri*, (Kansas City, Missouri, 1882)

Biographies from Biographical Record Book of March 1893 (?)

Broderbund Software, Inc. World Family Tree Vol. 23, Ed. 1, (Release Date, July 8, 1998), CD-ROM, Tree #1481+
Carroll County Scrapbook, 1905

Carroll County, Missouri, Cemetery records, Vol I, III-IV, Ancestry. com

http://www.rootsweb.com/~molinn/murders.html

Carrollton Daily Democrat, Monday, Mar. 18, 1895; Tuesday, Mar. 19, 1895; Saturday, Mar. 23, 1895; Wednesday, Mar. 27, 1895; Thursday, Mar. 28, 1895; Friday, Mar. 29, 1895; Saturday, Mar. 30, 1895; Sunday, Mar. 31, 1895; Tuesday, Apr. 2, 1895; Wednesday, Apr. 3, 1895; Thursday, Apr. 4, 1895; Friday, Apr. 5, 1895; Thursday, Jul. 1895; Friday, Jul. 26, 1895; Saturday, Jul. 27, 1895; Sunday, Jul. 28, 1895; Tuesday, Jul. 30, 1895; Wednesday, Jul. 31, 1895; Thursday, Aug. 1, 1895; Friday, Aug. 2, 1895; Saturday, Aug. 3, 1895; Sunday, Aug. 4, 1895; Wednesday, Aug. 7, 1895; Saturday, Aug. 10, 1895; Monday, Aug. 12, 1895; Nov. 17, 1950 (Carrollton, MO.)

The Chillicothe Constitution, Chillicothe, Missouri, July 13, 1926

Deposition of Amenda Harvy, Carroll County Courthouse, Carroll County; Carrolton, Missouri

Deposition of Mrs. Sallie Carter, Carroll County Courthouse, Carroll County, Missouri

Ellsberry, Elizabeth Prather, Cemetery Records Northwestern Linn County, Missouri, (Chillicothe, MO, n.d.)

Genealogy Researchers of Linn County, Missouri, Obituaries of the *Browning Leader-Record*, 1909-1919, Vol. I (Brookfield, MO, n.d.)
————, Obituaries of the *Browning Leader-Record*, 1920-1929, Vol. II, (Brookfield, MO, n.d.)
————, Obituaries of the *Browning Leader-Record*, 1930-1939, Vol. III, (Brookfield, MO. n.d.)
————, Obituaries of the *Browning Leader-Record*, 1940-1949, Vol. IV, (Brookfield, MO n.d.)

History of Carroll County, Missouri, "Colonel John B. Hale," electronic

The Complete History of Sullivan County Missouri, Volume 1, 1886-1900, Copyright 1977 by History Publications, Inc. in the United States of America.
or
History Publications, Inc., "The Meeks Murders of Linn and Sullivan Counties, MO," *The Complete History of Sullivan County Missouri, Vol. 1*, 1886-1900, web site, http://www.rootsweb.com/~molinn/murders.html

Kansas City Star, Kansas City, Missouri, May 13, 1894; June 10, 1894

Kirksville Weekly Graphic, Fri. 29 Jun 1894

The Linneus Bulletin, Linneus, Missouri, June 13, 1894; Dec 12, 1894
Marriage Records of Linn County, MO, Linn County Courthouse, Linneus, Missouri

Marriage Records of Sullivan County, Missouri, Microfilm

"Missouri and Missourians," *Kansas City Times*, Kansas City, Missouri; Friday, Aug. 3, 1894

Mexico Weekly Ledger, (Mexico, Missouri, 7 May 1896, May 1896 Motion for New Trial in State of Mo. vs. William P. Taylor and George E. Taylor, Circuit Court of Carroll County, Missouri, at the July term, 1895, Carroll County Courthouse, Carrollton, Missouri

Niblo, James A. & Mrs. C. B. Eubanks, "Bodies Under the Straw," *Master Detective*, July 1937.
Rootsweb's World Connect Project, Genealogy of Hugh and Marian (Yancey) Zorger, (http://worldconnect.genealogy.rootsweb.co)

Springfield Democrat, Springfield, Missouri, 24 May 1894

St. Joseph Gazette, Saturday, May 12, 1894; Tuesday, May 15, 1894; Thursday, May 17, 1894; Friday, May 18, 1894; St. Joseph, Missouri

The St. Joseph Weekly Gazette, St. Joseph, Missouri) · 17 Apr 1896, Friday

Stigall, Audrey Durst, *Linn County Will Records*, Excerpted, 16 Apr 1891 -23 Dec 1946, (Brookfield, Missouri, n.d.)

The Brookfield Gazette, Saturday Morning, May 12, 1894; Saturday Morning, May 19, 1894, (Brookfield, Missouri)

The Leader Jeffersonian, Jan. 21, 1904, (Norborne, Missouri)

The Meeks Murders, web site at: http://www.oseda.missouri.edu/ linncntyr1.k12.mo.us/LIB1/htm

The Milan Republican, Sept. 28, 1893; May 17, 1894; May 24, 1894; May 31, 1894; Jun 7, 1894; Jun. 28, 1894; Jul. 5, 1894; Jul 12, 1894;

Aug. 9, 1894; Feb. 7, 1895; Mar. 28, 1895; Apr. 4, 1895; Apr. 11, 1895; (Milan, Missouri)

The Milan Standard, Milan, Sullivan County, Mo. June 13, 1891; Oct. 23, 1891. (Milan, Missouri)

The State Republican, June 14, 1894, Jefferson City, MO
Transcript of the Record and Proceedings Had and Made in the Circuit Court of Linn County State of Missouri in the Case of The State of Missouri vs William P. Taylor and George E. Taylor. Carroll County Courthouse, Carrollton, Missouri

Trenton Morning Tribune, Trenton, Missoui; October 23, 1894; Dec.1894
United States Bureau of the Census. Eleventh Census of the United States, Linn County, MO: 1900, Microfilm, T623, roll #s 871 & 872

————, Tenth Census of the United States, Linn County, MO: 1880, Microfilm, T9, roll #s 699 & 700.

Wednesday Morning Democrat, Carrollton, Missouri, April 3, 1895.
Walker, Ryan, Murder of the Meeks Family or Crimes of the Taylors, (Kansas City, MO, 1896) (Brck & Clark, Printers, Kansas City, MO.

Descendants of Gus and Delora Page Meeks

...2 Gus Meeks b: Abt. 1863 in Ohio, d: 10 May 1894 in Linn Co, Missouri, USA

+ Delora Page b: 12 Sep 1867 in Sullivan County, Missouri, USA m: 29 Dec 1886 in Sullivan, Missouri, USA, d: 10 May 1894 in Browning, Linn County, Missouri, USA

......3 Nellie L. Meeks b: 23 Sep 1887 in Missouri, d: 04 Mar 1905 in Audrain, Missouri

+ Albert Ross Spray b: 29 Dec 1883 in Bute, Sullivan County, Missouri, USA m: 06 Jan 1904 in Milan, Sullivan, Missouri, USA, d: 02 Apr 1979 in Brookfield, Linn County, ,Missouri, USA

.........4 Harriett Pauline Spray b: 24 Feb 1905 in Fulton, Callaway County, Missouri, USA, d: 03 Dec 1977 in Detroit, Wayne County, Michigan, USA

+ Albert Lee Daniels b: 19 Aug 1904 in Kansas City, Wyandotte County, Kansas, USA, m: 02 Oct 1928 in Linneus, Linn, Missouri, USA, d: 23 Sep 1985 in Fort Dodge, Ford County, Kansas, USA

+ Wayne Ollie Jones b: 17 Feb 1902 in Milan, Sullivan County, Missouri, USA, m: 24 Nov 1919 in Milan, Sullivan, Missouri, USA, d: 01 Nov 1964 in Warsaw, Benton County, Missouri, USA

............5 Harold Dean Jones b: 16 May 1922 in Milan, Missouri, USA, d: Michigan

+ Bertha Irene Jones b: Abt. 1924, m: 18 May 1940 in Wayne

............5 Opal Kathleen Jones b: 21 Jul 1924 in Milan, Sullivan County, Missouri, USA, d: 14 Jan 2001

+ Hornik b: Abt. 1920 in Michigan

+ Phillip M Stein b: Abt. 1921, m: 28 Dec 1940 in Wayne

+ Fasano b: Abt. 1920, d: Michigan

+ Joseph R Temple b: 29 Nov 1918 in Michigan, m: 11 Mar 1942 in Inkster, Wayne, Michigan, USA, d: 03 Jan 2000

......3 Hattie Meeks b: 1890 in Missouri, USA, d: 10 May 1894 in Browning, Linn County, Missouri, USA

......3 Mamie Meeks b: 1893 in Missouri, USA, d: 10 May 1894 in Browning, Linn County, Missouri, USA

Annalou Mack

Descendants of James and Ruth Ann Phenis Niblo

......1 James Alexander Niblo b: Dec 1847 in Fayette County, Pennsylvania, USA, d: Abt. 1917 in probably, Oklahoma, USA

    + Ruth Ann Phenis b: 26 Nov 1846 in Franklin County, Indiana, USA, m: 17 Sep 1868 in Richland, Illinois, USA, d: 29 Dec 1898 in Milan, Sullivan County, Missouri, USA

........2 James A. Niblo jr b: 16 Apr 1869 in Illinois, d: 22 Apr 1930 in Kansas City, Jackson County, Missouri, USA

    + Ida May Coldwell b: Mar 1872 in Missouri, m: 1890 in Sullivan, Missouri, USA, d: 1931 in Jackson County, Missouri, USA

...........3 Hazel G. Niblo b: Nov 1896 in Missouri

    + Kenneth C Baird

    + Joseph W Brown b: Abt. 1895, m: 15 Sep 1922 in Jackson, Missouri, USA

    + Wm E Sands m: 22 Oct 1936 in Weber, Utah, USA

...........3 Maude Ber Niblo b: 16 Mar 1900 in Missouri, d: 20 Sep 1978 in Salem, Marion, Oregon, USA

    + Walter Oliver Pounds b: 07 Mar 1894 in Nebraska, m: 22 Feb 1932 in Clay, Missouri, USA, d:08 Mar 1974 in Oregon, USA

...........3 James A Niblo III b: 14 Jan 1903 in Missouri, d: 19 Sep 1986 in Kansas City, Clay, Missouri, USA

    + Rosie E Phoenix b: 16 Dec 1905, m: 13 Oct 1924 in Jackson, Missouri, USA, d: May 1978 in Kansas City, Jackson, Missouri, USA

    + Margaret W Niblo b: 04 Jun 1911 in Missouri, d: Jun 1993 in Kansas City, Clay, Missouri, USA

...........3 Harold Walter Niblo b: 05 Dec 1905 in Milan, Missouri, USA, d: 06 Mar 1963 in Kansas City, Jackson County, Missouri, USA

    + Mary Lucille Greenwood b: 16 May 1920 in Cloud Chief, Washita County, Oklahoma, USA, d: 23 Feb 2004 in Kansas City, Wyandotte County, Kansas, USA

    + Patricia I Bunnett b: Abt. 1909, d: Abt. 1998 in Newport Beach California, USA

........2 Samuel L. Niblo b: Abt. 1871 in Illinois, d: 05 Mar 1925 in Fresno, California, USA

    + Susan I Richmond b: 29 Feb 1880 in Missouri, m: 31 Aug 1909 in Jackson, Missouri, USA, d: 10 May 1970 in Fresno County, California, USA

.........2 Bessie Kate Niblo b: Jul 1877 in Illinois, d: 02 Feb 1924 in Bryan Oklahoma, USA

+ Edward S Bennett b: Apr 1874 in Missouri, m: 23 Nov 1899 in Sullivan, Missouri, USA, d:1943

...........3 Edward James Bennett b: 02 Feb 1901 in Milan, Sullivan, Missouri d: 1946 in USA

+ Norma Bell Brown b: Abt. 1909 in Texas, m: 18 May 1929 in Carter, Oklahoma, USA

...............4 Norma Carolyn Bennett b: Abt. 1932 in Oklahoma

...............4 Marian A Martin b: Abt. 1935 in Oklahoma

.... 3 Marjorie Joyce Bennett b: 24 Dec 1902 in Milan, Sullivan, Missouri, USA, d: 24 Nov 1964 in Sherman, Grayson, Texas, USA

+ William Andrew Tucker b: 04 Mar 1890, m: 12 Sep 1940 in Bryan, Oklahoma, USA, d: 11 Oct 1973 in Sherman, Grayson County, Texas, USA

...........3 Ruth Frances Bennett b: 15 Dec 1904 in Macon, Missouri, d: 23 Sep 1978 in Dallas, Dallas, Texas, USA

+ Hope Chisholm Daniels b: 21 Aug 1893 in Arkansas   m: 16 Jan 1921 in Bryan, Oklahoma, USA, d: 29 Nov 1961 in Dallas, Dallas, Texas

...............4 Hope Bennett Daniels b: 11 Mar 1922 in Oklahoma, USA d: 29 Dec 2005

+ Norma Gwendolyn Thomas b: 06 May 1923, m: 28 Jul 1942 in Bryan, Oklahoma d: 22 Dec 2000

...............4 Bessie K Daniels b: Abt. 1925 in Oklahoma

...............4 Joe Edward Daniels b: 13 Jan 1928 in Durant, Oklahoma, USA, d: 17 Apr 2007 in Dallas, Texas, USA

+ Dorothy

..................5 Peggy Alice Daniels

...............4 Billy Niblo Daniels b: 09 Mar 1930 in Durant, Bryan County, Oklahoma, USA d: 05 Mar 2014 in Dallas, Texas, USA

+ Linda Griffin

...............4 Bobby Daniels b: 26 Apr 1932 in Oklahoma, d: 24 Aug 1995 in Calera, Bryan, Oklahoma, USA

...............4 Patsy S Daniels b: Abt. 1937 in Oklahoma

...........3 Ralph Niblo Bennett b: 26 Apr 1908 in Oklahoma, d: 17 Nov 1986 in Fort Smith, Sebastian, Arkansas, USA

+ Jewell G Cullen b: 19 Nov 1905, m: 10 Feb 1934 in Sebastian, Arkansas, d: 27 Mar 2001 in Alexandria, Rapides, Louisiana, USA

...............4 Michaelae Bennett b: 06 Feb 1937 in Fort Smith S, Arkansas
d: 20 Feb 2003

         + William B Wilkinson b: 06 Apr 1929 in Chicago, Cook,
Illinois, USA, d: 29 May 2017

.................5 James Bennett Wilkinson b: 29 Dec 1962 in Richmond,
Virginia, USA, d: 26 Oct 2012 in Alexandria, Rapides Parish, Louisiana

...............4 Patrick Joseph Bennett b: 27 Apr 1940 in Ft Smith, Sebastian,
Co, Arkansas, USA, d: 16 Jan 1941 in Ft Smith, Sebastian Co, Arkansas

...............4 Ralph Cullen Bennett b: 29 Aug 1943, d: 26 Dec 2014 in Tempe,
Arizona, USA

        + Bobbie

...........3 Lola Bennett b: Abt. 1913 in Durant, Bryan, Oklahoma, USA

        + Buck Sallee b: Abt. 1913 in Texas, m: 03 Oct 1932 in Bryan,
Oklahoma, USA

...............4 Kenneth Dean Sallee b: 21 Jul 1933 in Durant, Bryan County,
Oklahoma, USA d: 12 Mar 2012 in Ardmore, Carter County, Oklahoma

        + Lutreca Vern Harris b: 21 Nov 1945 in Coleman, Johnston
County, Oklahoma, USA m: Texas, USA, d: 27 Mar 2018 in Coleman,
Johnston County,Oklahoma, USA

        + Sarah E Prichard b: 11 Sep 1866 in Mercer County, Missouri,
USA, m: 22 Feb 1900 in Sullivan, Missouri, USA, d: 29 Aug 1952 in Rural
Precinct 1, Wichita, Texas, USA

Descendants of George and Della Gibson Taylor

......1. George Edward Taylor b: Abt. 1864 in California, d: Abt.Sep 1926 in Tulsa, Oklahoma, USA

+ Serena Idella Gibson b: 18 Jul 1875 in Linn County, Missouri, USA, m: 08 Oct 1891 in Linn, Missouri, d: 17 Mar 1924 in Kansas City, Jackson, Missouri, USA

.........2 Flossie Vaughn Taylor b: 02 May 1893 in Linn County, Missouri, USA, d: 20 Feb 1923 in Browning, Linn, Missouri, USA

+ Guy Thomas Carter b: 18 Feb 1891 in Browning, Linn, Missouri, USA, m: 03 Dec 1912 in Kansas City, Jackson, Missouri, d: 30 May 1938 in Browning Linn, Missouri, USA

...........3. Della Laurie Carter b: 20 Jan 1915 in Browning Linn, Missouri, USA, d: 05 Feb 1986 in Toledo, Lucas, Ohio, USA

+ Wallace Moody King b: 02 Dec 1897 in Nashville, Davidson, Tennessee, d: 22 May 1984 in Rochester, Fulton, Indiana, USA

...........3 Gail Gertrude Carter b: 03 Oct 1920 in Browning, Linn, Missouri, USA, d: 06 Jan 1997 in Mendocino County, California, USA

+ Ira A. Rhodes b: 1916, m: 11 Oct 1941 in Cook, Illinois, United States, d: 1967

..............4. James Carter Rhodes Sr. b: 07 Mar 1943 in Chicago, Cook, Illinois, USA, d: 16 Oct 1991 in Santa Rosa, California

+ Sharon A Williams b: in California, m: 01 May 1964 in Mendocino, California,USA

.................5. Sharon S Rhodes b: in Mendocino, California

+ McCutcheon b: Abt. 1960 in California

....................6. Russell Wayne McCutcheon b: in Mendocino, California

....................6 Rachel Lynn McCutcheon b. in Mendocino, California

.................5.James Carter Rhodes Jr. b: in Mendocino, California

.................5.Jonathan Eric Rhodes b: in Ukiah, Mendocino, California,

+ Christina Marie Pruden b: in Caifornia, USA, m: 29 Aug 1992 in Douglas, Nevada, USA

....................6 Melissa Dawn Rhodes b: in Ukiah, Mendocino, California

....................6 Julie Rhodes

+ Robert Aaron Powell b: 26 Jun 1907 in Missouri, m: 28 Aug 1937 in Browning, Linn, Missouri, USA, d: 23 Sep 1980 in Idaho Springs, Clear Creek, Colorado, USA

+ Karl H Lemmerz b: 12 Sep 1915, m: 14 Dec 1959 in Mendocino, California, USA, d: 22 Aug 1969

............3. Mary Aragonia Carter b: 04 Apr 1922 in Browning Linn, Missouri, USA, d: 26 Feb 2005 in Saint Joseph, Buchanan, Missouri

.........2. Georgia Ethel Taylor b: 08 Jul 1894 in Linn County, Missouri, USA, d: Dec 1898 in Linn County, Missouri, USA

Descendants of David and Aragonia Johnson Gibson

... 1 David Green Gibson b: 12 Sep 1853 in Linn County, Missouri, USA, d: 26 Aug 1938 in Nevada, Vernon County, Missouri, USA

+ Aragonia Johnson b: 03 Feb 1850 in Daviess County, Missouri, USA, m: 1873, d: 26 Dec 1936 in Douglas County, Missouri, USA

......2 Clarence Beverly Gibson b: 09 Feb 1874 in Linn County, Missouri, USA, d: 22 Dec 1951 in Los Angeles County, California, USA

+ Florence Irene Merrill b: 30 Apr 1878 in Missouri, United States of America, d: 29 Dec 1980 in Los Angeles County, California, USA

.........3 Clarence Merrill Gibson b: 17 Aug 1908 in Alliance, Box Butte, Nebraska, USA, d: 09 Nov 1970 in Long Beach, Los Angeles, California, USA

+ Lila Mae York b: Abt. 1911 in Nebraska

............4 Gordon York Gibson b: 04 Apr 1938 in Bridgeport B, Nebraska, d: 28 Mar 2002 in Alta Loma, San Bernardino, California, USA

+ Sharon Marie Collins b: 11 Jun 1940 in California, m: 16 Jun 1964 in Orange, California, USA, d: 28 Jan 1991 in Orange

.........3 Violet Irene Gibson b: 31 Mar 1912 in Alliance Box, Nebraska, d: 02 Dec 1996 in Long Beach, Los Angeles, California, USA

+ Mervin Loyal Larson b: 15 Oct 1908 in Stromberg, Nebraska, USA, d: 09 Jul 1973 in Los Angeles, California, USA

......2. Serena Idella Gibson - see George and Della descendants)

......2 William Isaac Gibson b: 12 Sep 1877 in Linn County, Missouri, USA, d: 17 Apr 1932 in Linn County, Missouri, USA

......2 Ellis Waller Gibson b: Abt. Oct 1879 in Linn County, Missouri, USA, d: 20 Mar 1880 in Linn County, Missouri, USA

......2 Drue Green Gibson b: 19 May 1881 in Linn County, Missouri, USA, d: 02 Jun 1947 in Milan,
Sullivan, Missouri, USA

+ Nancy Ann Boyd b: 18 Jan 1881 in Green Castle, Sullivan County, Missouri, USA, m: 11 Mar 1906 in Milan, Sullivan, Missouri, USA, d: 29 Dec 1967 in Milan, Sullivan County, Missouri, USA

.........3 Clarence Beverly Gibson b: Abt. 1910 in Milan, Sullivan County, Missouri, USA, d: Abt. 1910 in Milan, Sullivan County, Missouri, USA

......2 Iva May Gibson b: 26 Jul 1889 in Missouri, d: 25 Aug 1969 in Winchester, Jefferson County, Kansas, USA

+ Vern Clinton Bartlett b: 20 Jun 1885 in Illinois, m: 12 Jan 1913 in Browning, Linn, MO, d: 18 Dec 1961 in Leavenworth, Kansas

........3 Vernon C Bartlett Jr. b: 14 Aug 1915 in Missouri, d: 30 Sep 1957 in Leavenworth, Kansas

+ Helen M. Bartlett b: 28 Jan 1920 in Willow Springs, Howell County, Missouri, USA m: 06 Jun 1938 in Howell, Missouri, USA, d: 27 Jun 1994 in Leavenworth, Leavenworth County, Kansas, USA

..........4 Sally Ann Bartlett b: 21 Jan 1939 in Willow Springs, Howell County, Missouri, USA, d: 26 Dec 2016 in Reno, Washoe County, Nevada, USA

+ Ronald C. Bergei b: 09 Jul 1935 in Beresford Un, South Dakota, m: 24 Jul 1957 in Yankton, South Dakota, USA, d: 05 May 1987

..............5 David G Bergei b:in South Dakota, USA

..............5 Angela S Bergei b:

..........4 Joanne Kay Bartlett b: 21 May 1940, d: 29 Dec 1940

..........4 Vernon C. Bartlett III b: in Kansas

..........4 Philip L. Bartlett b: in Kansas

..........4 David Leslie Bartlett b: 20 Aug 1945, d: 02 Aug 2014

..........4 Carl Bruce Bartlett b: Abt. 1947 in Kansas

..........4 Paul Eugene Bartlett b: 03 Nov 1948, d: 26 Jul 1970

..........4 Michael M. Bartlett b: 25 Aug 1950 in Kansas

+ Julie Bartlett

..........4 Patrick Dale Bartlett b. in McLouth, Jefferson, Kansas, USA

..........4 Patricia May Bartlett b: 11 May 1952 in McLouth, Jefferson County, Kansas, USA d: 15 Mar 2011 in Bossier City, Bossier Parish, Louisiana, USA

+ Paul W. Sollars Sr b: 01 Jan 1939 in Saint Joseph, Buchanan County, Missouri, USA, d: 24 Jul 2012 in Eudora, Douglas County, Kansas, USA

..........4 Harold L Bartlett b: in McLouth, Jefferson, Kansas, USA

..........4 Howard J Bartlett b: in McLouth, Jefferson County, Kansas, USA

..........4 Katherine June Bartlett b: 01 Jun 1954 in Kansas City, KS, d: 02 Jun 2014 in Topeka

+ Miller

..............5 Jamie Miller b: Kansas

..........4 Donis Jean Bartlett b: 25 Jun 1955 in Kansas City, Kansas, d: 27 Jun 1983 in Kansas, USA

+ Ronald Barker b: Kansas

..........4 Mary Bartlett b: in McLouth, Jefferson, Kansas, USA

........3 James David Bartlett b: 29 Jan 1918 in Browning Linn, Missouri,

USA, d: 15 Feb 1998 in Umatilla, Oregon, USA

   + Nina Mildred Lovan b: 12 Jul 1921 in Richland, Pulaski County, Missouri, USA d: 27 Jan 2009 in Pendleton, Umatilla County, Oregon, USA

............4 James William Bartlett b: 24 Jul 1939 in Willow Springs, Howell, Missouri, USA, d: 03 Jan 1994 in Wallowa, Oregon, USA

   + Marjorie Ann Trow b: 23 Aug 1939, m: 23 Aug 1959 in Union, Oregon, USA, d: 26 May 2008

............4 Charles Lee Bartlett b: 29 Nov 1947 in La Grande, Union County, Oregon, USA, d: 06 Jan 2011 in Pendleton, Umatilla County, Oregon, USA

Descendants of William and Maud Leonard Taylor

....1. William Price Taylor b: 22 Sep 1861, d: 30 Apr 1896 in Carrollton, Carroll County, Missouri, USA

+ Maud Leonard b: Mar 1868 in Missouri, d: Apr 1934 in Kansas City, Jackson, Missouri, USA

.........2 Frances L Taylor b: 11 Dec 1887 in Missouri, d: Apr 1972 in Kansas City, Jackson, Missouri, USA

+ Milos N Mikulic b: Abt. 1886 in Serbia, m: 21 Oct 1923 in Jackson, Missouri, USA

............3 Boyourd Milos Mikulic b: Abt. 1926 in Missouri, d: 01 Feb 2002

.........2 Bertha Alma Taylor b: 20 Feb 1891 in Missouri, d: 15 Jun 1984 in San Luis Obispo

+ Edward Earl Hoops b: 09 Jul 1887 in Henry County, Missouri, USA, d: 24 Dec 1973 in San Luis Obispo County, California, USA

............3 Mary Elizabeth Hoops b: 20 May 1918 in Missouri, d: 02 Nov 1961 in Fort Worth, Tarrant, Texas, USA

+ Curl

............3 George E Hoops b: Abt. 1922 in Missouri

.........2 Ada E Taylor b: 16 Feb 1892 in Missouri, d: 12 Oct 1971 in St.Louis, Missouri

+ Dudley Lynn Hoffman b: 11 Aug 1890 in Lincoln, Lancaster, Nebraska, USA, m: 15 Jun 1916 in Jackson, Missouri, USA, d: 24 May 1959 in Prince Albert, Saskatchewan, Canada

............3 John Lenoard Hoffman b: 05 Sep 1918 in Missouri, d: 17 Apr 2002 in Carlsbad, Eddy County, New Mexico, USA

+ Frances Evelyn Porter b: 22 Jul 1920 in Poplar Bluff, Missouri, m: 17 Mar 1942 in Butler, Missouri, USA, d: 22 Feb 1995 in Carlsbad, Eddy County, New Mexico, USA